DELILAH'S DAUGHTERS

Also by Angela Benson

Sins of the Father
Up Pops the Devil

DELILAH'S DAUGHTERS

ANGELA BENSON

WITHDRAWN

WILLIAM MORROW
An Imprint of HarperCollins*Publishers*

HarperCollins books may be purchased for educational, business, or sales promotional use. For information please e-mail the Special Markets Department at SPsales@harpercollins.com.

Library of Congress Cataloging-in-Publication Data

Benson, Angela.

Delilah's daughters : a novel / Angela Benson.

pages cm

Summary: "Delilah Monroe and her husband Rocky always dreamed of their three daughters making it big in show business as a musical trio. After Rocky's death, Delilah's determination is even stronger. However, her daughters—Roxanne, Veronica, and Alisha—aren't so sure. Roxanne is a cruiseline entertainer, while Alisha writes jingles for an ad agency by day and secretly composes her own songs at night. Veronica, whose dancing is better than her singing, is the one with the biggest opportunity due to her husband Dexter's grand plans—plans that are at the expense of her sisters'. Delilah wants to keep her daughters together, but they have minds of their own. Soon Roxanne, Veronica, and Alisha embark on their own paths, only to find that the price of fame might be more than they're willing to give. An inspirational family drama, DELILAH'S DAUGHTERS showcases Angela Benson as one of the strongest voices in African-American women's fiction today." —Provided by publisher.

ISBN 978-0-06-200271-6 (pbk.)

1. African American women—Fiction. 2. Mothers and daughters—Fiction. 3. Sisters—Fiction. 4. Performing arts—Fiction. I. Title.

PS3552.E5476585D45 2014

813'.54--dc23

2013025516

13 14 15 16 17   OV/RRD   10 9 8 7 6 5 4 3 2 1

To my nieces, Mia and Kersten.
Thanks for giving me a reprieve from our
Monopoly rematch so I could finish the
final chapters of *Delilah's Daughters*.

DELILAH'S
DAUGHTERS

Prologue

*O*n days like today, Rocklin "Rocky" Monroe hated being dead.

He eased down on the bench next to his wife, Delilah, who sat at the piano near the back of the stage, beaming with pride as their three daughters—"Delilah's Daughters," as he'd named their singing trio—took their bows to a standing ovation at the annual Gospelfest in Birmingham, Alabama. The sassy and upbeat rendition of "Revive Us Again," arranged by their youngest, Alisha, had brought the house to its feet. He put his arm around Delilah's shoulders. *You did good, sweetheart,* he whispered, even though he knew neither she nor those around her could hear him.

She shivered, rubbed her arms, and he knew she felt his presence. "These are our girls, Rocky," she murmured softly. "I'm so proud of them, and I know you would be too."

I am proud of them! he wanted to shout, but knew it would do no good. He could see her, touch her, smell her, but she could only sense his presence. As he'd learned in the three years since a blood clot in his lung led to his untimely and totally unexpected demise, being dead was certainly a limiting experience.

The applause grew amid chants of "Praise Him!" and "More, more!" The girls glanced back at their mother, whose fingers flowed across the keyboard as they launched into Alisha's rendition of "Take My Life and Let It Be." Their eldest, Roxanne, who had the best voice of the three, brought the lyrics alive. When she crooned, "Take my voice and let me sing," he jumped to his feet along with the audience. Who could keep sitting when his baby poured out her heart and soul that way? It was as though her words became the words of the hearts of her listeners. It wasn't her song anymore—it was everybody's song.

Alisha and Veronica backed Roxanne up in perfect harmony. Their choreographed movements, which he knew to be the work of Veronica, the born entertainer of the family, were every bit as powerful as the lyrics. The three of them were angels, singing and dancing with joy before their Lord.

The song ended with the audience on its feet in another ovation and moment of praise. He rushed toward his girls, his heart more full of love now than it had ever been. He wondered how that could be possible, since he had loved them with all that was in him when he was alive. Maybe his heart had grown larger in death.

He reached Alisha first. His baby girl was the shy one who had always been closer to her mother than to him. He brushed a kiss against her forehead and whispered, *I love you,* in her ear. When he pulled back, her eyes were full of tears. She missed him, he knew, but she also knew he loved her and that he was there with her.

He moved next to Roxanne, favoring her with a kiss and the same *I love you*. Parents weren't supposed to have favorites, but God help him, Roxanne had been his favorite. He guessed it was because she was most like him. While Alisha and Veronica enjoyed singing, Roxanne *had* to sing. The music gave her life and purpose. She sang when she was happy and when she was sad. He knew, too, that she sang when she missed him, sang until she felt him in every part of her being. In those times, he saw her heart in ways he hadn't seen it when he'd been alive. Sometimes he ached for Roxanne because along with sharing his love for music, she also shared his willingness to do anything for it. Praying she would make better choices than he had, he pressed a second kiss against her forehead, then moved on to his middle daughter.

Ah, Veronica, the child he least understood. She worried him more than the other two. He reached her as the trio moved down the stairs in front of the stage and toward the audience. He managed a whisper kiss against her cheek, so fleeting he was unsure she even felt it. His heart ached that Veronica was as elusive to him in his death as she had been when he was alive. Her thirst for the limelight scared him at times. While he was glad that she was so at ease with the spotlight, he didn't want it to consume her. He'd hoped her marriage would provide her with some much-needed perspective, but her husband seemed to fuel that fire rather than help calm it.

Shaking off his melancholy, Rocky stood back and watched with pride as his girls mingled with the audience, showing their appreciation with handshakes and hugs. Many of the audience members knew the girls—had known them since they were kids—which made the sharing now even more special. He glanced back and saw Delilah looking on them with pride as well.

He turned to go back to his wife, but a tall, slender man reached her first. *Who is that?* he wondered.

"Hey, Mrs. Monroe," the man said, causing Delilah to look up at him.

"Roy," she said, getting up to give him a hug. "It's so good to see you. I didn't know you were going to be here today."

Roy? Rocky thought. *That's Roy Stiles? Well, that boy sure has lost a lot of weight. How long has it been since I last saw him?*

Roy hugged Delilah back. "I missed Gospelfest the last couple of years because of *American Star* commitments, but I'm back now. I don't plan to miss another one."

"We understand, Roy," Delilah said. "We're all so proud of you. You're an example to all the young people. Us old ones too," she added with a twinkle in her eye.

"I can feel the love, Mrs. Monroe. Some people look at me and think I was an overnight success. I have to tell them that my overnight took fifteen years."

Delilah laughed. "You don't have to tell me."

Rocky agreed. He'd watched Roy's career, and he'd wanted what Roy had for his girls: to be given the opportunity to sing before a television audience of millions. Like Roy, his girls sang a blend of gospel and pop that he called "gospel for the world," and as with Roy, he hoped a television audience would embrace them and their sound. You couldn't pay for that kind of exposure.

Roy pulled a folded sheet of paper out of his shirt pocket. "Delilah's Daughters is special, Mrs. Monroe, really special. They've only gotten better over the years."

Delilah beamed. "That's nice of you to say."

Roy shook his head. "I'm not being nice. I'm being honest. They need the kind of exposure that I got on *AS*."

"If only there were an *American Star* for groups," she said.

Rocky had been thinking the same thing.

Roy chuckled. "Well, there is—or there will be." He handed her the paper he had pulled out of his pocket. Rocky moved over to stand behind Delilah so he could read it too. "It's a spin-off of *American Star* that's going to be filmed in Atlanta," Roy said. "They take solo acts and groups. I think Delilah's Daughters should try out."

I do too, Rocky said, forgetting that nobody could hear him. According to the flyer, the winners of the *Sing for America* competition would get a recording contract worth around $300,000. Right then, he began praying Delilah's Daughters would win.

"I can't believe this," Delilah said, still staring at the flyer. "This is perfect for the girls." She looked up at Roy. "I don't know if they're ready, though. Since their father died, they haven't had much of a rehearsal schedule. Getting ready for Gospelfest each year is a major effort."

What are you saying, Delilah? Rocky shouted at his wife. *The girls are more than ready! If they could pull themselves together for a Gospelfest performance a few short months after I died, they can certainly get ready for this contest.*

"Believe me, Mrs. Monroe," Roy said, "they're ready. Of course, more rehearsal time will help, but to be honest, I don't see how they can pass up an opportunity to try out. If they're chosen to compete, it can be a life-changing experience."

Not only will they compete, Rocky said, touching Delilah's arm and willing her his confidence, *but our girls are gonna win this thing.*

"I'll talk to the girls about it," Delilah said, with a little bit more enthusiasm. "What could it hurt?"

Roy smiled again. "That's exactly what I thought when I tried out for *American Star,* and look what happened." He hugged her again. "I need to head off to the green stage for my performance. I'll look for you and the girls in the audience."

"We wouldn't miss it," Delilah said. She stared at the flyer after Roy left. "If only Rocky were here," she murmured.

I am here, Rocky said, his frustration at being unheard growing. Though this was his third Gospelfest visitation, the boundaries between the living and the dead still grated on him. *The girls have to try out. They're going to win this thing. It's their destiny. I feel it, Dee.*

He watched his wife as a light chuckle escaped her lips. She felt the girls' destiny too. He knew she did. When she quickly sobered, he knew she was thinking about him and his dream for Delilah's Daughters to one day become a chart-topping gospel group. It was a dream that had begun forming early in their marriage, after they'd survived a major challenge to their love and recommitted themselves to each other and their family. It was a dream that later had been put on hold so the girls could complete their education. The plan had been for them to resume their careers after they finished college, but he'd died soon enough after Alisha's graduation that the dream had been lost in their grief over his death.

"Maybe it's time," Delilah murmured to herself. "The girls have to do this for Rocky—I have to do this for Rocky."

Rocky smiled, his heart full. He never knew what to expect during his yearly visits with his family, but this year was proving especially gratifying as he got to be a part of the moment when his daughters restarted the music careers he had always known were destined to be theirs. He pressed a kiss against his wife's forehead, thankful for her continued belief in their daughters' gifts. By the time he returned next year, Delilah's Daughters would be well on their way to bringing their brand of music to households all over the world.

Chapter 1

Six months later

*T*elevision commercials were a legal form of torture. Delilah Monroe was convinced of it as she sat in the front row of the studio audience of the hit show *Sing for America*. This had to be the tenth commercial they'd gone to since the show started forty-five minutes ago. The studio folks said the ad segments were a minute long, but when she checked her watch for what must have been the umpteenth time, she realized this last one had gone on for *at least* three minutes. She frowned, wondering where she should send her complaint. How could a live sixty-minute show have five hundred three-minute commercials? Okay, five hundred was an exaggeration, but still. . . .

She drummed her fingers on the armrest of her chair in a cadence that matched the beat of her heart. She hoped she didn't have a heart attack while she waited for the show to resume. No way did she want to miss the announcement of the three finalists.

"They're going to make the finals, Mom," said her son-in-law, Dexter Timmons, putting his hand atop hers to stop the drumming. "They made it through the quarterfinals last month. They're going to make it through the semifinals tonight. And then next month they're going to win it all. I can feel it."

Delilah gave him a fake smile. She'd never liked him and doubted she ever would. What Veronica saw in him she'd never know. All three of her daughters said he looked like Boris Kodjoe, the six-foot cutie from the television show *Soul Food,* but to her he looked more like Boris Karloff, the man who played the monsters in old movies now only seen on American Movie Classics. The way Delilah saw it, Veronica had only gotten involved with Dexter to escape the pain of her father's death. "I wish they'd get on with it," she said. "These commercials are going to be the death of me."

"They're drawing out the suspense," Dexter said in that know-it-all tone he always used with her, Roxanne, and Alisha. Let some folks get an advanced degree and they got a big head. She respected the MFA as much as the next person, but she didn't think it was a requirement to become a successful artist. She didn't have one and neither did Roxanne or Alisha, and Dexter looked down on them for it. Only Veronica had chosen to pursue graduate study in the arts, so he considered her his intellectual and professional equal. Well, almost his equal. Dexter was a professor, while Veronica was still a student. The good news was that she wasn't his student. Veronica was in the dance program, while he was on the creative writing faculty. At least, he had been until his recent tenure denial at the University of Alabama. She guessed a book every three years didn't cut it. Anyway, he had the upcoming school year to find a new position. By then, Veronica would have her degree, and there was no telling where he'd drag her baby. That was another reason she didn't like him. She liked her family close. Both Roxanne and Alisha still lived in Birmingham, though Roxanne did travel a lot in her job.

"I don't know if my heart will hold out until the announcement of the finalists," she said.

Dexter laughed. "I'm gonna tell you like you're always telling me and Veronica: have faith."

Delilah hated to admit it, but he was right. She didn't give him much credit for it, though, since even a stopped clock is right twice a day. "I have faith," she said. "I still want them to hurry up and announce the finalists."

Dexter chuckled. "Delilah's Daughters will make the finals. You saw them up there, Mom. Your three daughters tore it up. You were right to have them sing 'I Believe I Can Fly.' They brought the house down."

Delilah smiled in agreement. Her daughters had brought the entire audience to its feet with their rendition of the old standard. They made her proud. Her only disappointment was that Rocky wasn't here to share in this moment. He'd been the first to recognize their daughters' talent. And he'd been their biggest supporter and promoter. She also wished Tommy could be here, but she understood and agreed with his reasons for staying away.

The houselights came up then, and the crowd began a rousing applause, followed by chants of the names of the most popular acts. "Delilah's Daughters" rang out in the midst of about five other names, and Delilah's eyes grew damp with unshed tears of joy. Her daughters had developed a large fan base. Rocky would have loved it.

The skinny emcee, Morris Williams, came out onto the stage. "Are y'all having a good time?" he asked the crowd.

The yeahs and yays were so loud, Delilah almost covered her ears. Almost. She was one of the ones yelling.

"Well, the time you've been waiting for is upon us."

Delilah's heart raced as the crowd grew quiet.

"We're going to select three finalists from tonight's ten semifinalists," Morris continued. "My only regret is that all ten acts won't make it to the finals. So before we announce the final three, let's show some love to all of our semifinalists."

The crowd roared in cheers and applause.

As Morris introduced each semifinal act, they came on the stage, took a bow, and then went to their designated place on the dais. It seemed to take him forever to get to Delilah's Daughters.

"From the lovely city of Birmingham, Alabama, we have Delilah's Daughters," he finally said.

An explosion of applause rang out as her three daughters—Veronica and Roxanne, all long and lean like their father, and Alisha, her baby girl who, like her, was not as long and a bit on the thick side—joined the other finalists onstage. Tears welled in Delilah's eyes. She was so proud of them—beautiful, talented, and kind. That was the way she and Rocky had raised them. They had taught their girls that their beauty and talents were gifts from God and they should treat them accordingly. Egos were kept in check in the Monroe household. Rocky had seen to it. And after he died, she'd taken on the job.

As the applause for the tenth and last semifinal act died down, Delilah's anxiety rose.

Morris held up an oversized envelope. "In this envelope," he said, "I have the names of the three acts that have made it to the finals."

A hush came over the audience as he lowered the envelope and then opened it. He took a deep breath. "Our first finalist is Blue Heart."

The audience erupted into another round of applause as the country band from Nashville stepped forward, hugging and slapping each other on the back with joy. Delilah had to admit that they had been good and deserved to be finalists.

She held her breath as Morris read the name of the second finalist.

"Our second finalist is Annie Jones."

"What?" Delilah said aloud, caught herself, and gave a quick prayer of thanks that the cheers of Annie's fans masked her outburst. How had the cross between Madonna and Carrie Underwood become a finalist? There had to be some mistake.

"I can't believe it either," Dexter shouted in her ear. "It must have been her skimpy outfits that won over the judges and the voting audience. She dressed worse than Lindsay Lohan on drugs."

Delilah didn't say another word. She began to pray in earnest. "I don't believe you brought us this far to have us go home empty-handed," she told the Lord. "Delilah's Daughters will be the third finalist. I believe it and receive it."

Another hush came across the audience.

"The last finalist is . . ."

Delilah held her breath and squeezed her son-in-law's hand.

" . . . Delilah's Daughters."

Chapter 2

A lisha eased behind her older sisters and away from the flash of the cameras. She didn't like press conferences. Too much light, too many people, too much cross talk. She'd much rather be sitting on a couch talking to Oprah or the ladies of *The View* than dealing with this circus.

"Roxanne," a reporter yelled out to her oldest sister. "How does it feel to be a finalist?"

As her oldest sister took a step forward and flashed a smile that rivaled the cameras in its intensity, Alisha felt a bit of envy. Roxanne's experience as a shipboard entertainer for Dreamland Cruise Lines was paying off big-time. "It's our destiny," Roxanne said. "I only wish our father were here to share in the joy. He always believed in us, believed that our gifts were meant to be shared with the world."

Alisha reached for Veronica's hand as Roxanne spoke of their father. She held on tight, easing a bit from behind Veronica. Her father wouldn't want her hiding behind her sisters. "Don't hide your light under a bushel, Alisha," he'd tell her when he saw her withdrawing into herself. She eased to Veronica's side.

"What about you, Veronica?" another reporter yelled.

Veronica, always comfortable as the center of attention, stepped forward, hands on her hips. "I'll show you how I feel." Then she twirled in a combination holy dance-slash-Beyoncé-booty-shake that made the reporters laugh and the flashbulbs go crazy. "That's how I feel," she said.

Alisha sucked in her breath, hoping the reporters wouldn't call on her. But she knew they would. They always did. It was as if they felt sorry for her and didn't want to exclude her. She wished she could tell them she didn't mind being excluded.

"Your turn, Alisha," another reporter called out.

Seeing her father's encouraging face in her mind, she said, "We love music, and we're grateful for the opportunity to share our talent with the world. We thank *Sing for America* for giving us this chance."

She felt relief when she stepped back. Though her response had been boring compared to her sisters' responses, at least she hadn't made a fool out of herself.

A few more questions and the press conference was over. The girls headed to their dressing room. Alisha was the first to drop down in a chair. "I'm glad that's over," she said. "I thought we were going to be standing there all night."

Roxanne gave her a light kick in the shin. "Please, girl. We were only up there for about fifteen minutes."

Alisha didn't believe it. It had to have been an hour or more.

"You did fine," Veronica said. "You always do. I don't know why you let those things bother you so much."

Alisha rolled her eyes. "Easy for the booty-shaker to say. I don't even believe you did that."

Roxanne laughed. "I believe it. It was so like her."

Veronica repeated her booty-shake. "Don't hate," she said. "Appreciate. Anyway, that was a holy dance. I can't believe you two didn't recognize it. Heathens!"

Alisha tossed a pillow from the couch at Veronica. "You're the heathen. And a married one at that."

Veronica laughed. "Hey, how do you think I got Dexter to the altar?" She shook her booty again. "That shake works with boyfriends, husbands, *and* reporters. That shake is going to help us win this thing."

Alisha sat up straighter in her chair. "Do you really think we have a shot?"

"We have more than a shot," Roxanne said. "This is our moment, Alisha. Can't you feel it?"

"I don't know what I'm feeling." Alisha sank back into the couch. "I just wish we could perform one of my original songs."

Roxanne sat next to her and put her arms around her shoulder. "I know you do, sis, but I think Momma's right. This contest is as much about showmanship as it is about talent. To get votes we have to give the audience what they want. And what they seem to want are familiar songs with our special twist on them. And nobody puts a twist on a popular tune better than you, Alisha. The songs we've performed in this contest may not have been Alisha originals, but each one of them had your stamp all over it. Don't worry so. Hold on to your original songs for our first album. We're going to need them."

"I can see it now," Veronica added, using her hands to frame the headlines of a newspaper. "'Delilah's Daughters debut at number one on the *Billboard* charts.' Our first single to hit number one will be one you've written. Just hold on, sis," she said to Alisha. "Your day is coming."

Roxanne got up, laughing. "Please," she said. "*Our* day is now. Delilah's Daughters is about each of us using our gifts and creating something uniquely special together. That's our trademark. We're not Delilah's Daughters without all three of us and what we bring. And when we start singing your original songs, our brand will only be enhanced. Be patient, sis."

"You're right," Alisha said. She saw no benefit in continuing this conversation with her sisters. They didn't understand how much her music, her lyrics, her beats, yearned to be set free. Her music was self-expression, something she'd had to suppress each day of the last three years she'd worked at McKinley and Thomas Advertising, the biggest ad agency in the Southeast. The pay was good, but writing jingles for cars and sports drinks didn't exactly lend itself to self-expression. The job had been a godsend, though, when she'd first landed it. On the heels of her father's death, she'd needed a break from the music of the heart, and M&T provided it. But that wasn't the case any longer. Now she needed more. Even singing with her sisters didn't fulfill her. She was only in the group because their parents, their dad especially, had wanted their daughters to perform together. She'd be as content, if not more so, writing lyrics that others would sing.

Things were different with her sisters. As a student in a graduate dance program, Veronica got to explore the depths of her talent. The more she expressed herself, the more she excelled in her program. Roxanne was in a similar situation. While being an entertainer for Dreamland Cruise Lines didn't sound like a big deal, it was pretty close to being a Las Vegas act. DCL treated Roxanne like royalty. They recognized and appreciated her talent. Not only was she able to pick the songs she sang, but she even got her sisters in on the act. Veronica had choreographed a few routines for Roxanne, and every now and then Alisha had given her a song to test-drive with her Dreamland audience.

"Where's Momma?" Alisha asked, tiring of her personal pity party. "Shouldn't she have gotten back here by now?"

"You know Momma," Roxanne said. "She's probably out there wheeling and dealing with some unsuspecting reporter or record producer. I wouldn't be surprised if we ended up with a feature article in a major magazine or a record contract with a major label. Momma Delilah learned at the feet of the master."

Veronica nodded. "I want this for Momma as much as I want it for us. I haven't seen her so excited and alive since Daddy died. This contest has been good for all of us."

Alisha agreed, but with a caveat: it had been better for some than for others. Living the life of a *real* musician the past several weeks had only made her see the emptiness of the life she'd been living before. There was no way she could go back to her old life now.

Chapter 3

"*T*he answer is 'no,' Mr. Washington," Delilah told the A&R representative from Legends Productions. The young man, who was only about twenty-five, had intercepted her on her way to her daughters' dressing room and pulled her into the office that Legends maintained at the studio. She'd been in here last month for a reception after the semifinalists were named. "How many times do I have to tell you?"

"I can't believe you've thought this through," Charles Washington said, flicking at his mustache. He reminded her of a young Berry Gordy, as dark as chocolate but not necessarily good for you. "Nobody turns down Legends. We're not some fly-by-night record label; we have a stable of Grammy Award–winning artists, and we only take on a few new artists each year. Our success with those new artists is the best in the business. We know talent when we see it, and we know how to take that talent to its limits."

Delilah knew all of that was true, and she'd have been shouting with joy if the offer was for Delilah's Daughters, but it wasn't. "Delilah's Daughters is a group. We're not looking for contracts for solo acts."

The young man smiled at her as though she were a demented old woman in a nursing home. "The chance for stardom for Delilah's Daughters is 50 percent at best. The chance for Veronica is pretty close to 100 percent. She has what it takes, Mrs. Monroe. She could be as big as Beyoncé."

"Beyoncé is not our standard, Mr. Washington," she said. How could this man expect to build Veronica's career if he didn't even know what she and her music were about?

He pursed his lips, and she knew he was growing agitated with her. "You know what I mean," he said. "She could be bigger than CeCe Winans was at her peak. She could do what Yolanda Adams tried to do and failed. She could reach the heights of Beyoncé's success singing the crossover pop-inspirational tunes that CeCe and Yolanda sang. She has it all, Mrs. Monroe. We can give her the guidance she needs to reach the pinnacle of the recording industry."

Delilah couldn't help but take some pride in the words the young man spoke. Yes, Veronica was talented, but so were Alisha and Roxanne. "That only tells me what Veronica brings to the group," Delilah said.

Washington shook his head. "You're not hearing me," he said. "The group holds her back. I know you can see it. We only get a glimpse of her style, her personality, when the group is onstage. We see that superstar quality in her press briefings when the spotlight is on her. You saw the way she stole the show with the Beyoncé booty-shake. She loves the spotlight, and it loves her."

Delilah didn't bother to explain to the man that her daughter had done a holy dance. She'd also have to talk to Veronica about taking some of the "booty" out of the dance. "So you're saying you want to sign her because she has a big butt? I know we're not interested now."

Washington lifted his arms, clearly exasperated. "That's not what I'm saying, and I think you know it. That said, I won't deny that having a certain look, a certain style, can propel an artist up the charts. I've seen it happen, and it could happen with your daughter. She has the voice *and* the intangibles to make it."

Delilah smirked. "She's not even the strongest voice in the group."

Washington nodded. "I know she isn't. Roxanne has the best vocals, but she doesn't have the intangibles."

"That's why they're so good as a group," Delilah said, not welcoming his comparison of her daughters. "No one of my daughters is better than the other, Mr. Washington. Each one brings different strengths that make the group stronger."

"That might be true with some groups, but not with your daughters. Roxanne's vocals compete with Veronica's style, and I don't see either one of them playing down their strengths for the other. Do you see Roxanne taking a backseat to Veronica when it comes to vocals? Do you see Veronica toning down her personality any more than she already does? She's straining to break out. If you can't see that, you're not a very good manager."

Delilah did see it, and so had Rocky. But they had worked hard to find and maintain the balance that made the group work. Veronica had always been the one who blossomed in the limelight. All Roxanne wanted to do was belt out tune after tune, whether it was in the bathroom or as the opening act for a touring band in an outdoor concert before thousands. And Alisha, quiet Alisha, who Charles Washington hadn't even bothered to mention, would be perfectly content in a room with a piano and a pencil so she could write her music. "What you don't understand, Mr. Washington, is that Delilah's Daughters is about more than reaching the top of the charts. It's about family. It's about working together to achieve a goal. If you have a contract for all three of my girls, then we can talk. If you don't, this conversation is over."

Washington gave her the smile reserved for doddering old ladies again. "There's no need to make a decision right now," he said, as if sensing he'd pushed as far as he could today. "We'll talk again in a month, after they announce the winners."

Delilah lifted a brow. "Are you so sure Delilah's Daughters won't win?"

He now gave her a smile that she guessed he brought out for beloved pets. "I know they won't win, for all the reasons I've given you. Veronica would have had a better chance on her own than she has in the group. Your daughters have talent, but it takes more to make it in this business. Look at who's won and who's lost on *American Star* in recent years. Some of the losers went on to great success, while some of the winners made one album and were never heard from again. Even if Delilah's Daughters did win, they wouldn't achieve the commercial success that they deserve or that you want for them. I've said it once and I'll say it again. Talent alone is not enough to guarantee success. It also takes that special intangible that Veronica has and your other daughters don't.

I know this is hard for you to hear as their mother, but it's a truth you need to accept as their manager."

"It may be your truth, Mr. Washington, but my daughters and I listen to a higher truth."

Again he gave her that smile. "I believe in the man upstairs too, Mrs. Monroe. How about we make a deal?"

She lifted her brow. "What kind of deal?"

"If your girls win next month, I'll treat your entire family to a weeklong vacation on St. Thomas. Legends owns an estate there, and we'd give it to you for the week."

"And if they don't win?"

"Your family still goes on vacation and you let me talk to Veronica about what we can do for her. Sound fair?"

"I'll think about it," Delilah said, but her heart was already giving her the answer.

Washington shook her hand. "I'll see you in a month."

Delilah watched the young man pick up his briefcase and open the door for her. He wore his arrogance well. She guessed arrogance was a natural accessory when you sported a $1,500 suit and wore $500 shoes.

Chapter 4

A week later, Veronica sat with Dexter in the Silver Olympian dining room on the Dreamland Liberty cruise ship. She fingered their engraved names on the sterling silver Tiffany Heart tag choker he had given her earlier in the day, when they were alone together on a private beach owned by one of Roxanne's Dreamland colleagues.

"You love it, don't you?"

She could only shake her head. "I love you," she said. "The choker is gorgeous, but it's your faith and confidence in me that fills my heart."

"I've always known you were a star," he said, picking up her hand and bringing it to his lips for a kiss.

A tingling warmth spread down Veronica's spine. She knew her husband wasn't spouting empty words. His belief in her talent was something she could always count on. "I'm not a star yet," she said, enjoying their quiet moment together despite being in the crowded dining room. They'd wanted to dine in Harry's Supper Club, the ship's more exclusive dining room, but had been unable to get reservations. Her strapless turquoise minidress and five-inch heels were a bit of overkill for the Silver Olympian, but it didn't matter because tonight she had dressed to please her husband.

"Here we go again," Dexter said, inclining his head in the direction of the young woman in capris and sandals headed toward them with a camera in her hands.

"Be nice," Veronica said, giving the young woman a welcoming smile. "She only wants a picture. She won't be here but a minute."

He released her hand. "She won't, but her boldness will open the floodgates. You may as well prepare yourself for a cold dinner."

Dexter's negative attitude toward fans who approached her was disconcerting. She'd have to talk to him about it later. For now, she ignored his pique and sent the woman another smile that said it was fine for her to come to the table.

"Aren't you on *Sing for America?*" the young woman asked when she reached the table.

Veronica nodded. "I sure am. Do you watch?"

The woman bobbed her head. "Every week," she said. "I'm pulling for Delilah's Daughters all the way. You're the best act on the show. You're the only reason I watch."

Veronica didn't miss the roll of Dexter's eyes. She was glad the woman couldn't see him. "How nice of you to say that," Veronica told her. "Be sure to vote for us on the finals show."

"You can count on it," the woman said. "Would you mind taking a picture with me? My friends back home will never believe I met you if I don't have a picture. They love you too."

"I'd love to take a picture with you," Veronica said. Dressing to please Dexter had an unexpected upside. The look he liked on her was the look the public expected from a budding music star. She was more than ready to take pictures with her fans. "In fact, my husband here will do us the honors." She took the woman's camera and handed it across the table to Dexter. "You don't mind, do you, sweetie?"

Veronica knew he very much minded, but she couldn't let that bother her right now. While she tried to be sensitive to his need for private time with her, she welcomed the attention of the fans and the support of people who knew them. To celebrate the group's success on the show so far, Dreamland had given the family a complimentary cruise. She meant to enjoy every minute of it before they got back home and back to rehearsing for the finals show. And meeting fans like this young lady was part of her fun. She wanted Dexter to enjoy it too. He should be glad people recognized her and wanted to vote for Delilah's Daughters. Instead, he resented the intrusion and pouted like a little girl. Men could be such babies!

"Why don't you take two pictures of us, sweetie?" she said, her words dripping with honey.

For the first picture, the young woman stooped next to her chair. "What's your name?" Veronica asked her.

"Melody," the girl said.

For the second picture, Veronica stood and put her arm around the woman's shoulder. "Now take one of me and Melody looking like old friends."

Dexter took the picture, and then he handed the camera back to Melody. Just to irritate him, Veronica said to Melody, "Be sure to check that they came out all right. I'd hate for you to get back to your stateroom and find out my husband is no good with cameras."

Dexter winced and Veronica smiled broader.

Melody checked her pictures in the camera's viewfinder. "They came out great," she said and then turned to Dexter. "Thanks." Turning back to Veronica, she said, "Thanks again. I'll go now so you can get back to your meal."

"No problem at all," Veronica said, sitting back down. "Don't forget to tune in to the finals show now."

"I won't," Melody said, backing away from the table. "Enjoy the rest of your cruise."

As soon as the woman was out of earshot, Dexter said, "People can be so rude. Can't they see that we're eating?"

Veronica sipped her tea. "Please, Dexter. These are fans, and fans help determine the winner of *Sing for America*. If we want to win, we have to be nice to them. You know that."

He stabbed his fork into his dinner salad. "It goes both ways. You should be nice to your fans, and they should be considerate of you. They just don't seem to have boundaries."

She took another swallow of tea. "They're only being supportive. That's a good thing, don't you think? They want us to win, and they're walking in faith with us that we will win. We both think Delilah's Daughters is going to win, don't we?"

"Of course I think Delilah's Daughters is going to win," he said. "You're the best act on the show. Who else could win?"

Dexter's never-wavering faith in her doused some of the irritation she was feeling toward him. Putting down her glass, Veronica said, "If you're right, we have to get ready for the changes in our lives, Dexter. You're going to have to share your wife with her adoring public, so you'd better start getting used to it." She said the latter as a joke, but the downturn in Dexter's lips told her he didn't receive it as such. "Lighten up," she told him. "This cruise is supposed to be a relaxing time for us."

"Tell that to your fans," he muttered.

"I'm telling you," she said, wanting him to understand. "What's this about anyway? Please tell me you're not jealous of the little attention I've been getting."

"I'm not jealous of anything," he said, cutting his eyes away from her.

She thought her husband needed an attitude adjustment, but before she could tell him so, a couple more fans came over, wanting pictures and autographs. She obliged them with a smile while Dexter begrudgingly took the pictures. The stream died down after about twenty minutes.

"That wasn't so bad," she said.

He shook his head. "Our food is cold."

She rolled her eyes. "Dexter, it's a cruise. Order more food." She lifted her arm to get the waiter's attention. When he came over, she told him what had happened, and he graciously took new orders from them. In return, she took a picture with him.

"I hope that's the last picture," Dexter said.

She glanced around the room, and seeing no faces turned in their direction, said, "I think it is."

Dexter sipped his wine. "Look, I don't mean to be a spoil-sport, but I wanted this evening to be about us, away from your 'adoring fans.'"

She reached across the table for his hand. "This cruise can

be whatever we want it to be, Dexter. We have reservations at Harry's tomorrow night, which will be much more private. And we have a large suite with a whirlpool tub and a huge balcony. We can have all the privacy we want right in the suite. We can even have our meals delivered there. But when we're out like this, we have to accommodate the fans. That's the business we've chosen. That's the business you've said you'd support me in. Are you changing your mind?"

He shook his head. "I'm behind you 110 percent, but I already have to share you with your mom and sisters, and now there are all these fans. I just don't want to get lost in all the people who flock around you."

Her heart softened a bit toward him. "That'll never happen," she said. "This business will never become more important than our marriage. I won't let that happen, and neither will you."

"How can you be so sure? Your career is about to take off, and I'm still looking for another faculty position."

"The folks at UA were wrong not to tenure you, Dexter," she said. "You'll get another position, a better position. I know you will. And if you don't, then it's time for you to focus full-time on your writing. We'll both be working in our dream careers."

"You make it sound so simple."

She reached across the table and squeezed his hand. "It is, if we allow it to be. We have to keep our heads on straight, though, and remember our priorities. We can't let little stuff like fans wanting autographs and pictures make us crazy, okay?"

He nodded.

She slipped her foot out of her shoe and rubbed it up his leg. "Now that we've settled that issue, why don't we head back to our wonderfully large suite and its wonderfully large king-sized bed? I think you need reminding that our marriage really does come first with me."

"What about the dinner order that you just placed?"

She lifted a brow. "What about it? This is a cruise. They can deliver it to the room. That is, unless you want to stay here and wait for it."

Dexter placed his napkin on the table and pushed back his chair. "I'm not a fool," he said, giving her a leer. "Let's get out of here."

Chapter 5

"Stop looking at your watch," Delilah told Alisha, who had recently joined her at the Lucky Sevens slot machines near the entrance of Czar's Palace Casino on the ship's promenade deck. "I warned you not to play those dollar slots."

Alisha sighed. "Don't rub it in. I've learned my lesson."

Delilah pulled the lever on her machine, hoping for Lucky Sevens. Not surprised when she didn't get them, she inclined her head toward the nearby Gloves Sports Bar, where Roxanne, looking gorgeous in a midthigh black sequined sheath, stood signing autographs for the small crowd of about twenty gathered around her. "You should follow your sister's lead," she told Alisha. "Mingle. Meet people. It'll only enhance Delilah's Daughters chances in the finals."

Alisha frowned. "You're kidding me, right?" She pointed to the Batman T-shirt and worn jeans she had on. "I came on this cruise to relax, not to spend time grinning nonstop at folks I don't know and who don't know me."

Delilah pulled the lever again and then scanned her daughter from head to toe. "I've been meaning to speak to you about that outfit. The T-shirt and jeans are bad enough, but do you really need to wear that silly Braves baseball cap?"

Alisha leaned in and kissed her mom on the check. "Face it, Momma. You have two daughters who are fashion plates, and then you have me."

"What am I going to do with you?" Delilah asked, shaking her head and pulling the lever.

"Love me," Alisha said with a big old monkey grin.

Delilah grunted and pulled the lever again. If she hadn't recognized Alisha's stubbornness as matching her own, she might have gotten angry with her. As it was, she accepted her daughter for who she was, quirks and all, as she did with Roxanne and Veronica. Though the girls were in a group together, they were still individuals. As she'd tried to make Charles Washington understand, their individuality was what made them so special as a group.

"Uh-oh," Alisha said, spinning around on her stool like a kid. "Roxanne the rock star is making her way over here. Seems her fans have all been satisfied."

Delilah looked in her oldest daughter's direction. "Hi, sweetheart," she said when Roxanne reached them. "I love that dress, and I love you in it."

Roxanne kissed her mother's cheek. "You would," she said. "You picked it out."

Delilah and her two daughters laughed. "What can I say?" she said. "I have excellent taste."

Roxanne pointed to Alisha. "Except when it comes to this one."

"Moi?" Alisa said, eyes wide with mock innocence. "I can't believe you're insulting me after I've waited all this time to get your autograph." She picked up the napkin under the cup next to the machine that Delilah was playing and handed it to Roxanne.

"Yeah, right," Roxanne said, pushing the napkin back in her sister's direction. "Maybe if you didn't dress like a homeless person, someone would ask for your autograph."

Delilah laughed. She enjoyed the playful banter between her daughters, always had. "Don't be too hard on your sister, Roxanne. She's in a bad mood because she's lost about a hundred dollars."

"You lost a hundred dollars?" Roxanne asked her sister. "Why didn't you stop before then?"

Delilah understood Roxanne's surprise. Neither she nor her girls were big gamblers. They typically played somewhere between $20 and $50 each time they visited a casino, which wasn't that often. So it was rare for one of them to lose $100.

Alisha rolled her eyes. "Because I felt *the win* in me."

Delilah and Roxanne laughed. "So much for that feeling," Delilah said. "You know better than to come to a casino thinking you're going to win anyway."

"Momma's right," Roxanne said, adding, "I've been around enough cruise ship casinos to know that your odds of winning are slim, even slimmer than if you were in Vegas. Heck, they're slimmer here than they are at Greenetrack back home."

"Don't talk badly about Greenetrack," Delilah said, defending the small casino about seventy-five miles from their home. "I have fun going there. The cost is no more than going to a concert and having dinner. If you throw in a Greenetrack dinner, it's cheaper."

"Well, I'm not going to debate you about casinos," Roxanne said. "How long are you two going to be at it?" she asked.

"I'm ready to go now," Alisha said, taking another spin on her stool, "but Fast Eddie here can't pull herself away from the machine."

Ignoring her youngest daughter, Delilah said, "I am getting sorta tired. Let me play out this fifty dollars. Then win or lose, I'll head in."

"I'm gonna hold you to that," Alisha said. She turned to Roxanne. "What are you doing for the rest of the evening?"

"I'm meeting a friend for dinner," Roxanne said, looking above Delilah's head.

"I'll bet you're meeting your secret lover," Alisha said, grinning. "Come on, you can tell us. After all, we're family."

Delilah wasn't sure Roxanne was meeting a secret lover, but she knew something was up. Why hadn't her oldest looked at her or Alisha when she'd answered the question? It wasn't like her girls to be secretive about their relationships. Alisha rarely dated, so there wasn't much room for secrets with her. Roxanne, on the other hand, dated frequently. Delilah didn't get to meet many of the guys, but she'd never known Roxanne to deliberately hide one from her. She hoped her oldest wasn't doing so now. A hidden man was the wrong man. That she knew for sure.

"Mind your business, Alisha," Roxanne said.

"I don't have any business to mind," Alisha said, spinning on her stool. "I don't have a secret lover, or a public one either for that matter."

"And whose fault is that?" Delilah said, pulling the lever again. "Sometimes you can be so childish."

"Me, childish?" Alisha asked, poking a finger in her chest and into Batman's eye. "I'm not the one hiding my boyfriend from the family like some shy, lovesick teenager."

Delilah took a break from the slot machine and turned to her youngest daughter. "I'm sure we'll meet Roxanne's guy when the time's right." She turned to Roxanne. "Isn't that right, Roxanne?"

"That's right, Momma."

"I hope it's during this century," Delilah added, just for fun.

Alisha burst out laughing. "Good one, Momma."

Roxanne slapped her sister on her shoulder. "Girl, you're too silly. Are you gonna stay here with Momma?"

Alisha nodded. "It's called hiding in plain sight. Nobody's approached me about an autograph since I've been sitting here. I may spend the rest of the cruise between here and our cabin."

"The autograph seekers aren't that bad," Roxanne said.

"You must like root canals too," Alisha muttered.

"Don't start, Alisha," Delilah said, heading off another argument between the girls. "Why don't you pull up a chair and join us, Roxanne? This really is relaxing. What time are you meeting your friend?"

Roxanne checked her watch. "I'm about fifteen minutes late now."

"You go on then and enjoy yourself," Delilah told her. "We'll see you later in the suite."

"Yeah," Alisha said, winking at her sister, "we'll see you

later in the suite. Why don't you bring your man by so we can meet him? We'll be up late."

Roxanne winked back. "I will as soon as you put on some makeup and a dress."

Delilah laughed. Then she pulled the lever again.

Chapter 6

$\mathcal{G}$uilt settled on Roxanne's shoulders as she made her way down the passageway on the Empress deck. By the time she reached Gavin Yarborough's suite, a heavy weight pressed down on her. She stood at the stateroom door, staring at the key card in her hand for several minutes, debating whether to enter. *What am I doing?* she asked herself. *Why am I seeing a married man?* With every fiber of her being, she knew it was wrong. What she and Gavin were doing went against all the values her parents had instilled in her. Her mother would die of disappointment if she knew. As Roxanne turned to leave, the door opened and she stood face to face with the blond, blue-eyed Gavin.

His eyes widened in surprise, and then he pulled her into the suite and into his arms. "I've missed you," he said.

Stepping out of his embrace, she said, "It hasn't been that long."

He laughed and extended his arms. "It has been for me. I'm a fool for love. I can't stand for you to be out of my sight."

She smirked. "What you are is dramatic."

He smiled. "But you love me anyway."

She met his eyes. He'd told her several times that he loved her, but she never took him seriously. How could she? He probably repeated the same words to his wife. She wondered if his wife believed him. "If you say so," she finally said. The droop in the corners of his lips told her she hadn't said the words he wanted to hear. When he sank down on the couch, she knew she'd hurt his feelings.

"Sometimes I hate that music you love so much," he said.

She understood. Sometimes she did too. She sat next to him, put her arms around his shoulders. "We wouldn't have met if not for the music."

He looked up, met her eyes. "I still remember the first time I caught your show. You mesmerized me with 'The Wind Beneath My Wings.' I could have sworn you were singing only to me, and I bet everyone else in the audience felt the same way."

Roxanne remembered that night three years ago well, coming so soon after her father's death. How often did the ship's captain make it to a show, much less invite a temporary entertainer out for a nightcap? "That was one of the best evenings of my life," she said, settling in next to him.

"Mine too," he said, kissing the top of her head. "I knew Dreamland had found something special, and I made sure they didn't let you get away."

Roxanne realized now how young and naive she'd been back then. And desperate for something that would lessen the pain of her father's death. She often wondered if her fondness for Gavin was more about what he had done for her career than about the man himself. She didn't like to ponder that question too long, though, because she didn't like what the answer revealed about her own character. Finding a steady singing gig had been hard to do back then. And out of nowhere Gavin made a call to someone at Dreamland headquarters, she was called in for a series of auditions, and voilà, she was hired as a salaried Dreamland entertainer. It was as though she'd been given a great gift without even having to ask for it. She couldn't help but develop warm feelings for Gavin as a result. He was handsome, funny, intelligent, and interested in her singing career. What more could a girl want? Unfortunately, it was only much later that she'd found out he was married.

"A penny for your thoughts," Gavin said.

She gratefully accepted his intrusion into her thinking space. "Nothing and everything. Tonight I need to decompress. The contest is taking its toll."

"Delilah's Daughters is going to win," he said, rubbing her shoulders. "I don't know why you're worried."

She pressed a kiss against his neck. She could always count on Gavin for support. He believed in her and her talent. "And you're biased."

He pulled her closer. "Maybe, but that doesn't mean I'm wrong. I've watched the show since you first made the cut, and I know what I see and hear. You and your sisters get better with each round."

"From your mouth to God's ears," she said. "I want this so badly," she admitted. "I don't know when it went from being a tribute to my father and a way to make my mother happy to being something that means so much to me, even more than it means to my sisters. Alisha's real interest is in songwriting, while Veronica just wants to be in the spotlight. For me, it's all about performing the music. It's in my blood the way it was in my dad's blood."

He tipped her face up to his. "Then I'm not sure it's ever been a lark to you," he said. "Maybe it just took you a while to admit how much you wanted to win."

She nodded into his chest. "Or how disappointed I'll be if we don't. How can I go back to my life as it is when I've spent the last couple of months hoping for a major change?"

"I hope you don't want to change everything," he said.

She turned her head up so she could see his face. "No, not everything," she said, but she knew deep in her heart that Dreamland and Gavin would both become part of her past if Delilah's Daughters won the contest.

Chapter 7

*T*hree weeks later, Veronica Monroe Timmons stood with her two sisters on the stage in the NBS television studio in Atlanta waiting for the winner of *Sing for America* to be announced.

"And the moment we've all been waiting for is now upon us," Morris Williams, the show's announcer, said.

Veronica's stomach roiled with anxiety. She wanted so badly to win, for herself, her sisters, her mom, and her husband. Even though he'd never admit it, Dexter needed this win as much as she did. Every day he grew more and more discouraged by his inability to find a suitable faculty position. If Delilah's Daughters won the contest, he could focus his energies on writing the commercial best-seller she knew was in him. This win would be the fresh start they both needed for their careers and their marriage.

"The second runner-up in *Sing for America* is Blue Heart."

Veronica breathed a sigh of relief when Delilah's Daughters wasn't called. Roxanne, who stood next to her, squeezed her hand. She squeezed back. She and her sisters thought Blue Heart was much stronger competition than Annie Jones, who was left standing with them. Their odds of winning had improved considerably.

The second runner-up group left the stage to loud applause.

"The first runner-up is—"

Veronica hated this part. The good news was that, when announced, the winner would step forward and the curtain would go down to hide the first runners-up from the audience. That way, the losers could mourn in private. She felt a bit sorry for Annie. The woman had been nothing but kind to them.

"Delilah's Daughters," the announcer said. "That means the winner of *Sing for America* is Annie Jones!"

Veronica's emotions exploded in a loud "What?" as the curtain came down and shuttered them from the audience. She couldn't believe that Annie Jones had won over them. There had to be some mistake.

Roxanne covered her sister's mouth with her hand to prevent another outburst. "Calm down, Veronica," she said, "before you make a fool of yourself and us in front of a nationwide television audience."

Veronica kept her mouth closed as she stomped back to their dressing room. "We were robbed," she said, pacing around the dressing room after they had closed the door. "I can't believe that no-talent Annie Jones won. How in God's name could they pick her over us?"

"It's not the end of the world, Veronica," Alisha said. "Being in the contest did us a lot of good."

"Don't start with me, Alisha," Veronica warned, her ire ignited more by Alisha's nonreaction to their loss. "You know as well as I do that we should have won this contest. How can you be so calm about it? This was our chance. We should have won."

" 'Should have' doesn't really mean much right now," Roxanne said. "What are you going to do? Write a letter of protest to the fans and judges? I doubt it. Alisha's right. This contest has been a big boost for us. We can build on it."

Veronica stomped around the room. "I don't want to build on it. I want that guaranteed recording contract. We worked hard. We deserve it."

"Look," Alisha said, again speaking too calmly given the injustice the group had been handed. "This contest opened my eyes. I don't want to be a jingle-writer. I want to write songs and have them performed, so I've decided that's exactly what I'm going to do. I'm giving notice at my job next week. I'm going to devote myself full-time to my music."

Veronica folded her arms across her chest. "You can't be serious. You're not going to quit your job after we *lost* the contest. You quit when you *win*."

Alisha shook her head. "You quit when the time is right for you to move in a new direction. The time is right for me. I'm going to make a move of faith. I've saved a bit of money, so I haven't totally lost my mind."

Veronica looked at Roxanne. "You'd better speak some sense to your sister. I think losing the contest has made her delirious. I initially mistook her reaction for disinterest, but I see now it's not."

Roxanne shrugged. "If anyone's delirious, it's you. It

sounds like Alisha's thought this through. If it's what she wants, I want it for her."

Veronica's eyes widened. "Are you quitting your job too?"

Roxanne shook her head. "No, but I'm going to figure out how to leverage the exposure we've gotten by being on this show to elevate my career. I don't want to be a shipboard entertainer for the rest of my life. That's for sure."

Veronica dropped down in a chair. "You two have certainly surprised me. You're taking our loss well. Much better than I am."

"Well, you've behaved true to form," Roxanne said. "If we all went off the way you do, we'd never get far in this business."

Alisha laughed. "Tell it, sister."

"We're down, but we're not out," Roxanne said to Veronica. "And you'd better pep up before Momma gets here. She's going to be disappointed enough as it is, and I don't want you adding to it. Be mature for once."

Veronica opened her mouth to take exception to that when the door opened and their mother entered.

"Well, girls," Delilah said, taking a moment to meet each of their eyes. "We didn't get the big prize tonight, but we did get a prize."

Veronica stood, wondering what Kool-Aid her mother and sisters had been drinking. How could there be this much cheer after such a wretched loss? "What are you talking about, Momma? I didn't hear about any prize going to the first runner-up."

Delilah sat on the couch next to Alisha. "There are a lot of benefits to being on a show like this, Veronica. And at the top of the list is the exposure. A lot of folks got to see you and hear you over the last ten weeks, and you made a strong impression."

Veronica knew good news was coming, but she might be dead before her mother got around to it. "Come on, Momma, tell us the news already."

"All right," Delilah said, grinning from ear to ear. "Delilah's Daughters has been offered a contract by Magic City Records here in Birmingham."

"That's it?" Veronica said, her hopes dashed. Tommy Johns, the owner and founder of Magic City, was a family friend. "That's your good news? No offense to Mr. Tommy, but Magic City isn't even close to being a major player. Signing with them would be starting at the bottom. It'll take us forever to attain any kind of success if we go with them."

"Veronica—" Roxanne warned.

"It's all right, Roxanne," Delilah said. "Your sister has a right to her opinions. She just happens to be wrong in this instance."

"How am I wrong, Momma? Did Magic City become a player overnight?"

Delilah smiled at her the way she had smiled at her when she was a kid asking a silly question. "You underestimate what Tommy has done at Magic City, Veronica. If you hadn't, you'd be more than pleased with this offer. Delilah's Daughters is going to be Magic City's main priority. Tommy thinks you are the perfect act to broaden Magic City's reach into the growing gospel-pop arena. He has that kind of faith in you, and he's willing to put his money on the line to show it. He wants to build a new label around you and your brand of gospel-pop. The upfront money is only half of what you would have gotten had you won, but the contract terms are much better. Delilah's Daughters actually gets a percentage of the new label's profits for the next ten years. That's how much Tommy believes in you."

"That's unheard of," Roxanne said.

"What about my songs?" Alisha said. "What will happen with them?"

What a dumb question, Veronica thought. A dog could get a contract writing music for Magic City. Sure, several artists had gotten their start with them, but they had wisely moved on to bigger, more influential labels as soon as they could.

Delilah smiled at Alisha when she answered her question. "Not only will you have the opportunity to write for Delilah's Daughters, but your songs will also be considered for other artists at the new label. Tommy wants to leverage all your talents." She scanned her daughters' faces. "Girls, this is a great deal. It's a blessing from God. I don't see how we can turn it down."

Alisha's nod said she agreed. *Well, she would agree,* Veronica thought. *She got what she wanted, an opportunity to write songs. That's all she cares about.*

"I can think of a reason to turn it down," Veronica said, hoping to bring some reason into the conversation. "The deal looks good, but 10 percent of nothing is still nothing. Magic City is not a major player in this business. We'll probably do more for them than they'll do for us."

"I like the deal," Roxanne said. "What are we going to do if we don't take it? It's not like we have other offers raining down on us. Besides, we know Mr. Tommy, and I believe he'd do right by us."

"Of course, he would—" Delilah began.

"There's at least one other offer."

Veronica turned at the sound of her husband's voice. She hadn't heard him enter the dressing room. "What are you talking about, Dexter?" she asked.

Her husband turned to her mother. "Why don't you tell them about the other offer, Mom?"

Chapter 8

*D*elilah met Dexter's gaze. The smug look on his face reminded her why she didn't like him. It also told her he knew about the second offer. No doubt Charles Washington had tracked him down and given him the contract pitch for Veronica.

"What are you talking about, Dexter?" Veronica again asked her husband.

He inclined his head toward Delilah. "Ask your mother."

Delilah's dislike of Dexter grew. She'd always known that one day he'd sow discord in her family. Today was that day, it seemed. She took a deep breath. "Dexter is talking about an offer from Legends Productions in Atlanta."

"Legends Productions!" Veronica exclaimed. "Momma, they're one of the top recording studios in the country. They offered us a contract?"

Delilah glared at Dexter. "Not exactly."

"And you turned it down?" Veronica completed.

"Did I get to write?" Alisha asked.

"Okay, let's all calm down," Delilah said to her daughters, ignoring Dexter. "The offer was not as good as you might think. This offer wasn't for Delilah's Daughters. It was for one of you as a solo act."

"Which one?" Alisha asked.

"Isn't it obvious?" Roxanne said, glancing from Dexter to Veronica.

"Me?" Veronica said, pointing to herself. "Legends Productions offered me a contract?"

Delilah nodded.

"And you didn't tell me?"

"I didn't see any need," Delilah explained. "You're a group, not three solo acts. That deal is not for us."

"It may not be for Delilah's Daughters," Dexter interjected, "but it might be the very opportunity Veronica needs. I've always thought she'd be stronger as a solo act. It seems I'm not the only one thinking along those lines."

His selfishness gave Delilah heartburn, while the expressions on her daughters' faces broke her heart. "This doesn't concern you, Dexter," she said. "This is about my daughters, the group."

"It does concern him, Momma," Veronica said. "It concerns him because it concerns me. It concerns our future. You should have told me. You should have let me decide what I want to do."

"You'd leave the group?" Roxanne asked.

"Admit it, Roxanne," Dexter said, before Veronica could speak. "You'd leave too if you had an offer from Legends. You're lying if you say you wouldn't."

"That's enough, Dexter," Veronica said. "Why don't you leave us alone for a few minutes? We need to talk."

"But—"

She shook her head. "No buts. I can take care of this."

Dexter scowled, making it clear he didn't like being told to leave. "Okay, but don't make any decisions before we talk. This is our future."

Veronica nodded.

When he was out of the room, Delilah said, "You can't be thinking about leaving the group. I told you about the offer from Magic City. It's a better offer."

"Better for whom?" Veronica asked.

"Better for the group," Roxanne said. "We're a group, remember?"

"What I remember is that we're a group who just lost a contest," Veronica said. "What I remember is that we're a group that's been offered a contract by a third-tier recording studio. That's what I remember."

"You three girls have always been Delilah's Daughters," Delilah said, hoping a history lesson would help clarify their present situation. "That's who you are. That's who your father made you."

"It's not fair to bring Daddy into this, Momma," Veronica said.

"Can't help it," Delilah shot back. "Your father is right here in the midst of us. Are you telling him you don't want the dream he had for you?"

"I don't know what I want," Veronica said, "but I know I should have been given a choice. You shouldn't have turned down the deal without talking to me."

"I did what was best for the group, and I don't apologize for it. I won't."

Roxanne went and sat next to her mother. "I know you had the best of intentions, Momma, but you should have told us about the second offer, all of us. It's in my best interest for us to stay together as a group, but Veronica should have the opportunity to think about what's best for her."

Delilah looked at her youngest daughter. "Do you agree, Alisha?"

"I agree that you should have told us and let us figure out the right answer together."

Times like this Delilah wished Rocky were still alive. She was sure he could make the girls understand her decision and be thankful for it. "Well, I'm sorry if I let you all down. I didn't want to make you decide, so I took on that burden myself. How can one sister leave the others high and dry? How can two sisters hold back a third? I didn't want you to have to make those choices. I did what was best for the family, not for any one of you." She turned to Veronica. "And that's what you should do, Veronica. Think about the family, not just yourself."

"I hear you, Momma, but my family is bigger than you three. It also includes Dexter, and he has a say."

Delilah brushed off those words. "Dexter doesn't have the family history that you do. He doesn't appreciate what we have, what we've built together. You girls are your father's legacy. You can't put a price tag on that."

"I'm not trying to put a price tag on it, Momma," Veronica said. "I only want my shot. Let's be honest. I don't sing as well as Roxanne, and I can't write music like Alisha. If Legends thinks they can make me a star despite that, I have to think about it. This is a once-in-a-lifetime opportunity."

"The easy way is not always the best way, Veronica," Delilah warned, not liking the direction of her middle daughter's thoughts.

"I know that, but neither should I walk past an open door without at least looking in."

"You've decided then?" Roxanne asked, her question tinged with a disappointment that Delilah shared. "You're going to go with Legends?"

Veronica shook her head. "The only thing I've decided is that I want to talk to them, see what they have to offer. I owe it to myself to do that." She looked at her sisters. "You understand, don't you? You have to understand."

"You have to investigate it, Veronica," Alisha said.

"Alisha's right," Roxanne added, with a little enthusiasm in her voice this time. "You have to."

Delilah didn't agree, and she couldn't pretend she did. The stakes were too high. Veronica didn't know it, but her decision could cause a fracture in their family that might never heal. "And after you do all your investigation," she told Veronica, "you're going to have to make the biggest decision of your life. I hope you're up for it."

Veronica met her mother's eyes. "I hope I am too."

Chapter 9

"Your mother was so wrong for what she did," Dexter said for the tenth time. He'd been yapping nonstop about how her mother had betrayed her since they left the studio.

"Stop talking, Dexter," Veronica said. "My mother loves me. She did what she thought was best for the family. I'll never believe anything else." Of course, she'd been angered by her mom's secrecy, and she still was, but she didn't believe her mom was trying to cheat her out of anything. She'd never believe that. She could see how Dexter believed it, though, since he hadn't had the stable family life she'd had. After his mother's death from drug abuse when he was twelve, he'd been shuffled around to live with various family members. Because of his discipline problems, he'd never stayed with any relative for an extended period of time.

"Well, you must not be an equal member of the family because I don't see how what she did helped you at all."

"She made a mistake, Dexter. We all make them, even you. But her heart was in the right place."

"Doesn't that Bible your mom's always quoting say something about knowing the heart by the actions? Well, I think that applies here."

When Dexter turned their Buick Lucerne onto the street of the Inman Park rental house they'd occupied since the contest began, she immediately saw the black Hummer parked in their drive. "Who can that be?" she asked.

"It must be Charles Washington, the A&R rep from Legends," Dexter said, pulling up next to the Hummer. "I told him to meet us here."

Veronica turned to him. "You've got to be kidding. You invited him here and didn't bother to tell me?"

"I'm only looking out for you, babe," he said, unbuckling his seat belt. "I believe in you, and so does Mr. Washington. Now put on the shine and confirm for this guy that you have the talent, charm, and professional training needed to make it as a Legends artist."

Veronica so wanted to slap Dexter upside his head. Had her whole family gone mad? Didn't anybody think she deserved to be consulted about anything, especially those things that impacted her life and career? Dexter was no better than her mother in that respect. Tamping down her anger, Veronica slipped off her seat belt. Before she could open the door, Charles Washington pulled it open for her. She took his offered hand and got out, a firm smile on her face. "Thank you, Mr. Washington," she said.

The man shook his head. "No, thank you for agreeing to meet with me tonight. I know it's been an emotional evening for you."

"No problem," Dexter said. "We're happy you were able to

find me and let us know about your interest in Veronica. Her mother didn't think it was information worth passing along."

Veronica shot a *shut up* glare Dexter's way. She would not allow him to malign her mother in front of this stranger, recording contract or no recording contract.

"Mrs. Monroe is a fine woman," Washington said to Dexter. "I'm sure she had a reason for her decision. She's very protective of her daughters." Then he turned to Veronica. "Any loving mother would be. In this case, I think she made a decision with a mother's heart that deserved a manager's head."

Veronica gave Washington a sincere smile this time. "That's exactly what I think happened," she said. "Momma always has our best interests at heart, but like you said, sometimes the head needs to overrule the heart."

"Let's finish this inside," Dexter said, heading toward the front door.

Washington took Veronica's arm. "I'm honored to meet you," he said. "I've had my eye on you since the contest started. Delilah's Daughters is a wonderful and talented group. I wish I could have taken you all on, but Legends only goes after stars. And you, dear lady, are a star."

While a part of Veronica knew Charles Washington was giving her the hard-sell, she still felt herself being sucked in by his words. "Thank you," she said. "But I'm not a star yet."

"That's where we come in," he said. "You have star quality. We'll showcase that quality so that everyone else will see it. Give us a year, eighteen months, and you'll be a household name."

By the time they were seated in her living room and Washington had laid out his plans for her, Veronica was a believer.

She was fully convinced that Legends could make her a star, first in the music world and then later in movies. Washington had laid out a full program.

"So what do you think?" he asked.

"We like what we hear," Dexter said. "We like it a lot, don't we, Veronica?"

Veronica could only nod. "It's more than I ever dreamed," she said. "More than I could have asked or thought. It's like a miracle."

Washington shook his head. "You're the miracle," he said. "We're lucky to have found you. It was only a matter of time before someone discovered the jewel that you are."

The ongoing barrage of compliments began to make Veronica uneasy. She didn't know what to say, so she said nothing. Thankfully, Dexter wasn't at a loss for words. "So when would all this begin?"

Washington opened his briefcase and pulled out a contract. "We need you here in Atlanta within a month after signing this contract, sooner if possible."

"We have to move here permanently?" Veronica asked.

"There is a cost to being a star, Veronica," he told her. "We can do everything for you that I've outlined here tonight, but it's going to take a 150 percent effort from you. Once you sign this contract, you no longer have a job; you have a career. So forget about nine-to-five, forget about vacations. Until your first album drops, your life will consist of nothing but work."

Veronica frowned.

Washington laughed. "You'll have leisure time," he said, "but even that will be planned for maximum benefit. You'll play, but you'll play with the right people in the right places and at the right times. You're going to have to put yourself in our hands completely."

Her thoughts immediately turned to Dexter and the concerns he'd expressed about time together when they were on the cruise. "What do you think about all of that?" she asked him. "It doesn't sound like we'll have a lot of time together."

Before Dexter could answer, Washington said, "Dexter has a look we like too. We want to weave him into our promotions for you. You're a writer, aren't you, Dexter?"

Dexter nodded, though a bit slowly. She read the question in his eyes.

"Well, how about you charting the rise of Veronica Y in a book that will drop around the same time as the album?"

"Veronica Y?" Veronica echoed.

Dexter's eyes lit up, question erased. "Are you serious?"

"We don't say things we don't mean at Legends, Dexter. We've thought this through completely. With our guidance, Veronica will become the face of Generation Y. Before we're done, she'll own social media *and* the top of the music charts. And you'll be right there with her as a *New York Times* best-selling author."

Veronica could feel Dexter's enthusiasm for Washington's plans, while she had to resist the urge to pinch herself. Could this miracle really be happening to them? "What about my sisters?" she asked, addressing the missing component that would make her dream complete. "Isn't there something you can do for them?"

Washington shook his head. "I'm sorry, but we only take on one or two artists a year so we can give them the attention they need. We don't have the resources for your sisters."

Veronica wasn't convinced that a big production company like Legends couldn't find room for two more artists, but she let it drop for now. She didn't want to be too demanding before she'd even cut her first album. She'd take care of her sisters after Legends took care of her. "I'd like to submit a couple of my sister Alisha's songs for my album."

Washington's lips curled a bit. "I know you love your family, Veronica, but this deal is about you, not your sisters. We have a stable of well-known, award-winning songwriters and producers on our staff who will be dedicated to your album. We don't need or want another songwriter."

"She understands, Mr. Washington," Dexter said, "but old habits are hard to break."

Washington met Veronica's eyes. "Sometimes you have to break free completely of the past in order to build a bright future. That's where you are, Veronica."

Veronica didn't like what she was hearing now. The more Washington talked, the more she felt as though she were deserting her sisters. Well, she wouldn't desert her mother. "I want my mother to look over the contracts."

"That's fine with us," Washington said, "but I'll also leave you the cards of a couple of the top entertainment lawyers in the business. You need experienced people looking out for you."

Before Veronica could respond, Washington dropped several business cards on the coffee table and stood. She and Dexter followed suit. "I hope to have you on the Legends team soon," he said to her. "We can work miracles together."

"Thank you," Veronica said. "We have a lot to think about."

"But I think you know what our answer will be," she overheard Dexter add as he escorted Washington to the door. She dropped back down on the couch. Her mother had been right about one thing: this would be one of the most difficult decisions she ever made.

Chapter 10

*A*lisha tugged at the hem of her sleep shirt as she studied the laptop screen in front of her. "This is exactly what I need," she murmured.

"I should have known you'd still be up."

Alisha looked up to see Roxanne standing next to her. "I didn't wake you, did I?" she asked.

Roxanne pulled her pink robe close around her torso. "Please," she said. "I couldn't sleep either."

Alisha closed the laptop cover and moved over to make room for her sister on the couch. "I know what you mean. It's been that kind of day."

Roxanne sat on the couch and folded her legs under her body. "You didn't say much tonight."

Alisha shrugged. "Too much had happened. I was on overload."

"I know what you mean."

Alisha looked up at her sister. "You didn't seem to need a

lot of processing time. You seemed pretty sure about what you thought Veronica should do."

Roxanne rolled her eyes. "Well, yeah, it's a clear case of Veronica choosing either to go for herself or stick with the group. The group comes first; it always has."

Alisha smiled. "Now you're sounding like Daddy," she said, recalling her father's oft-spoken words to his daughters. "He drilled that into us from day one."

"I can't believe he's been gone three years. I miss him," Roxanne said. "Every day."

"Me too," Alisha said. "The first Gospelfest after his death was the most difficult day of my life, after his funeral. It didn't seem right to be up there singing without him."

"Believe it or not, Gospelfest wasn't hard for me. I can't explain it, but I feel him closest each year at Gospelfest." Roxanne shrugged. "It's like he's there with us."

Alisha nodded. "He's always with us in spirit."

"I know that," Roxanne explained, "but Gospelfest is different. It's like he's actually there."

Alisha smiled. "You were always his favorite, so maybe he is there for you."

"Daddy didn't have favorites."

Alisha lifted a brow. "I loved Daddy, and I knew he loved me, but you were his favorite." When Roxanne would have interrupted, Alisha added, "It's okay. I figured it was because you were the oldest child. And because you could hold your own when you sang with him."

Roxanne laughed. "Do you remember those duets he and I used to do?"

Alisha joined in the laughter. "How can I forget? You two were a mess. You and Daddy would go at it every time you sang together. Why did everything have to be a competition between you two?"

"We weren't really competing with each other," Roxanne said. "It's more that we were challenging each other, forcing each other to dig deep for the heart and soul of each lyric. Daddy understood how I feel about music and singing because he felt the same way."

"And Momma understood me and my need to compose. I guess that's why you being Daddy's favorite didn't bother me—I always felt I was Momma's favorite. At least, I always felt that she understood me best."

Alisha was quiet as she thought about the family dynamics of the Monroe clan. As the oldest, Roxanne had been Daddy's girl, and as the youngest, she had been Momma's baby. Where had that left Veronica? She was surprised she had never considered that question before. "I wonder how Veronica saw things."

Roxanne turned up her nose. "Please. She always thought she was the favorite of both of them. Veronica has a pretty big ego. I'm sure you've noticed."

Alisha laughed but quickly sobered. "Maybe that's why Legends chose her. She's special. Always has been."

Roxanne poked her on the shoulder. "Yes, Veronica's special, but so are you. And so am I."

Alisha knew Roxanne was channeling their father again. The unique specialness of each of them had been his mantra. Delilah's Daughters was great because of the individual talents and strengths they brought. No one of them was any better than the other two. Their greatness was as a group. "You think Daddy was right about the group coming first?"

"Don't you?"

"I don't know," Alisha said. "This situation with Veronica is making me rethink a lot of things."

"What do you mean?"

Alisha shrugged. "What's wrong with each of us developing our individual talents?"

"There's nothing wrong with it, but we develop individually to build the group, not to tear it apart. I hope Veronica doesn't forget that."

Alisha wasn't so sure. Maybe there was more to be mined from their individual talents than what was required for the group.

After a few minutes of silence, Roxanne pushed at Alisha with her foot. "What's going on in that big head of yours?"

Alisha flipped open her laptop. When the browser appeared, she turned the screen to Roxanne. "Take a look."

Roxanne leaned closer. "What am I looking at?"

"It's the conference schedule for the 'I Create Music ASCAP Expo.' This is *the* conference for songwriters, composers, and producers." Alisha directed the laptop's pointer to the Panelists button and clicked. "Look who's going to be there."

"I don't know many of these names," Roxanne said, skimming the page.

"That's because everybody always focuses on the artists who sing the songs. Nobody cares about the behind-the-scenes work of the songwriters, composers, and producers.

Well, not unless those songwriters, composers, and producers are household names like Sean Combs or Simon Cowell or Smokey Robinson. Believe me, if I listed the songs these panelists helped create, you'd know who they are."

Roxanne looked at her, a little too closely. "You certainly sound excited about this conference."

"I am," Alisha said. "It's being held in Los Angeles in a couple of weeks. I had planned to go this year, and then I put the idea aside because of the way we advanced in the contest."

"And now that we didn't win, you're going to go?"

Alisha hadn't fully decided until now. She knew going to this conference was more than merely attending a conference. It was her first step in working toward her own dream rather than the group's dream. "Yes, I'm going to go."

Roxanne caught her sister's eye. "So you think Veronica is going to take the Legends deal?"

Alisha let out a short sigh. "I really don't know what she's going to do, but I know I have to have a fallback position. I can't go back to my job, Roxanne, not after all we've experienced with this contest. I know singing for Dreamland isn't your ultimate goal, but at least you're doing what you love every day. Veronica is in school studying dance, doing what she loves. And I'm writing jingles. Well, I don't want to write jingles anymore. I've figured out what I want to be when I grow up, and I want to get started on that path. I'd love for that to be with Delilah's Daughters and Magic City, but if it's not, I have to have a backup plan. You understand, don't you?"

Roxanne nodded. "Of course I understand, but don't give

up on Veronica yet. She may surprise all of us. I'm praying she will."

Alisha didn't respond. She believed in prayer as much as her sister did, but she couldn't pin her future on somebody else's decision, even if that somebody else was her sister. She had to forge her own path.

Chapter 11

Veronica stabbed into the waffle that came with her Midnight Train, a menu favorite at Gladys and Ron's Chicken and Waffles Restaurant in midtown Atlanta. "Enough already, Dexter," she said to her husband, who was sitting across the table from her. He'd yammered at her all night about the decision they needed to make. Then he'd started up again as soon as she'd awakened this morning. "You've made your point. Now eat your food before it gets cold."

He lifted a brow. "You mean before your mother gets here, don't you?"

Well, he had her there. "I need to talk to Momma, and your being here is not going to make it any easier."

Dexter shook his head. "Just remember that she does not have your best interests at heart. If she had her way, you wouldn't even know about the Legends offer. Just remember that."

"I know what Momma did, Dexter, and I know why she did it. In her own way, she was doing what was best for me."

Veronica willed herself to believe her words and forgive her mother, but it was hard when she considered everything Legends was offering her. And Dexter's constant harping wasn't helping. "She's my mother."

Dexter picked up a chicken wing from his plate. Before he put it in his mouth, he said, "I think I should stay here for your talk with Delilah. I'm afraid she's going to guilt you into doing what's best for her and your sisters rather than what's best for us."

Veronica shook her head as her husband chewed. "I want to do what's best for all of us: you, me, Momma, and my sisters."

Dexter wiped his mouth with his napkin. "That's not going to happen, Veronica. This is one time when you'll have to make a choice. You either do what's best for the two of us as a family or you do what's best for your mom and sisters." He reached across the table and put a hand on top of one of hers. "Think what this could mean to us. This deal could launch your recording career and my writing career. It's a double blessing."

Veronica considered her husband's words as the strains of R&B flowed from the restaurant's sound system. *If only we had won that contest,* she thought, *then I wouldn't be faced with this choice.*

"Uh-oh," Dexter said, pulling his hand away. "Your mother is coming our way." He met his wife's eyes. "I can stay."

She shook her head. "I need to do this alone. Trust me."

Standing, he said, "It's not you I don't trust." When Delilah reached the table, he leaned in and brushed her cheek with what Veronica knew was an empty kiss. She didn't know why the two of them chose to fake caring about each other. Everybody knew they didn't like each other. "Good morning, Mom," Dexter said, his fake smile firmly in place.

"Yours must have been better than mine," Delilah said, not joining in the standard pretense. "I've been worrying about the future of my family all night and all morning."

Across Delilah's head, Dexter shot a knowing glance at Veronica. Ignoring him, she said, "Sit down, Momma. You'll feel better after you get something to eat."

"That's right," Dexter said. "Take my seat. I'm leaving you two alone so Veronica can tell you her decision. I hope you hear her out with an open mind."

Delilah slid into the booth across from Veronica. "I think we all need an open mind," she said, looking into her daughter's eyes.

Dexter leaned over and kissed Veronica on the cheek. "I'll see you later at the house. Don't be too long. We have an appointment this afternoon with the attorney."

Delilah glanced after Dexter as he left the table before turning to her daughter. "You have an appointment with an attorney? It's too much to hope it's about a divorce, I suppose."

Veronica couldn't help but chuckle. "Momma, you're a mess. You know that, don't you?"

Delilah waved off her comment with the rose-colored napkin, and then she placed it in her lap. "I'm just talking. I don't want you to get a divorce. You know better than that. What I want is for you to have a happy and fulfilling life."

"I know you do."

"And that's why I didn't tell you about the Legends offer. No good can come of it, Veronica. The price is too high."

"What if I don't think it's too high?"

Her mother's eyes widened. "You only say that because you have stars in your eyes. You see yourself as the next Whitney, the next Beyoncé. But at what cost?"

Veronica pushed her plate away and folded her elbows on the table. It was now-or-never time. "I've seen the contract, Momma. Mr. Washington came over to the house last night. He explained everything to me and Dexter." She reached for her mother's hand. "It's a great deal, Momma, and you'd be the first one to say so if it were a contract for Delilah's Daughters and not one just for me."

Delilah squeezed her fingers. "I could understand your taking this offer if there wasn't another one for the group on the table, but this I don't understand. How can you betray your sisters, your father, this way?"

Veronica pulled her hands away. "I'm not betraying anybody, Momma. I'm being true to myself. This deal could be a life-changer for me and Dexter. Do you know they want him to write a fictionalized account of my rise to stardom?"

Delilah turned up her nose. "I should have known there was something in it for him," she said. "What's in it for your sisters, the women who have struggled with you this far? What's in it for them?"

"Nothing now," Veronica said, "but once I make it big, I can help them. I promise I will."

Delilah looked at her with disappointment. "I wonder if that's what Malcolm Knowles and Beyoncé told Kelly Rowland and that other one from Destiny's Child. You can see how well that worked out."

"This is different. Alisha and Roxanne are my sisters. I'll always look out for them."

Delilah lifted a brow. "The way you're looking out for them now? I'd like to see you explain that to them."

Veronica leaned forward. "You can make them understand, Momma. I need your help."

Delilah shook her head. "Not this time. This is your decision. If you're big enough to make it, then you're big enough to defend it to your sisters."

Veronica sank back in her chair. "It's not like they have nothing. They still have the contract with Magic City."

Delilah leaned forward, across the table. "Don't play dumb with me, Veronica. That deal was for Delilah's Daughters, all three of you, not two of you. It's going to vanish as soon as I tell Tommy you're out. He's a family friend, but he's also a businessman."

"You don't know that," Veronica said, though deep in her heart she knew her mother was right.

Delilah looked at her, and Veronica felt her compassion. "I didn't want you to have to make this decision, Veronica. I tried to keep it from you. I know you and your sisters think I was wrong. I don't know. Maybe I was. Maybe this really is your moment and your decision. This is your time to figure out what you want your life to be, what God wants your life to be."

"I didn't ask for this opportunity, Momma. It was given to me. God gave it to me. How can I turn it down?"

"You have two opportunities, Veronica. What God has given you is a choice. It's up to you to decide which road is the right road."

Chapter 12

"You're still the best cook in Alabama," Tommy Johns told Delilah as he put the last of the dishes in the dishwasher of his recently remodeled kitchen." He turned around to face her. "And the most attractive."

Delilah leaned up on her toes and pressed a soft kiss against his cheek. "You're biased."

Tommy pulled her closer. "Marry me, Delilah. We've waited long enough. It's our time now."

Delilah let herself enjoy the strength of Tommy's arms around her. He'd been her friend for a very long time, since before she met Rocky. In fact, she had met Rocky through Tommy. And then she'd married Rocky, and Tommy had been forced to keep his feelings for her hidden. He'd been her rock after Rocky's death. Over time, their feelings of friendship had deepened. Now here they were at fifty and very much in love, but now wasn't the time to think about marriage. She eased out of his arms and looked up into his eyes.

"You know I can't. Not right now, Tommy. There's too much going on with the girls."

"We're not getting any younger, Delilah," he said, putting his arms around her shoulders and guiding her to the living room. When they were seated next to each other on the upholstered sofa, he continued. "How long are we supposed to wait? Your daughters will always be your daughters, and they'll always have something going on in their lives. There'll never be a perfect time. We have to pick a time that's good for us and go with it."

Delilah leaned her head on his shoulder. "I'd agree with you at any other time, but what's going on with Delilah's Daughters right now is different. Veronica is about to make a decision that will split the family."

"So you think she's going to take the Legends offer?"

Delilah nodded. "She hasn't said so directly, but that's where her heart is. I'm praying she changes her mind, but I have a feeling it's a desperate prayer. She wants what Legends is telling her they can give her."

"Can you blame her? She's young. At twenty-six, fame and fortune are very enticing."

"At twenty-six, she has to know that nothing comes without a cost," Delilah countered. "She hasn't considered the cost. If she goes with Legends, she'll regret it down the line. I know she will. She can get to where she wants to be by taking your generous Magic City offer."

Tommy picked up her hand and kissed her fingers. "There's a big difference between Magic City and Legends. From a purely business perspective, going with Legends is the best option for Veronica, and that's coming from the owner of

Magic City. The companies operate on different levels, Delilah. You know that. I consider it a success when a Magic City artist is picked up by a major label like Legends. They can do more for Veronica's career than I ever could at Magic City. That's the truth of the matter."

"But what about her sisters? What happens to them while Veronica is off becoming a star? Your contract offer was for the group. I don't expect you to try to launch Delilah's Daughters in competition with Legends' launching of Veronica."

Tommy nodded his head in agreement. "That wouldn't be fair to Alisha and Roxanne. We'd either be in a race to get them out first or we'd be trying to find a place for them after Veronica's splash. We'd lose in either case because of Magic City's limited resources. All is not lost, though. We'll find a way to work out something at Magic City. I care about the girls too, Delilah. I won't leave them hanging."

Delilah appreciated that Tommy was willing to take Roxanne and Alisha on, but there was little value in that if he didn't have a plan to launch them as a duo. The only plan he had now was for the entire group. "If Veronica would just think this thing through to its final end, we wouldn't have this problem. Why can't she see the damage she's about to do?"

Tommy pressed a kiss against her head. "She's a grown woman, Delilah. You have to let her make her mistakes. It's called life. You have to let her live it. On her terms."

A part of Delilah knew Tommy was right, but another part of her was convinced that the cost of a mistake in this instance would be too high. "I could go along with it better if Veronica's decision only affected her, but it doesn't. She's making a decision that also affects her sisters. Why can't she think of them as well as herself? If Rocky were here, he could help her make the right choice. She's not listening to me."

"She's listening, Delilah, but she doesn't agree. Your girls are no longer children. They're women with their individual goals and interests. Veronica has sisters, but she also has a husband. Her decisions have to take into account Dexter and their plans for the future."

Delilah sat up next to him. "You sound like Veronica. She said practically the same thing to me."

He rubbed her neck with his hand. "You need to listen to her."

"This is not what Rocky wanted for them."

Tommy dropped his hand from her neck. "Is this about the girls, or is this about Rocky?"

From his tone, Delilah knew what he believed the answer to be. How could she explain it in a way that he would understand? "Yes, it's about Rocky, because Delilah's Daughters was his creation. It was his dream to see the girls blossom together as a group. I bought into that dream, and so did the girls."

"And you want to see his dream come to fruition?"

She nodded.

He rested a palm against her cheek and looked into her eyes. "Rocky forgave you, Delilah. You no longer have to do penance. He's not looking down from heaven, waiting for you to make up to him for past sins."

Delilah batted her eyes to hold back tears. This man sitting next to her was her best friend, and he knew all her secrets. He knew them all, and he still loved her. How could she be so blessed to have found two good men to love her?

"You're right," she said, "but it's more than penance for me. It's me holding this family together the way he did. Rocky could have walked away back then, and nobody would have blamed him, but he stayed. He put the family first, and we were able to work through our problems. It was hard, but it was worth it. That's the way I feel, and I believe he felt the same way."

"He did," Tommy said. "Nothing was more important to Rocky than you and the girls. Rocky forgave and he forgot, Delilah. He loved you and he loved his girls, all three of them."

Delilah blinked back more tears. "I know he did. The girls never doubted his love. He never gave them a reason to question his feelings for them. He was the perfect father."

Tommy pulled her closer. "But he wasn't the perfect husband," he added. "He started on the road to becoming one when he forgave you. There was a time in Rocky's life when you and the girls came *after* his music. By forgiving you, he changed his priorities, and in doing that, his life was enriched beyond measure."

"I had a good marriage," Delilah said.

"Yes, you did. And you could have another good one if you'd give us a chance."

Delilah knew he was right.

"I need to know that you want to move forward with me, Delilah."

She looked up at him. "You know I do."

"I need you to show me. We're too old to be hiding our relationship like there's something wrong with it. Your girls need to know that we're more than friends. I feel as though we're lying to them. They're not children, and we shouldn't treat them like they are."

Delilah knew this was a point on which she couldn't waver. "Okay, we'll tell them. Veronica's going to tell us her decision about the Legends contract next week. Let's pray that we can tell the girls our news at the celebration of Delilah's Daughters joining Magic City Records."

Chapter 13

A week later, after meeting with her new entertainment lawyer and signing the Legends contract, Veronica arrived back in Birmingham with Dexter. Their first stop was her mom's house. Veronica didn't want to wait to tell her sisters what she had done. While she knew she had made the right decision for her future, she also knew it was going to hurt them. She'd prayed for an easier answer, but none had come.

When Dexter pulled into her mother's driveway, she took a deep breath. She knew what she was about to do could change her relationship with her sisters for a long time. She'd make it up to them, she promised herself. As soon as she made it big, she'd pull them up right behind her.

"It's going to be all right," Dexter said. "You made the only decision you could make. If they love you, and I know they do, they'll understand."

Even though she knew Dexter was trying to be helpful, she wished he would keep quiet. He agreed with her decision because it was the one he wanted her to make. Of course he would be magnanimous toward her mother and sisters. "They're going to be hurt, Dexter."

"They're grown-ups," he said. "They'll get over it."

Now she really wanted to pop him. "How would you feel if I had gone the other way and chosen to stay with the group?"

His lips turned down in a frown. "Let's not even think about that. You made the right decision for both of us." After he turned off the ignition, he turned to her. "You put us first, Veronica, and you'll never know how much that means to me."

"I think I know," she said, pressing a hand against his cheek. "Just show a little compassion for my mom and sisters. That's all I ask."

He pulled her hand to his mouth and kissed her palm. "I can do that."

"Thank you," she said. Then she got out of the car and headed for the front door, her husband behind her. Her mother opened the door before they reached it.

"We've been waiting for you," Delilah said. "Did you have a good drive over?"

"Fine," Veronica said, pressing a kiss against her mother's cheek.

"Good," Delilah said, leading them into the house. "I've been praying for you, for all of us really." She squeezed her daughter's hand. "Your sisters are in the living room. Are you ready?"

Veronica squeezed back, thankful for her mother's unexpected support. Maybe this would go better than she had imagined. "I'm ready," she answered.

Delilah escorted them into the living room. Alisha and Roxanne sat on the sofa, anxiousness etched on their faces. These were her sisters. Veronica didn't know if she could break their hearts this way.

"You and Dexter take the loveseat," Delilah said, taking the armchair between the loveseat and the sofa.

After she and Dexter were seated, Delilah cleared her throat. Then she said, "There's no sense beating around the bush. Why don't you tell us the decision you've made, Veronica?"

It was Veronica's turn to take another deep breath. She stared down at her hands before looking back up at her sisters. "The Legends offer is a great offer," she began.

"For you," Roxanne said. "But the Magic City offer is best for the group."

Veronica glanced at her hands again. She'd hoped her sisters would let her plead her case without interruption, but that was not to be. She lifted her eyes and met Roxanne's stare. "I know Magic City's offer is best for the group, but I'm not sure it's best for me."

"You've decided to take the Legends offer, haven't you?" Roxanne said accusingly.

Veronica forced herself to hold her sister's gaze, though it would have been easier to turn away from the pain she saw there. Roxanne had struggled for so long. Even though she had that gig at Dreamland, Veronica knew she wanted more and knew she hoped to achieve that something more with the group. "I'm sorry, Roxanne," she said. "I know how much music means to all of us. I wish so much that we had won that contest and gotten a contract as Delilah's Daughters. But we didn't win, and we have to play the hand life has dealt us."

"It seems some of us got better cards than the rest of us," Roxanne said, not giving an inch.

Veronica felt Dexter about to say something, so she squeezed his thigh to stop him. This was between her, her sisters, and her mother. She didn't need him adding his two cents' worth and making things worse. If they could get worse, that is. She looked to her mom for help. When Delilah only shook her head slowly from side to side, Veronica knew not to expect any more support from her. As despair began to consume her, she felt Dexter's soft caress on her knee and remembered that she was not alone. She rested a hand atop his, accepting the comfort and support he offered.

"Look," Dexter said. "This is not the end of the world." He glanced from Roxanne to Alisha. "You two are still Delilah's Daughters. There is no reason you can't build on the exposure the group gained in the contest. You'll just have to do it without Veronica."

Veronica winced. Her husband had good intentions, but the grimaces on the faces of her mother and sisters told her that his words had not been received in the spirit they had been given. Their nonreaction to his words spoke volumes. "What Dexter means," she said, before her mother and sisters gave voice to their emotions, "is that the group is still viable even though I'm not a member."

"Viable?" Roxanne repeated. Then she gave a dry laugh. "You've got to be joking. Momma already told us that Magic

City's offer is off the table if the deal doesn't include the three of us."

Dexter cleared his throat. "I'm sorry about that, but one rejection is no reason to give up."

Veronica knew Dexter's reasoning was going nowhere. "I know my leaving the group has lessened the opportunities for Delilah's Daughters." She squeezed Dexter's fingers, knowing he disagreed with what she was about to say. "That's why I'm prepared to offer financial restitution for the loss."

"No way," Dexter said, his voice stern. "We've talked about this, Veronica."

"You want to pay us off?" Alisha asked.

Veronica sighed. Why couldn't they understand? "I'm not trying to pay you off. You're my sisters. I want to do the right thing by you."

"Doing the right thing would be staying in the group," Roxanne said.

She met her sister's eyes. "I can't do that, Roxanne, but I can replace the money Magic City was going to give each of you and Momma."

"You don't have to do this, Veronica," Delilah said, finally speaking.

Veronica nodded. "I know I don't have to do it," she said. "I *want* to do it."

"Guilt money," Roxanne said, folding her arms across her chest. "You're using your money to ease your conscience. Well, I want no part of it."

"If that's the case, we'll keep our money," Dexter said.

Veronica shook her head. "No, we won't," she said to him.

"The money is theirs." She turned back to her mother and sisters. "You'll get half the money when Legends cuts my first check, and the other half after I finish the first album, which is when they'll cut my second check. It's the best I can do."

"It's something," Delilah said.

Veronica couldn't tell if her mother thought it was a good something or a bad something. She hoped for the former, but decided not to ask in case she was wrong. "What about you, Alisha?" she asked her younger sister. "If you're serious about quitting your job, the money will come in handy."

"You're right about that," Alisha said, "but I'm with Roxanne. This feels like a payoff."

"Think of it as a buyout," Delilah said. "This is Veronica buying her way out of Delilah's Daughters. Veronica has been able to put a price on membership in the group, something I'd never thought to do. So now we know the price of a family legacy."

Delilah's words cut Veronica deeply.

Roxanne stood. "I'm glad Daddy is not here to see this day. It would break his heart to see how mercenary you've become."

"That's enough, Roxanne," Delilah said.

"It's the truth," Roxanne said to Delilah. "Veronica has gone from a member of a family group to a solo artist surrounded by folks only interested in the money she can make for them." She turned to Veronica. "I hope you know what you're doing. You're giving up a lot for your shot at stardom."

"It's not just for me," Veronica tried to explain. "Don't you see? If I make it big at Legends, I'll be in a position to help you and Alisha move ahead with your own careers."

"So can I submit a couple of songs for your album?" Alisha asked, hope in her voice.

Veronica wished she had a better answer. "I already asked. I'm sorry, they want to go with an established writer-producer team with a history of hits for this first album, but I'm sure there'll be a chance with the second."

"Of course there will be," Roxanne said, her voice full of sarcasm. "After one album, you'll be a star, and then you can tell the label what to do. Sure. It happens all the time."

Veronica again looked to her mother for help. Delilah's lips didn't move, but her eyes clearly said, *I told you so.*

Sadly, Veronica shook her head. "I don't know what else to say."

Dexter stood. "There's nothing left to say. It's clear to me that your mother and sisters don't want what's best for you."

"Don't speak for me, Dexter," Delilah warned. "Everything I do and everything I've done is for the good of this family, and that includes Veronica."

Veronica stood when Dexter reached for her hand. "You haven't shown any support for Veronica today," he said. "You've all stood against her and the opportunity God has given her. Why can't you stand with her and support her?"

"Because it's the wrong decision," Delilah said.

"So what if it's the wrong decision?" he countered. "Veronica's a grown woman. She's allowed to make her own decisions, wrong or not."

"She's not allowed to walk away from her family," Delilah shot back.

"I'm not walking away from the family," Veronica shouted. "I'm taking on a new opportunity. Can't you see that?"

"Okay," Delilah challenged. "Will you still perform with your sisters as Delilah's Daughters on occasion?"

Again Veronica had to shake her head. "I asked, but the label thinks doing so would dilute my brand."

"What brand?" Roxanne said with a dry laugh. "All anybody knows about you is Delilah's Daughters."

"What about the Gospelfest?" Delilah asked. "Can you do the Gospelfest with your sisters?"

"I don't know," Veronica said, but deep down inside she did know. She just didn't have the courage to give another negative answer. "My schedule in preparation for this first album is jam-packed. I don't see getting away for the concert, much less practicing for it."

"But we've always done the Gospelfest," Alisha said. "It's tradition. We've been doing it since we were kids. How can you not do the Gospelfest?"

Before Veronica could answer, Dexter said, "Things are changing. We're going to have to establish new traditions."

Delilah met Veronica's eyes. "Have you thought this out, Veronica? Is it truly what you want?"

Veronica glanced from her mother to her sisters. Though she knew they were disappointed in her, she knew she couldn't change her mind. Opportunities like the one Legends offered only came along once in a lifetime. One day her mom and sisters would understand this. Her eyes stung with unshed tears as she realized that day might be far into the future. She bit back her tears and answered her mother's question. "It's what I want, Momma. I'm sure of it."

Chapter 14

Delilah kept her seat after Veronica and Dexter left. She didn't have the words to express her disappointment. Veronica was making a huge mistake. She was sure of it. And there was no way Delilah could fix it. Not now. Not after her brash daughter had signed the contract.

"Well," Alisha said, interrupting her thoughts, "that was fun."

Roxanne smirked. "Only if you like root canals. I can't believe Veronica turned her back on us."

"It's Dexter," Alisha said. "No way would Veronica have made this decision on her own. You could see that he didn't want her to give us any money."

"We're not taking that guilt money," Roxanne said.

"Speak for yourself," Alisha said. "That money is going to come in handy when I quit my job. I have some money saved, but every little bit will help."

Delilah felt as betrayed as she knew her daughters did, but

she couldn't give in to those feelings now. She hadn't been able to keep the group together, but she wasn't ready to give up on Rocky's dream for Delilah's Daughters. She hated to admit it, but something Dexter said had rung true in her heart: Delilah's Daughters could go on without Veronica. "Veronica has made her decision," she told her two daughters. "Now we have to make ours."

"What are you talking about, Momma?" Roxanne said. "Veronica made the decision for all of us. When she chose Legends, she had to know Magic City was going to withdraw their contract offer. The only opportunity we had is gone." She got up and paced in front of the loveseat where Dexter and Veronica had sat. "I still can't believe she did this to us. I don't know what's come over her."

"Fame," Alisha said simply. "Veronica sees her name in lights, adoring fans at her feet, and her pockets full of cash. It's what she's always wanted."

Roxanne shook her head. "Sure, Veronica has dreams of fame, we all do, but she loves her art."

"Come on, Roxanne," Alisha said. "I know Veronica loves dancing, but she loves the spotlight more. Maybe the contract with Legends is the best thing for her. They'll give her the chance at fame she wants."

"What about our chance, Alisha? Did she have to go for hers at our expense? I could have understood it if she had a deal and we didn't have one. But we had one together, and she chose to go for hers alone rather than work together for all three of us to achieve our dreams. Would you have done that?"

Alisha shrugged her shoulders. "I don't know."

Roxanne rolled her eyes. "I do. You wouldn't have, and neither would I. You might have wanted to, but in the end you would have stayed with the group. Somewhere down the line we might have parted, but you would have given us a shot together. I'm sure of it."

"Enough," Delilah said, growing tired of the bickering between her daughters. "Neither of you know what you would have done in Veronica's situation," she said. "This was a hard decision. That's why I didn't want Veronica to have to make it. That's why I didn't bring it to the group."

"I didn't think she'd leave us," Roxanne finally admitted. "Deep inside I thought she would stick with us. It hurts that she didn't. It's as though she pushed us aside in her rush to fame. Does fame mean more than family?"

"You can't look at it that way, Roxanne," Delilah said. "This is one decision in Veronica's life. She wasn't pushing you and Alisha to the side. She was doing what she thought was best for her and Dexter. She has a husband, so her decisions aren't really all about her. They're about him too."

"Dexter has never wanted to be a part of this family," Roxanne said. "Not really. He wanted Veronica, but I think the rest of us were too much for him. I'll bet he's glad to have her to himself for once."

Delilah was sure Roxanne was right about Dexter's intentions. "That boy doesn't know what he's in for. If he thought he was losing his wife to us, then that label's hold on her is going to come as a major shock. Legends promised Veronica fame, and they may deliver, but it will be on their terms every step of the way. Veronica and Dexter are both going to find that out." She slapped her palms on her thighs. "But enough about them and their decision. Let's talk about the future of Delilah's Daughters."

Roxanne stopped pacing and stared at her mother. "What future? What are you talking about, Momma? We have nothing without Veronica."

"I'm still leaving my job," Alisha said.

"Stop talking crazy," Roxanne said. "Veronica was right about one thing. You don't quit your job when you lose the contest, or the contract. You quit when you win."

"That's enough," Delilah said. She knew the harsh words Roxanne and Alisha were exchanging now were born out of frustration. "You two are so caught up in Veronica's decision that you aren't listening to me. Delilah's Daughters can still live without Veronica. You two are Delilah's Daughters."

"What good does that do us?" Roxanne asked. "Magic City wants three daughters, not two."

Delilah waved off the comment. "That's easy to remedy," she said. "We'll find a third sister."

Alisha giggled. "Are you trying to tell us something, Momma? Did Dad have kids out there somewhere that we don't know about?"

Delilah frowned at her youngest daughter. "Be serious," she said.

"I am serious." Alisha lifted her eyes to her mother. "You don't have a secret daughter, do you?"

Delilah couldn't help but smile at Alisha's foolishness. She slapped her on the shoulder, and Roxanne laughed. "You two need to get serious. I'm talking about your future here. All we have to do is find a third member to replace Veronica."

"Not to douse cold water on your idea, Momma," Alisha

said, "but the group won't be Delilah's Daughters if the third woman is not your daughter."

"Delilah's Daughters is our name, and we can apply it as we see fit. Besides, the third woman will be a daughter."

Roxanne raised a brow. "Okay, now you're making me nervous and I'm thinking like Alisha. Are you sure you or Dad don't have any other daughters we don't know about?"

Delilah shook her head. "You girls should have paid closer attention in Sunday school. The third daughter won't be a daughter by birth but a daughter by adoption, much like the Gentiles were adopted into the body of Christ." She looked from Alisha to Roxanne. "It'll be the perfect hook and will only bring more attention to the group."

"I don't know, Momma," Alisha said. "We couldn't keep Veronica in line with the plans for the group, and she's our blood sister. How can we count on an outsider sticking with us for the long haul?"

"Alisha's right," Roxanne said. "We'll never find anyone who shares our commitment to the group. How could they? They don't have our history or our family connection. I don't see how it could work."

"I don't believe this," Delilah said, lifting her arms in frustration. "You two are the young ones who should be coming up with new and innovative ideas, but I'm the one who's thinking outside the box. Veronica is gone and she's not coming back. That ship has sailed—if not forever, then for the foreseeable future. We have to go on without her."

"I know," Roxanne said. "I just don't think going on as Delilah's Daughters and finding a replacement for Veronica is the answer."

Alisha jumped up. "I do," she shouted.

"What are you talking about?" Roxanne asked. "A minute ago you were agreeing with me."

"I know, I know," Alisha said, grinning at her mother like a chimpanzee. "I'm still agreeing with you."

"You're not making sense, Alisha," Delilah said.

"That's an understatement," Roxanne muttered.

Alisha held her palms up. "Hear me out. I agree with you, Momma, that we need to add a third person to the group." She turned to Roxanne. "And I agree with you that we can't just add a third body."

"Then what do you propose we do, Ms. Genius?" Roxanne asked.

"I say we find a third person who is as committed to this group as we are, if not more."

Roxanne folded her arms across her stomach. "And who would that be?"

Delilah knew what Alisha was going to say before she said it.

"We can add Momma as the third person," Alisha said.

"No way," Delilah said.

"Momma?" Roxanne said at the same time.

"It's the perfect solution, Momma," Alisha said. "Think about it. The Judds got started as a mother-daughter group and look at their success. We can make this work."

"But the group wouldn't be Delilah's Daughters," Delilah said, searching for the words to make her youngest see the futility of her suggestion.

"Like you said, Delilah's Daughters is whatever we want it to be, and I want it to be the three of us." Alisha turned to Roxanne. "It'll work, won't it?"

Roxanne tapped her chin with her forefinger. "I think Alisha may be on to something."

Alisha clapped her hands. "I knew it," she said. "Momma's voice will mean we have a greater range of approaches we can take with our songs. I can't wait to get started. This is going to be great."

Delilah raised her palm. "Hold up," she said. "I haven't agreed to anything."

"You will," Alisha said, her eyes flashing confidence. "Once the idea sinks in, you'll be fully on board."

"I think Magic City might be intrigued by a Delilah's Daughters that includes the actual Delilah," Roxanne added. "How'd you like to take that idea to Mr. Tommy?"

The idea wasn't one that Delilah wanted to take to Tommy. He was thinking marriage and building a life together, not her taking on an even larger role in Delilah's Daughters. She wasn't sure how he'd take the news. "We have to be smart about this," she told the girls. "We need to present Magic City with a plan, not an idea."

"But you'll think about the idea, won't you, Momma?" Alisha pleaded.

"I'm with Alisha on this one, Momma," Roxanne added. "The more I think about it, the more I like the idea. Delilah's Daughters could easily become Delilah & Daughters."

"Come on, Momma," Alisha coaxed. "You wanted innovative ideas from us, and now you have one."

"It's just the three of us, Momma," Roxanne added. "We can't do this without you."

"Yes, you can," Delilah said, but as she looked at her daughters she wondered what another disappointment would do to their commitment to the group. Earlier today their hopes and dreams had been dashed. Now they were filled with excitement and possibilities. She couldn't let them down again, could she? Surely, she could make Tommy understand. "I'll think about it," Delilah said, but she knew where her heart was leaning. The smiles on her daughters' faces told her that they did too.

Chapter 15

"Surprise!" a group of about fifty friends called out to Veronica as she and Dexter entered the backroom of Justin's, her favorite Birmingham restaurant.

Veronica turned to her husband. "What is this?"

"Surprise, Veronica!" he said, kissing her full on the lips. "Your friends are here to celebrate your new contract and new life."

"You did this?"

He grinned down at her. "With a little help."

"Hey, you two," Glo, one of her Alpha Kappa Alpha sorority sisters, called out to them. "This is a party, not a hotel room, so save that lovey-dovey stuff for later. We're here to give you a grand send-off to HOTLanta," she said to Veronica. "We don't want you to forget us when you're a big star so we've got a memory-filled evening planned for you. Come on over here and sit down, guest of honor, and let the party begin. You too, hubby."

Dexter followed Veronica over to her friends. They directed her to the King's chair at the table in the middle of the group. "Sorry," Glo said to him. "You have to be Queen today, 'cause our girl is the king."

Dexter gladly obliged. He could take this good-natured teasing from Veronica's friends. The smile they had put on her face was more than worth it. His wife had been glum-faced since their talk yesterday with her mother and sisters. Her family had really done a number on her. So much so that the guilt she felt over leaving them behind—which she really wasn't doing—had overwhelmed the joy she'd felt at being given the opportunity to pursue her dreams. He wanted to give her that joy back.

After they were seated, Glo said, "First we're going to feed you, and then we're going to remind you of some of the things we know about you, things that we'll be offering to the tabloids—for a price, of course—should you try to go all diva on us after your first chart-topper and pretend you don't know us."

"I'd never do that," Veronica said.

"We know you won't," Glo said, giving her a wink. "Especially not after we remind you of some of your most outrageous antics. Can anybody say Essence Music Festival in New Orleans?"

"Don't even go there, girl," one of her sorors called out. "A lot of us could get in trouble."

"Yeah," another one called. "Too many husbands are in this room. We need to keep it clean. Veronica might decide to turn the tables on some of y'all. Of course, I have nothing to hide."

"Right," Glo said. "I'm sure your husband believes you."

The entire group began to laugh, including Veronica. She was getting her joy back. And just as quickly it faded. "What's wrong?" Dexter whispered.

"My mom and sisters," she murmured. "They're not here, and I'm missing them."

Dexter wanted to pound his fist on his knees. Even now, Delilah, Roxanne, and Alisha were ruining his time with his wife. "Don't think about them. Think about the folks who are here to celebrate with you."

"They're my family, Dexter. How can I not think about them? Did you invite them?"

Dexter looked her directly in the eyes and lied. "Of course I invited them. Delilah thought it was too soon for your sisters. They need a bit more time to get used to the changes."

"They're still angry with me?"

He brushed her shoulder-length hair back over her ear. It was more that he was still angry with them for not being more supportive, but he saw no value in sharing that bit of news. "They're disappointed, but they'll get over it. Think about it this way. This celebration might be too much for them to handle right now. Your career is about to shoot into the stratosphere, and they don't know where theirs are going. They need some time to adjust."

"What if they don't?"

"They will," he said, all the while hoping they wouldn't. In his opinion, he and Veronica were better off without them. He'd always thought she was cut from a better grade of cloth than her sisters and mother. That she was the only one of them to pursue graduate study to extend her professional training was the only proof he needed. Veronica had class and style, even the folks at Legends could see that. She needed to get away from her family, who dimmed her light by their very presence in her vicinity.

"I hope so," she said. "I really do miss them."

He pressed a kiss on her palm. "You won't have much time to miss them starting tomorrow. Our new life in Atlanta begins then. You're going to be too busy to think about anything but work." He wriggled his brows. "And me, of course."

Her smile came back. "You're so crazy."

"Crazy about you," he said, with all seriousness. He meant it too. Veronica was the most important thing in his life. He counted his blessings every day that they'd found each other. He couldn't imagine life without her. That was one of the reasons he was glad they were moving away from her family. He knew they didn't think much of him. Delilah thought he was pretentious and not a good provider. Alisha and Roxanne thought their sister could have done much better than an academic with an unsteady work history. But all that was about to change. He and Veronica were going to have a chance to share their lives with each other, without her family's interference. He welcomed the change and knew it would only strengthen the bond between them. By the time they came back to Birmingham, if they ever did, their bond would be so strong he wouldn't have to worry about her family coming between them.

Chapter 16

Alisha practically floated through the doors of Carlile's Barbeque in downtown Birmingham. She grinned at the waitress who greeted her. "There'll be three of us," she told the young girl. "I'm meeting my mom and sister."

"Do you want to wait or be seated now?" the girl asked.

"I'd like to be seated now," Alisha said. "I want a nice cold glass of sweet tea."

"Follow me," the girl said, taking menus from the stack on the counter and leading Alisha to the tables near the windows on the left side of the restaurant. "Is this all right?" she asked.

"Perfect," Alisha said. "I can watch for my lunch companions from the window."

"Good," the girl said. "Now I'll get that tea for you."

"Thanks," Alisha said, still grinning. If she had known it would feel this good to be unemployed, she would have quit years ago. Her new life was off to a great start. Quitting her job had been her first step; heading off to LA for the ASCAP conference was her second.

"Alisha, is that you?"

Alisha looked up at the sound of her name. One of Veronica's sorority sisters stood next to her table. She couldn't remember the woman's name.

"You probably don't remember me," the woman said. "I'm Cassandra Taylor, one of Veronica's sorors. She introduced us at the Gospelfest a couple of years ago."

"I'm sorry," Alisha said. "I don't know where my mind was. Of course, I remember you. Nice to see you again."

"You too. I thought I'd see you last night. You missed a good time. Veronica's going-away party was seriously off-the-chain."

Going-away party? Alisha asked herself. She didn't know anything about a party. "Well, I'm glad you all had a good time. We're very proud of Veronica."

"I'm proud of all three of you. Delilah's Daughters represented Birmingham well on *Sing for America*. I'm expecting good things from all three of you."

"From your mouth to God's ears," Alisha said.

Cassandra chuckled. "I heard that. Well, did Veronica get off okay? I remember Dexter saying they were leaving for Atlanta early this morning."

Leaving for Atlanta? Today? Alisha couldn't believe her sister would leave without telling them. "They got an early start," she said, hoping she was right. "They're probably in Atlanta now."

"Yeah, I guess so." When the waitress brought Alisha's tea

to the table, Cassandra glanced at her watch. "I need to get back to work. It was good to see you. And congratulations again."

"Thanks," Alisha said. Then she sipped her tea, wishing she had ordered something stronger. She couldn't believe it. She put down the glass, opened her purse, and pulled out her cell phone. She scrolled through her contacts to Veronica's name. She needed a word or two with her sister.

"Hey, put that phone down," Roxanne said as she and Delilah reached the table. "Haven't you heard that it's bad manners to talk on the phone during a meal?"

Alisha closed the phone. "Hi, Roxanne," she said. "Hi, Momma."

Her mother pressed a kiss on her forehead. "Hi to you too, sweetie."

After her mom and sister were seated, Alisha asked, "Have either of you spoken to Veronica?"

"It'll be a few days before I talk to her," Roxanne said. "I'm still upset with her for kicking us to the curb."

"It might be longer than you think."

"What are you talking about, Alisha?" her mother asked.

"Have you spoken to Veronica, Momma?" she asked again.

Delilah shook her head. "Not since we were all together the other day. I figured we all needed some space. I was planning to call her in a couple of days."

"Well, it's going to be a long-distance call. I think Veronica and Dexter have left for Atlanta."

"Unbelievable," Roxanne said. "She's really cut us out, hasn't she?"

"Look, this may not even be true," Alisha cautioned. "I was about to call her to confirm." She picked up her phone again.

"Put the phone away," Delilah said.

"But, Momma—"

Delilah shook her head. "Veronica needs her space. We all do. For the first time in our lives, we're on different paths. We need to respect Veronica's path and get started on ours."

"Dexter gave her a party last night," Alisha blurted out. "Invited her friends and sorority sisters but didn't invite us. What do you think about that?"

"I've never liked that boy," Delilah said. "I knew he would try to come between us and Veronica at some point."

"I wouldn't have gone even if he'd invited me," Roxanne said. Alisha shot her a glare. "I'm being honest. Veronica wanted the spotlight all to herself. I say let her have it."

"I'm with Momma," Alisha said. "This is not Veronica. It's Dexter. We have to do something about him."

"Do what?" Roxanne asked. "Veronica chose Dexter. She knew our objections before she married him, but she married him anyway. She made her choice a long time ago."

"You can't help who you love," Delilah said. "Veronica loves him. She sees something in him that we don't see."

"He's going to let her down," Roxanne said. "I'll bet my last dollar on it."

"We really shouldn't be surprised," Delilah said. "He didn't grow up the way Veronica did. He always saw us as intruders on their relationship. He never saw us as his family too. He wouldn't let us be a family to him, not really."

"So what are we going to do about it?" Alisha asked. "The man can't just take Veronica from us."

"He's not taking her," Roxanne said. "She's a grown woman, making her own decisions."

"But—" Alisha began.

"Roxanne's right," Delilah said, cutting her off. "Veronica's made her choice. We have to respect it. When she needs us, she'll call, and we'll be there for her."

"Why would she need us?" Roxanne asked. "Legends is going to make her a star. That's all she wants."

Delilah turned to Roxanne. "I know you're upset with Veronica's decision, Roxanne." She glanced toward Alisha. "You too. I'm disappointed myself, but she's still my daughter and she's still your sister. We're still family. We're going through a rough patch, but we're still family."

"I guess we're a long-distance family now," Alisha said. "I still think we should call her."

"I'll get in touch with her in a couple of days," Delilah repeated. "Let's give them some time to get settled."

The waitress chose the perfect moment to come take their orders. Alisha's appetite had faded quite a bit, so she only ordered a pulled pork sandwich like her mother and sister.

After the waitress left, Alisha said, "I have some news."

"Please," Roxanne said, "let it be good news."

"It is," Alisha said, feeling her happiness return. "I turned in my resignation today."

Roxanne's eyes widened. "You really did it?"

Alisha nodded. "I told you I was going to."

"Good for you," Delilah said, squeezing her hand. "Good for you."

"So how much notice did you give?" Roxanne asked.

Alisha grinned. "I gave them two weeks, but they sent me packing today."

"What?" Delilah asked. "Why'd they do that?"

"Apparently I'm not as indispensable as I thought. The good news is that they're paying me for the two weeks."

Roxanne shook her head. "I can't believe you really did it."

"I'm not looking back," Alisha said. "I'm leaving for the ASCAP conference on Thursday. And when I get back, I've got to get to work on those hit tracks for the new Delilah's Daughters. Mr. Tommy and Magic City are going to be blown away. They're going to be begging us to take their contract."

"What's this about you going to the ASCAP conference?" Delilah asked.

Alisha lifted her shoulders in a slight shrug. "I figured it's about time, Momma. If I'm serious about becoming a professional songwriter, which quitting my job proves, then I need to start connecting with other professional songwriters. Maybe make some contacts, get a better understanding of the business side of songwriting."

"I see," Delilah said. "I wish you had told me you were interested in conferences. I could have helped you research them."

Alisha reached for her mother's hand. "I know that, Momma, but this is something I wanted to do for me. I hope you understand."

Delilah lifted a brow. "Are you thinking about leaving Delilah's Daughters too?"

Alisha shook her head. "That's not what I'm thinking at all, but Veronica leaving the group got me to thinking about what I want in my career and how much I'm willing to do to achieve my dreams."

Delilah looked over at Roxanne. "Are you thinking the same way?"

Before Roxanne could answer, Alisha said, "Roxanne started to find her own place when she took the job at Dreamland. I want a career apart from the group like what she has, like what Veronica is embarking on. You can understand that, can't you?"

Delilah's eyes brightened a bit, but Alisha knew her spirit was dampened. "Things are changing," Delilah said. "I guess that's inevitable, since nothing really stays the same." She took a deep breath. "Well, I have some news of my own to tell you."

Roxanne leaned forward. "Please don't tell us you're no longer going to be our manager."

Delilah laughed. "It's not that. I'm sticking with Delilah's Daughters as long as you all want me." She cleared her throat. "No, my news is a bit more personal. I'm not sure if you girls are aware, but Tommy Johns and I have come to be a little more than friends. In fact, we've been seeing each other socially for quite a while now."

Alisha almost choked on her sandwich. Roxanne patted her on the back. "You and Mr. Tommy," Alisha said. "I had no idea." She turned to Roxanne.

"I had no idea either, but it makes sense. You've known him forever, so you know what you're getting. Congratulations, Momma."

"Thank you, sweetheart," Delilah said, relieved her news had been accepted so well. "We had planned to tell you together when Tommy gets back to town from his trip, but now seemed as good a time as any. Tommy wants to have us all over for dinner soon."

"You and Mr. Tommy," Alisha said. "I like it, but it's going to take some getting used to. I've never really considered you with anybody other than Daddy. I guess that was naive of me, and even a bit selfish."

"Not at all," Delilah told Alisha. "Your father and I had a strong and loving marriage. If it weren't for you girls, I would have been lost after his death. But you helped me through, and so did Tommy. He could relate to what I was going through because he loved your father too."

"I think Daddy would approve," Roxanne said. "He'd trust Mr. Tommy with your heart."

"I think so too," Delilah said. "Tommy and I are lucky we found each other. You know, a lot of men my age and in this business prefer much younger women. Tommy's different. He walks to his own beat."

"He's a smart man," Alisha said. "You're a great catch. He could go younger, but he couldn't get any better. He's got the best in you."

"That's nice of you to say, sweetie."

"It's true," Roxanne said. "Mr. Tommy has good sense. And he's in the music business so he fits right in."

Delilah smiled. "That certainly helps," she said.

"In more ways than one," Alisha said. "Now I know we can get Magic City on board with the new Delilah's Daughters. Mr. Tommy can't turn down his girlfriend, can he?"

"Leave it to you to say something so outrageous," Delilah said.

"I don't know, Momma," Roxanne added. "Alisha may be on to something. I can't help but wonder if the reason Mr. Tommy offered us the contract in the first place was because of your relationship. Was that the reason?"

Delilah shook her head. "No," she said to Roxanne. "Tommy recognized a good opportunity for Magic City. He wasn't doing us any favors. This business is too tough for that." She looked at Alisha. "Actually, it could go either way. My relationship with Tommy could help Delilah's Daughters, or it could make things more difficult. Probably both, at different times. We'll have to see how it plays out."

"Personally, I don't mind having an inside contact," Alisha said, grinning. "I'm not above having our Delilah play the role of the biblical Delilah and work her magic on Mr. Tommy for our benefit. Tommy and Delilah. I like the sound of it."

Delilah laughed. "You're outrageous, Alisha. You know that, don't you?"

Alisha winked. "A woman's gotta do what a woman's gotta do."

All three women laughed.

Chapter 17

As Dexter steered their Buick Lucerne over the bright yellow Seventeenth Street Bridge leading to midtown Atlanta's Atlantic Station community, Veronica felt a bit like Dorothy in *The Wizard of Oz*. There were differences, though. At the end of Veronica's yellow brick road was the fame and stardom she had only dreamed one day would be hers. Unlike Dorothy, Veronica didn't want to get back home, but she did wish that she could have brought a bit of home with her.

"We're almost there," Dexter said after they had crossed the bridge and entered into The District, flanked on one corner by a Dillard's department store and on the other by a high-rise office building. He reached over and squeezed her knee. "In more ways than one. This is our chance, babe. It's what we've always wanted."

Veronica put her hand atop her husband's and smiled. She didn't want to tell him she was thinking of her mother and sisters. Until a week ago, all of her dreams of fame had been with them beside her.

"Legends is going to make you a star, and you're going to make my book a best-seller. Before you know it, we'll be the hottest couple since Jay-Z and Beyoncé."

She laughed. "Jay-Z and Beyoncé?"

He cut a grin at her. "We'll see who's laughing a few years from now when we're sitting on Oprah's couch telling her about our new movie."

She wanted so much to be as confident as Dexter was about their future, but she just wasn't there yet. "By the time we make it big, Oprah may not even have a show."

He turned and smiled at her as he navigated the car to the right onto Atlantic Square, followed by a quick right onto Sixteenth Street, where their new home was located. "She'll come back just to interview us."

Veronica leaned over and kissed him on the cheek. "I love you," she said. "Even though you're crazy."

"Crazy in love with you."

She laughed again at his words, the lyrics from one of Beyoncé's song. "Just focus on the building numbers," she said. "I'm ready to see our new home. The studio's taking care of everything. Can you believe they're providing us with a place to live?"

His lips turned down in a frown. "They're not that generous. The cost of these accommodations will come out of your future earnings."

"Still—"

"I'm not complaining," he said. "Legends has done well by us. For this first year, at least, we won't have many out-of-pocket expenses at all. We shouldn't have to touch much of the advance money they gave us." He cut a glare at her.

"Which is good since you decided to give so much of it away to your mom and sisters."

"Not again, Dexter," she said, not wanting to revive an old argument. "I had to give them that money. It was only fair."

"Whatever," he said, turning his attention back to the street. "We need to watch the addresses closely now. We just passed 400 Sixteenth Street, so 384 should be coming up on the right."

"I'm glad 400 isn't ours," Veronica said, studying the row of three-story townhouses with art deco facades. "That's one ugly building. An art deco rowhouse." She shook her head. "The southern girl in me doesn't get it."

Dexter laughed. "At this price, they're called brownstones. I sorta like them. They remind me of the SoHo area in New York City. You've got to get with the program, babe. Atlantic Station is a haven for artsy types who love the facade of that 400 building."

"Whatever you say. I'm still glad we're not living there."

"No," Dexter said. "Our building is farther down."

Veronica grinned as the red brick and white oak structure came into view. It was another row of townhouses like 400, but the facade looked more like what she was used to in the South. She especially liked the French doors leading into the first two floors and the white columns on the second-floor balcony. "Now this is my type of townhouse. It has a porch."

Dexter shook his head. "That's a balcony."

She slapped his arm. "Okay, smarty-pants, slow down. We're coming up on our townhouse." She pointed to the corner unit. "That's it," she said. "I hope it has a garage. From what I've read about Atlantic Station, we won't have much need for driving."

"I have no clue," Dexter said, pulling into a space on the street in front of the unit. "I hope we beat Mr. Washington here. I don't like the idea of him waiting around for us." After Dexter parked the car and cut off the engine, he turned to her. "Ready to start your new life?"

Before she could answer, a bright red convertible with the top down pulled up behind them and a thin woman in a black miniskirt, black thigh-high boots, and red halter stepped out. Veronica glanced at Dexter. "If she's our neighbor, I have a feeling we're a bit out of our league."

"That's impossible," Dexter said, opening his door. "The league will be defined by us. Now, let's get out so we can meet her."

Veronica looked in the side-view mirror. "She's coming toward the car." By the time Veronica opened her door and got out, the woman was waiting for her.

"I'm Tia Martin, your personal assistant from Legends," she said. "You must be Veronica." She turned to Dexter after he made his way to the sidewalk. "Tia," she repeated to him. "And you must be Dexter."

Dexter grinned at her and extended his hand. "How'd you guess?" he asked, a big flirty grin showing off his pearly whites.

Tia inclined her head toward the car. "Alabama tags. Plus, I've seen pictures of the both of you."

"You have?" Veronica asked before she gave in to the urge to smack her flirting husband upside his head.

"Don't look so surprised," Tia said. "There's not much about you two that I don't know. Legends does its homework and I do mine. You belong to them now. They had to know what they were buying."

Veronica didn't like Tia's phrasing. She didn't consider herself bought. She was under contract. She was about to make that clarification when Tia added, "Like I said, I'm going to be your personal assistant." Then she glanced at Dexter. "I'll work primarily with Veronica, but you're included too, since you're part of the package."

Dexter hugged Veronica from the side. "And she's a beautiful and talented package too. I'm one lucky guy."

Veronica patted the wrist Dexter had placed around her waist. He'd just made up for the flirting.

"I'll ask you about that 'lucky' comment after your first week," Tia said. "Your time here won't be a party, but I'm here to help you through it. I'll manage your schedule, get you to all your appointments, and track whether you're meeting the goals we set for you. My job is to make sure Legends gets a solid return on its investment in you. That means our relationship is bound to have its rocky moments. We're all adults, so I'm not going to sugarcoat anything I have to say. I don't have time for it, and frankly, neither do you if you want to be successful in this business. We each have a job to do, and while a friendly relationship between us will help, we don't have to like each other to get them done. Are we clear?"

Veronica felt like she was in army boot camp and Tia was her drill sergeant. She resisted the urge to snap to attention and salute. "We're clear," she said.

"And for the record," Dexter added, "we're on the same

page. We also want Legends to make a healthy return on their investment. They win, we win."

Tia nodded and flashed them a smile. Then she pulled some keys out of the pocket of her black miniskirt and waved them in the air. "Now let's take a look at your new home."

Veronica followed Tia and Dexter up the sidewalk to the double doors of their new home. Her husband seemed to have fallen under the woman's spell, but Veronica was still trying to figure her out. She'd have to keep an eye on Drill Sergeant Tia.

Chapter 18

*T*ia ended the townhouse tour in the kitchen, with its huge stainless steel side-by-side refrigerator and matching double-oven and industrial-sized island stovetop. Even the double sinks were impressive. Were they a tiny bit larger, Veronica was sure she and Dexter could take baths in them.

"I know this place can be overwhelming," Tia said, as if reading her mind. "Of Legends' five properties here in Atlantic Station, this is one of the best appointed. It was bought and furnished to make a statement about the artists assigned to live here, usually someone major from another label collaborating on a Legends project. Alicia Keyes has stayed here. So has John Legend. Consider yourself lucky. Rarely, if ever, does a new artist get a place this nice."

"Not lucky," Dexter said, flashing his flirty grin again. "Special."

Tia chuckled. "Don't count on it. Nobody's special at Legends until their album goes gold, preferably platinum. You'd both be wise to remember that fact."

Whatever warmth Veronica had begun to feel toward Tia during the tour vanished with those words. She cast a quick glance at her husband to gauge his reaction. He was still grinning like an idiot. *Just like a man,* she thought. She took a bit of comfort from seeing that Dexter had his eyes on Tia's face instead of her ample chest (probably fake) or her extremely long legs. While she knew her husband was only trying to charm their new personal assistant, she'd have to speak with him about toning it down a bit. They were no longer in the small towns of Birmingham and Tuscaloosa. This was the Atlanta music scene, and she had read and heard enough to know that the rules for fidelity and monogamy were much more relaxed here than back home. The last thing she needed was for Tia to mistake Dexter's flirting for an invitation to something more.

Tia looked at her watch and then checked her iPhone. "I thought Mr. Washington would be here by now. Apparently something has come up, so we'll have to carry on without him." She pulled out a stool from the granite bar that separated the kitchen from the breakfast area and sat down. "Take a seat," she said, thumbing through the screens on her iPhone. "We need to go over your schedule for the coming week."

Dexter pulled out the stool facing Tia and waited for Veronica to sit on it. Then he sat on the stool next to hers.

Tia placed her iPhone on the counter, opened the drawer under the bar countertop, and pulled out two folders. She handed one to Veronica and one to Dexter. Veronica wondered what else Tia had hidden in the townhouse. "I have a question," Veronica asked. "What about keys to the house?"

Tia opened the drawer again and pulled out two key rings, each with a single key. She handed one to each of them. "There are four keys to the residence. The two you have, the one I have, and one in the Legends office."

Veronica glanced at Dexter and waited for him to complain. When he didn't, she asked, "You'll have full access to our home at all times?"

Tia gave her a condescending smile. "Look at it this way. This townhouse is your home, but it's also your workplace. Like a property manager, I'll use my key only when there's a need. And even then, I'll always ring the bell before entering. That's the best I can do. It's probably not the level of privacy that you'd prefer, but that's the way it has to be. There have been times when I've had to drag drunk artists out of bed or break up all-night parties. I need access if I'm going to do my job and make sure you meet all your commitments. Can you two live with that?"

"Of course we can," Dexter said. "We don't plan to give you any need to access our home, so there's no problem." He put his arm around the back of Veronica's stool. "Is there, babe?"

Veronica shook her head. "None at all."

"Good. Now let's get back to the calendar."

Veronica opened the folder Tia had placed before her. She skimmed the pages, noting there was a schedule for each day of the next two weeks.

"Let's start with the good news," Tia said, pulling out the top sheet in her own folder. "You'll have the rest of the afternoon and evening free after we finish going over the schedule. I advise you to use the time to get settled. The kitchen is not fully stocked yet, so you'll probably want to go out for dinner. There are several great restaurants within walking distance, so that shouldn't be a problem."

"No problem at all," Dexter said. "We like to explore new places."

Tia nodded. "There's an envelope in the back of your folder with a Legends credit card for your meals and incidentals. You have a per diem as indicated on the accompanying paperwork. I'll need you both to complete and sign the company credit card use agreement before I leave tonight."

Veronica glanced at Dexter. He was grinning, but it didn't bother her this time since she was sure her own grin matched his. Legends was really taking good care of them. Maybe Dexter was right and they wouldn't need to touch her advance after all.

"Okay," Tia said. "Now back to the schedule. The real work starts tomorrow."

The day didn't appear too demanding to Veronica. All she had listed was an all-day spa session, which sounded more like vacation than work.

"Tomorrow, Monday, is going to be one of your toughest days," Tia said. "You're going to be poked and prodded by somewhere from eight to ten people, each of them analyzing and criticizing some part of your hair, face, and body. It's going to be tough to hear some of the things that are said, but you'll have to bear it. Just remember that whatever anybody does, they're doing to perfect your image, the brand that we want to sell the public. You're going to be a performer, and your look has to be exactly right."

"You can handle it, babe," Dexter said to her.

"Veronica won't be the only one who's poked and prodded," Tia said, looking at Dexter. "You will be as well."

Dexter's eyes widened. "Me?"

Tia nodded. "If Veronica is going to be a star, you have to look the part of the star's husband."

Veronica patted him on his two-pack. "You can handle it, babe," she said, throwing his words back at him. She grinned broadly because her husband was no longer smiling.

"As for the rest of the week," Tia continued, looking at Veronica, "you'll spend Tuesday with your trainer, nutritionist, and chef."

"Thank goodness for the chef," Veronica said. "This kitchen was built for someone whose culinary talents greatly exceed mine. I'd be lost in here."

"You won't be spending much time in here at all," Tia said. "The chef will prepare your meals each day." She looked back down at her folder. "On Wednesday, you'll make the rounds to several of the fashion designers who dress Legends clients. Here, again, expect to be poked and prodded. And criticized."

So far, so good, Veronica thought. She had a thick skin anyway. Having two sisters meant she'd developed one a long time ago. She had no doubt she could handle everything they threw at her, though she did wonder when they'd get to the music. After all, they'd signed her to be a singer and performer, right?

"Thursday will be another tough day," Tia said. "You'll spend it with your public relations assistant, photographer, and videographer. This will be a grueling day from a mental and physical perspective. The PR person is going to seem more like a psychologist, poking and prodding into your psyche. It'll be intense. We need to prepare you for the media, and we need to be prepared for the media and anything they know or may find out about you that could be harmful to your career or to Legends." She tapped the tip of her iPhone stylus on the counter. "You must take each of these meetings very seriously, and you must be forthcoming. We can deal with practically any indiscretion if we have time to come up with the proper spin. What we can't deal with is being caught off-guard. Understood?"

"Understood," Veronica said.

Dexter nodded.

"Finally," Tia said, "on Friday you'll get to do what you came here to do—sing. You'll spend the day with your voice coach and have meetings with several different producers we've lined up to work on your first album."

"I can't wait," Veronica said, wanting to pinch herself to make sure all this was real and not a dream from which she'd soon awaken.

"You don't get weekends off," Tia continued, "so on Saturday you'll meet with your dance instructor. This probably won't be an all-day meeting, but knowing him, he's going to give you homework, which typically includes making you watch film of concert performances of some top acts. Saturday night will probably include a trip to a dance club."

"I think Saturday is going to be my most enjoyable day," Veronica said. "I love dancing."

Tia eyed her. "Well, there's dancing and then there's performance dancing. Don't kid yourself. Working with the choreographer will be hard work."

Veronica considered explaining to Tia that dancers knew

and enjoyed the work of dancing. She didn't bother because the concept was usually foreign to nondancers. "The dance club should be fun," she said instead. "I can't imagine how even you can turn that into work."

Tia grimaced. "You'll soon learn that every public event is work for you. I hope the dance club is an enjoyable and relaxing experience, but you can't ever forget that you're always performing because people are always watching. You always have to be on your best behavior. Got it?"

"Got it," Veronica said. *Drill sergeant,* she added silently.

"Will I tag along with Veronica on Friday and Saturday?" Dexter asked.

Tia shook her head. "Usually your schedule will follow hers, but this week will be a little different. On Friday and Saturday, our publishing group is sponsoring a retreat for our authors and publishing team, and you're invited. The publishing team will shepherd your book. I'm not sure of the details yet, but I promise to get a full schedule to you by Wednesday."

"No problem," Dexter said. "I'm eager to meet the team and get a better understanding of their vision for the book. I want to get started right away."

"So will Sunday be a free day?" Veronica asked.

"Like I said," Tia reminded her, "there are no off days. Sunday will be a structured day of social events. First, you'll attend a church that many of our artists attend. Afterward, you'll be Mr. Washington's guest for a working lunch. He'll talk to you about the reports he's gotten from each of the people you're meeting with this week. I can't emphasize enough the importance of this meeting. Finally, later Sunday evening, I'll meet with you here to go over your schedule for next week." Tia closed her folder. "That's it. Are there any questions?"

"None," Dexter said.

Veronica knew she had questions, but her brain couldn't process them now. Tia hadn't given her just a schedule, she'd given her a pattern for a new life. How could she be expected to come up with a rational question when everything that had been said to her seemed unreal? "None," she said, repeating after her husband.

"Good enough," Tia said, getting up from the bar. "Why don't you two complete those credit card forms while I make a few phone calls? Once that's done, I'll leave you for the evening and you won't see me again until eight tomorrow morning."

After Tia left the kitchen, Veronica released a breath. "This is really happening, isn't it?" she asked her husband.

"It certainly is."

"I can't believe it." Squeezing her eyes shut, she said, "It's like a dream. Pinch me so I'll know it's real."

Dexter obliged her with a pinch on her forearm and her eyes popped open. "You're not dreaming," he said. "This is our new life, and I couldn't be more pumped about it." He glanced in the direction Tia had gone. "That Tia is a dynamo. I'm glad she's on our team. If anybody can keep us on track, she can."

Veronica nodded. She still had her reservations about Tia, but like Dexter, she'd rather have her on the team than not. *Team*, Veronica thought. Now she was going to be surrounded by a team, when before she'd been surrounded by family. She still missed her mom and her sisters dearly. Roxanne and Alisha would get such a kick out of the schedule Tia had planned for her. But she couldn't share that schedule with them yet, or anything else about her new life. It was too soon, and her good news would only make them sad because they couldn't share in it. Soon, she told herself, she'd make good on her promise to help them and they'd all be back together again as one big happy and successful family of musicians.

Chapter 19

Wrapped in a plush white terry-cloth robe and sipping on a large cold glass of iced lemonade, Veronica looked out of the wall of windows in Michael's Spa and Nail Salon onto the street two stories below while Yanni and Michael debated whether to cut her hair. She had her own opinion, but no one was asking for it, so she contented herself with soaking in the ambience of Atlantic Station. It was around noon, and The District was alive with workers on lunch break, lunchtime walkers and runners, and midday shoppers. Though she had yet to explore all of its nooks and crannies, she was already in love with her new neighborhood.

She and Dexter had ventured out the night before to have dinner at Copeland's Cheesecake Bistro, a short four-block walk from their town house. The crawfish eggrolls and barbecue shrimp linguine had been perfection. They'd capped the meal off with a huge slice of chocolate cheesecake. They figured they'd better get the good eating out of the way.

Something told her their chef wouldn't be preparing any such dishes.

"She needs a weave," Yanni said again. "About twenty to twenty-four inches, something that will hang about midway down her back. And we need to lighten the color a bit. A lighter shade of brown, but not blond, would definitely bring out her big brown eyes."

"Great eyes," Michael said. "But I'm not sure about the weave. Given the curly texture of her hair, wigs might be a better way to go. We could cut off a couple of inches and supply her with an array of wigs and hairpieces for ease in changing styles. We have to think efficiency here."

Veronica kept sipping on her lemonade. This morning Tia had told her to keep her mouth shut unless somebody asked her a question, and she was doing as she was told. While she'd never thought much of weaves, she was even less disposed to wearing wigs. She had too many childhood memories of shouting churchwomen and flying wigs to ever be comfortable wearing one.

As Yanni and Michael continued their evaluation, she wondered what Dexter's stylists were telling him. She hadn't seen her husband since they'd arrived at the spa early this morning and been shipped off to their respective stylists. *Men have it so much easier than women,* she thought. She'd bet that his stylists hadn't suggested either a weave or a wig for him. Maybe they wanted him to shave his head or grow a mustache. She smiled as she imagined him reacting to the idea of a mustache, wondering if he'd be able to withhold comment on such a suggestion.

Yanni jotted something down on a clipboard. "We're not

going to agree, so let's table the hair discussion for our report to Mr. Washington and his team at the end of the week."

"Fine," Michael said. He glanced at his watch, big and gold. Veronica didn't know much about jewelry—that was Dexter's department—but she knew expensive when she saw it. Apparently, the spa business was a lucrative one. "Look, I've got to run," Michael said. "Can you take care of her for the rest of the day?"

Yanni nodded. "I'll get it done."

He leaned over and brushed a kiss against Yanni's cheek. "You're the best."

"Yeah," Yanni murmured as Michael hurried out of the room. "I'm the best."

Veronica watched as the younger woman looked after the older man going out the door. So, were Yanni and Michael a couple, or did Yanni only wish they were? Veronica's inquiring mind wanted to know. Maybe Tia had the scoop. As quickly as that idea crossed her mind, she rejected it. She knew she and Tia would never be close enough to share gossip.

"Do you need anything?" Yanni asked her.

Veronica lifted her almost empty lemonade glass. "A refill?"

Yanni chuckled. "You have a long day ahead of you. You'd better slow down on that stuff, or you're going to find yourself having to run to the bathroom at the most inopportune time."

"It's delicious," Veronica said. "And I have a strong bladder."

"You win," Yanni said, taking her glass. "Monica takes over next. She'll do your body treatment and massage. She'll also make sure you get lunch and some more lemonade."

Yanni extended her hand. "I'll see you later in the week. It was nice meeting you. Good luck with your new career."

Veronica shook her offered hand. "You too. And thanks." After Yanni was gone, Veronica sank into the folds of her luscious robe. Her new career was off to a great start. Being comfortable with being talked about like she wasn't there would take some time, but being pampered was definitely something that could grow on her. She knew her sisters would love this as much as she did. How she wished they could share this experience with her!

Like a kid, she twirled around in the leather styling chair. She was about to do it again when a very tall—almost six-foot—woman entered the room. "I'm Monica," the woman said, handing her a fresh glass of lemonade. "Are you ready for your body treatment?"

Veronica nodded. "I can't believe they call this work."

Monica laughed, and her face lit up. "It's only work for me," she said. "It's heaven for you."

"I like heaven," Veronica said.

"And I like you," Monica said. She leaned close to Veronica and whispered, "I rooted for Delilah's Daughters on *Sing for America.* You and your sisters should have won."

"Thanks for saying that. We thought we should have won too." *If we had won,* she thought, *my sisters and I would be sharing this experience together.*

Monica leaned back against the stylist station. "Well, you didn't make out too badly. Legends is a great studio. We deal with a lot of their artists. They're all treated very well."

Veronica shook off the wave of disappointment that threatened to settle around her. Her sisters weren't here with her now, but soon they would be. She just had to work hard and become the success she knew she could become. "If today is any indication," she said, giving Monica her best smile, "I'm going to be spoiled before this is over."

Monica folded her arms across her stomach. "Just don't turn all diva on me," she said. "I've seen that happen before. The first time I meet the artist they're down to earth and as friendly as can be. Then I see them several months later and they don't remember me. Neither do they remember common courtesy. It's a shame, really."

"You won't have to worry about that with me," Veronica said. "My mother raised me well."

Monica studied her. "That's the sense I got about Delilah's Daughters. I felt like I knew each of you. I hope all of this doesn't change you. Are your sisters here with you?"

Veronica shook her head. She really didn't want to have this conversation. "Not this time."

As if sensing her discomfort, Monica changed the subject. "This body treatment is going to include a body review and analysis," she said, dropping her arms to her sides. "Michael or Yanni or maybe both of them will come in and do an evaluation of your form and figure. It'll be totally professional and detached, but you'll have to be naked or close to it. What do you have on under that robe?"

"Nothing."

Monica nodded. "Good. We can supply you with a skimpy bathing suit if that makes you more comfortable, but being naked is best."

Veronica wasn't sure how to respond. She wasn't a prude, but neither was she an exhibitionist. How did she feel about

Yanni and, especially, Michael poking and prodding her naked body?

"You can decide later," Monica said. "We have a lot of work to do before we call them in. I know you're probably hungry, so I'll get you a menu and we'll order lunch in. You can eat while your first treatment is setting. Are you ready?"

Veronica gulped down the rest of her lemonade, hoping she'd find some courage at the bottom of the glass. When she put the empty glass down, she said, "As ready as I'll ever be."

Chapter 20

As Delilah entered the converted storage building that housed the offices and studios of Magic City Records, she checked the bracelet watch that Tommy had given her for her fiftieth birthday last year. She was running a little late, but not enough for Tommy to complain.

"Good afternoon, Mrs. Monroe," Tommy's young secretary called as soon as Delilah pulled open the double doors that led to Tommy's office suite.

"Hello, Marie," Delilah said, having given up long ago on getting the younger woman to call her by her first name. "Is Tommy here? He's taking me to lunch."

Marie shook her head. "He was, but he was called out to Studio 7. He should be back any minute. You can wait in his office."

"Thanks," Delilah said, walking past the young woman's desk and through the open door leading to Tommy's office. The feeling of pride that she felt each time she walked into his domain surrounded her again as she entered the seat of

Tommy's empire. The decor reflected his comfortable masculinity and was a tribute to his success. Magic City might be a small studio, but Tommy's talents were anything but small. The dark-paneled wall of his office was covered with plaques representing his success—most from his days as a musician and producer—although there were a growing number acknowledging the success of the baby he had founded with his own money and sweat equity, Magic City. The most prized item in Tommy's collection was a gold-framed mounting of a copy of the first royalty check that Magic City had issued. That check represented the goodness and heart of Tommy. He hadn't mounted the first check he'd been paid, but rather the first check he'd paid out. He counted his success in being able to help artists reach their dreams. He had a gift for spotting and developing talent that others overlooked.

The girls were right when they said Magic City wasn't in the same league as Legends. But for Delilah and for Tommy, it didn't need to be. Tommy could have become a major player in the recording business had that been his goal, but he'd turned down so many offers for his studio that suitors had stopped calling. Everybody in the business knew he wasn't going to sell. Some called him shortsighted and small-minded, but she knew better. Unlike many in the business who found their identity in how much they acquired, Tommy's confidence came from doing what he loved and what he felt he'd been called to do.

Not that he hadn't done well for himself. In fact, Tommy had made a bundle over the last decade or so selling the contracts of his artists to major studios like Legends. He was in no way hurting for money.

"I'm sorry I'm late."

Delilah turned at the sound of Tommy's voice. "No problem," she said, walking over to meet him. When she reached him, she pressed a kiss on his cheek. "Everything okay in Studio 7?"

He grinned. "Yeah, that producer I brought in to work with the new guys wanted me to hear their latest track. They accomplished a lot during the week I was away."

"So you liked what you heard?"

He shook his head, but he was grinning. "I loved it. There's nothing like putting the right pieces together. You get the right artist and producer together and magic happens."

"Magic at Magic City."

His grin broadened. "It's more than a name," he said. "It's reality. We really do work magic here."

She leaned into him. "And you're the magician?"

Pulling her closer, he said, "I'm only a player doing my role, like all the other players. Together we make the magic."

Delilah pulled back to look at him. Though he and Rocky were totally different men, they shared a common belief that teams could accomplish more than individuals. She'd thought that she and Rocky passed that perspective on to their girls, but apparently they hadn't.

He tapped her on her nose. "Your nose is crinkling. What dismaying thought just passed through your mind?"

She shook off the dour thoughts. "Let's talk about it later. Where are we going for lunch?"

"The guys in Studio 7 want me to hang around for a while," Tommy said, taking her hand and leading her to the leather couch in the corner of the room. "So I called Roscoe and asked him to bring up a couple of specials. You don't mind, do you?"

"You know I don't," she said. "Roscoe has the best pasta and chicken in the Southeast."

Tommy settled back on the couch and pulled her close. "Now tell me what's on your mind? I'm guessing it's the girls."

"How'd you get so smart?"

He patted her shoulder. "Like fine wine," he said. "I get better with age."

She gave him a light punch in the side. "You're going to need a bigger office to hold you and your ego."

"Tell me," he said, his voice serious. "I know something's on your mind. Our short phone conversations over the last week haven't cut it. You don't have to hide your concerns from me."

"You're too good for me," she said.

"Delilah—" he coaxed.

"Well, the good news is that I told the girls about us." Tommy's eyes brightened, and Delilah felt the load around her heart lighten in response. "I'm sorry I took so long."

He kissed the top of her head. "Better late than never. I hope that's not what had your nose crinkling."

She shook her head. "Of course not." She sighed. "I love my girls, but sometimes I wonder if they learned any of the lessons Rocky and I tried to teach them."

"Are you talking about Veronica?"

"All three of them. Now that Veronica's charting her own path, Alisha thinks she needs to do the same. And Roxanne has her job at Dreamland. Delilah's Daughters is not a priority for any of them. Maybe it shouldn't be a priority for me."

He squeezed her shoulders. "Don't give up yet. There's still a chance for the group to grow."

"I don't know," she said. "Things changed when Rocky died. He was the heart and soul of Delilah's Daughters. Now it feels empty. I think that's why it was so easy for Veronica to leave. And now Alisha wants to chart her songwriting career. She's turned in her resignation from her job, and she's getting ready to attend the ASCAP conference. She thinks she needs to immerse herself in her new career. It just looks to me like she's giving up on the group."

"I think you're getting carried away," Tommy said. "Veronica's decision wasn't an easy one, and it's only natural for Alisha to explore her interests. This contest was a blessing for the girls, Delilah. You said things changed with the group when Rocky died. Well, I believe this contest breathed new life into the group and into each of the girls' hearts. You've got to trust that God knows what He's doing and that He's watching over them, whether they make good decisions or bad ones. Trust Him to take care of them."

She looked up at him and pressed a hand against his cheek. "And that's why I need you," Delilah said. "You keep me grounded. What would I do without you?"

"I don't ever want you to find out. We're going to have a long and happy life together, Delilah. And Delilah's Daughters is going to be a big part of our life together. I don't know how it's all going to work out, but I know that it will."

"From your lips to God's ears," Delilah murmured.

Tommy picked up one of Delilah's hands and pressed it to his lips. "I think something else is on your mind. And I think I know what it is."

Sometimes it irked her that Tommy knew her so well. This was one of those times. *Can't the man leave well enough alone?*

"You're going to have to tell her," Tommy said, when she didn't respond. "She needs to know. She deserves to know."

Delilah shook her head. "I can't. She'll hate me. They'll all hate me."

"No, they won't."

"You don't know that."

"But I know you," Tommy said. "You can't—"

Delilah was grateful for the knock at the door.

"Come in," Tommy said.

Marie stuck her head in. "Mr. Roscoe's here. Should I let him in?"

Delilah gave Tommy a stern look. Then she said to Marie, "Yes, you should. I'm starving."

"This conversation isn't over," Tommy said, before he got up to go meet Roscoe.

Yes, it is, Delilah thought as she watched him walk away from her. All she had to do was keep Roscoe here for lunch. She didn't think that would be a difficult task. At this point, she knew she could rise to any challenge if it meant she could delay what she knew was becoming more inevitable every day.

Chapter 21

"I'm not talking to you," Veronica told her husband. Unlike yesterday's spa day, she and Dexter had been together all day today. Tia had a car service drive them to Emory University Medical Center on West Peachtree Street, where they had spent the morning with a doctor who took a medical history and did a health screening on each of them. Now they were back in Atlantic Station at Jim's Gym for their fitness assessments.

"You can't ignore me all day," Dexter said from the treadmill next to hers.

Veronica checked the time on her treadmill. Eight minutes down, four minutes to go. She couldn't wait for this twelve-minute stress test to be over. She already knew she had a high cardiovascular endurance level. She was a dancer, for goodness' sake.

"They're not going to force you to have breast augmentation surgery," Dexter said for the hundredth time since she'd told him that she'd heard Michael, Yanni, and Monica commenting on the size of her breasts and suggesting that breast enhancement might be necessary. "It'll be your decision."

Veronica wished she had her iPod or something so she could tune Dexter totally out. His lack of understanding of how their suggestion made her feel disappointed her and made her sad. In all the time they'd been married, he'd never expressed any problem with the size of her breasts. He'd always told her that her "handful" was plenty for him. Now all of a sudden he was right there with Michael and Yanni talking about a boob job.

"Stop being childish," he told her, exhaustion from the run making his words disjointed. "They only want to put the best you forward."

When the final four minutes were up, Veronica got off the treadmill and headed for the refrigerated case where the bottled water was stored. She took out a bottle, twisted off the cap, and took a long swallow. Dexter stumbled behind her to get his own bottle. Though she knew it was petty, she took a bit of satisfaction in knowing she had endured the run better than he had. "Somebody needs to get in shape," she said to him. "I wonder what suggestions the trainer will have for you."

After getting his bottle of water, Dexter dropped down on the nearest bench. "Don't be cruel," he said.

She jabbed a finger toward her chest. "Me being cruel? What about you telling me I need a boob job?"

"I said no such thing."

Technically, he was right, but that was beside the point. "But you didn't say I shouldn't do it."

Sighing, he took another swallow of water, stood up next

to her, and put a hand on each of her shoulders. She lowered her head so she wouldn't have to look at him. "This is not about us personally," he said. "This is about business. Left to me, I would change nothing about you because I think you're perfect. But I'm not the expert here. All I'm saying is that we need to think carefully about each recommendation they give us. Like Tia said, everything they do is to make sure Legends makes money from their investment in you." He removed one hand from her shoulder and tipped her chin up. "That's what we want too, right? Remember, what's good for Legends is good for us."

To Veronica, Dexter was sounding more like a business partner than a supportive husband. She needed someone to care about her, Veronica Monroe Timmons, and her interests, not another member of Team Veronica Y. She needed her mother and her sisters. They would understand and support her. They always had. Well, they had until losing the contest had ruined things between them.

Clap! Clap!

Veronica turned at the sound, as did Dexter.

"I need to talk to both of you," Jim, their trainer and the owner of the gym, said. "Follow me to my office."

Already used to doing what she was told, Veronica dutifully followed Jim into his office, Dexter behind her. When told, they sat in chairs in front of his desk.

"You both did well on the cardiovascular endurance tests," Jim said. He turned to Veronica. "You did exceptionally well."

"I'm a dancer," she said.

"You're a very fit dancer," Jim said. "Which is good for us since it means you're ready to race."

"Race?" Veronica repeated.

"Yes," Jim explained. "The Peachtree Road Race. It's a 10K event held on the Fourth of July each year here in Atlanta. Legends always fields a team. This year they want you and Dexter to participate."

"But I've never run a race, 10K or otherwise," Veronica said.

"Neither have I," Dexter said.

Veronica bit down on her bottom lip while she waited for her ever-accommodating husband to add that, nevertheless, they were willing and ready to do it for the Legends team. When he didn't, she thawed a bit toward him. Even Dexter had his limits.

"It doesn't matter," Jim told them. "We host a ten-week training program here at the gym to get you ready for the race. Tia already has it on your schedule. Don't worry. You'll both do fine." He looked at Veronica. "The training for the race is similar to the program I put artists through in preparation for going on tour. It's all about endurance."

Veronica nodded. She understood the endurance needed to sing while keeping up with a dance routine. She welcomed the hard work of training for the race since she knew it would only help her during performances.

Finished with her, Jim then turned to Dexter. "Your case is a bit different. Endurance is not as important for you, but if you're going to keep up with your wife, you'll appreciate the results of the hard work we're putting you through. What we want more from you, though, is strength building and definition. We want to see your body more defined. Legends has big plans for your wife. If the future unfolds as they envision, she'll soon become a regular in the media, with you at her side. So you need to look the part. Male artists are very competitive about their bodies. You need to be in that competition."

Veronica took a little satisfaction in Dexter's weak nod. While her husband wasn't out of shape and took reasonably good care of his body, he considered himself more a mind man than a body man. Jim hadn't exactly told Dexter he was a slob, but the trainer had made it clear that his body wasn't up to the standards that Legends demanded. She was sure those words rubbed against Dexter's grain. *Good,* she thought. *Now maybe he'll understand a little bit how I feel about the boob job comments.*

"So Legends always has artists participating in this event?" Dexter asked, going back to something Jim had said earlier. The body comments must not have irked him that much after all.

Jim nodded. "It'll be great exposure to the local community. All the local television stations cover the event, and Legends will make sure you two get a few interviews out of it. Also, it doesn't hurt that by running you're both showing support for the city. That's like goodwill in the bank you can draw on in the future."

"Mr. Washington and his team think of everything," Dexter said.

"They have to. The music industry is not for the fainthearted. You're either in it to win it or you're not in it at all. Which are you two?"

"We're in it to win it," Dexter said.

"And you, Veronica?" Jim asked. "Are you in it to win it?"

Veronica gave the answer she knew she was supposed to give, but still thinking about the breast augmentation, she wondered exactly how much would be required of her.

Chapter 22

Roxanne watched Alisha shove her hands into the back pockets of her jeans as she gave that hunky coworker who had come to help her move the brush-off.

"Thanks, Jeff," Roxanne heard Alisha say. "I thought I was going to be finished tonight, but the packing is taking longer than I thought. Can you and your friends come back tomorrow afternoon? With my sister's help, I'll be ready then."

"We can help you pack," the hunk offered.

Alisha shoved her hands deeper into her back pockets. Roxanne was pretty sure her sister wasn't aware that the action caused her breasts to push forward in the stupid Braves T-shirt she was wearing. Not that the T-shirt was bothering the hunk. He was doing all he could to keep from staring. *Poor guy,* Roxanne thought. *He's picked the wrong woman to fall for.* Alisha didn't have a clue.

"That's okay," Alisha said. "We've got it covered. Tomorrow is good."

Having no other recourse, the hunk said, "See you to-morrow."

After Alisha closed the door, Roxanne called out, "You could have shown the man a little appreciation."

Alisha came back and plopped down on the floor next to a stack of books. "Appreciation for what? He hasn't done anything yet." Alisha began putting books in a box. "I'll thank 'em tomorrow after they get me moved."

Roxanne chuckled. "You, my dear sister, are a trip. You do realize that guy is interested in you, right?"

Alisha looked up, a question in her eyes. "Jeff? You're kidding. Jeff's not interested in me. We're work buddies."

Roxanne didn't think trying to convince her sister otherwise was worth it. "If you say so."

Alisha leaned her head to the side and looked at Roxanne. "Speaking of men," she said, "when are we going to meet your new guy?"

Roxanne turned to pick up another box. She folded it and then reached for the tape gun. "It's complicated."

"How complicated can it be? You're dating someone who seems to be someone special. Me and Momma want to meet him."

Roxanne knew her mother and Alisha would both die if they knew about Gavin. "I don't want to scare the guy off," she teased. "He's not ready for you and Momma."

"Why didn't he come to see us during the finals competition? He wasn't there, was he?"

He didn't come because he was celebrating his wife's birthday. "He had to work. He's on a ship to South America."

"Have you spoken to him since we lost?"

She had wanted to hear from him, but obviously he hadn't been able to steal a few minutes for a phone call. That was the price she paid for being his mistress. "Yes, we spoke for a few minutes. He was able to watch the show. He wanted to be here in person, but he was here in spirit. That was enough." It really wasn't, but she was in no position to make demands.

Alisha folded the tops of a full box, grabbed the tape gun, and in three broad swipes, taped the box closed. She pushed the box to the side and reached for an empty one. "I'm happy for you, Roxanne. It's obvious you care about this guy. He seems to be good for you."

If you only knew, Roxanne thought. "He's good to me too," she said. Needing to change the subject, she said, "You need a man in your life."

Alisha shook her head. "I don't need a man. What I need is to write a hit song for a major artist."

"You really are on a roll, aren't you, little sister? You quit your job, you rent your condo, and then you move back home with Momma. When you make a move, you make it big."

Alisha shrugged. "I feel like I've been waiting for this moment forever. Do you remember how you felt when you got the Dreamland gig?"

Roxanne nodded. The memory had been dimmed by more recent goals, but she still remembered the joy she'd felt at getting paid to do what she loved.

"Well, I'm feeling something like that now. I have this escalated sense of excitement mixed with urgency. I feel that this is my moment and I can't let it slip by."

"That's the way I felt too," Roxanne said, "until we lost the contest. Then we lost the Magic City contract. I'm not feeling really hopeful right now. I'm feeling more lost than anything. For the first time in a long time, I'm not excited about going to work. Dreamland can't be the limit for me. It can't be, but right now it is. And I find that more depressing than anything."

Alisha put her hand on her sister's knee. "Don't be depressed, sis. There are good things in store for us. I really do feel it. I'll write your first hit. You believe that, don't you?"

Roxanne put her hand on top of her sister's. "I want to, but it's hard right now."

"I know, but you have to hang in there. You can't give up. We can't give up." She grinned. "Look at Momma. If she'd given up after Daddy died, she wouldn't have found Mr. Tommy."

Roxanne smiled. "You have a point. What do you think of that relationship, really?"

Alisha shrugged. "I only want Momma to be happy. If he makes her happy, then I'm happy for her. She deserves some happiness. She really had to step up for us after Daddy died. Now she can let somebody take care of her. Mr. Tommy is that kind of guy."

"Momma and Mr. Magic City. I still don't know if I believe he offered us that contract solely because of our talent. I'm sure his relationship with Momma had something to do with it."

Alisha shrugged. "So what if it did? This is a tough business, Roxanne. We're going to need all the help we can get. If it takes preferential treatment from the man who's courting our mother to get us on the road to accomplishing our dreams, I'm all for it."

Roxanne thought about the cost she'd paid for the Dreamland job. "I hear what you're saying, but I don't like the idea of mixing business with pleasure. I don't want Momma to get hurt."

Alisha taped another box. "I don't think that's going to happen. Mr. Tommy seems to be taking a professional approach with us. Now, if Momma was really working some magic, he would have given us the contract without Veronica. No, Mr. Tommy is a businessman first."

"But I'm not sure Momma is a businesswoman first. She thinks about family first."

Alisha looked up at her sister. "Are you finally ready to admit that Veronica made a wise choice by going with Legends?"

No, Roxanne thought, *I'm not ready to admit any such thing.* "I never said it wasn't a smart choice for her and her career," she said to Alisha. "A blind man could see that it is. But look where it left *us.* Nowhere."

"Speak for yourself," Alisha said. "I can look at my situation as being out of a job and homeless or I can look at it as embarking on a new adventure. I'll choose the latter, thank you very much."

Roxanne knew Alisha wasn't merely spouting words. She was genuinely excited about what the future held. While Alisha was excited, though, Roxanne was scared. She was getting older every day, and the idea of herself as a middle-aged woman singing on a Dreamland cruise ship sparked dread in her heart, not excitement. Her career was going nowhere, and she was in a dead-end relationship. How had she let this happen to her?

Chapter 23

"Veronica, you make my creation sing," Victor Meggan said, beaming with pride from across the main salon of his Buckhead suite of offices. Victor was a tall, attractive guy who looked like he'd stepped out of the pages of *GQ* magazine. In fact, he looked more like a male model than a designer of high-end women's fashions.

The simple dress Veronica wore made her feel like breaking out in a song and dancing around the salon. The design was a bright red, off-the-shoulder sheath that fell just below her knees. The light material hugged her upper body and flowed from her hips, making her feel sexy and beautiful and strongly capable at the same time.

"And your breasts are perfect-o," he added, using his thumb and forefinger to make an "O." When he reached her, he said, "Michael and Yanni have a fetish for large breasts, but that is their issue, not yours, and not mine. Your body is perfect as it is. I will be honored to have you wear my collection during Atlanta's Fashion Week. I will let Tia know today so that she won't book you with anyone else. Nobody can dress you the way I can. You agree, don't you?"

After his comments about her breasts, Victor could have convinced her to agree to anything. "I'd be proud to wear your designs," she told him, "but I've never modeled before."

"Who cares? You will be a vision of beauty that all the women envy and all the men desire. You will sell my designs better than any model. I know of what I speak."

Who was she to disagree with one of the top designers in the world? After Michelle Obama chose one of his designs for the second inaugural ball, Victor had shot from "up-and-coming" to "there" in a matter of days. It really was a coup for her to be chosen to wear his designs at Fashion Week. "Your designs make me feel beautiful," she told him. "Beautiful and strong."

"And that is why Victor Meggan and Veronica Y will be a hit. And Mr. Washington will be more than pleased with the free publicity our merger will yield for you and Legends."

"Stop filling her head with visions of greatness, Victor," Tia said. She had left a couple of hours ago to check on Dexter's experience with the designers he was visiting, and now she was back. "You know these newbies can go from grateful to diva in nothing flat."

Victor lifted one of Veronica's hands to his lips and pressed a kiss against it. "Not my Veronica," he said.

"We'll see," Tia said, unmoved by Victor's declaration. "Are you finished with her for today?"

Victor nodded. "With her, yes. With you, no. We must talk about my plans for Veronica."

Tia shook her head. "Not today," she said. "We have a full schedule."

"When don't you have a full schedule?" Victor asked, walking toward Tia. When he reached her, he put a hand on her cheek. "I wish Mr. Washington had let me dress you," he told her. "But you were too special for me back then."

Tia stepped back so his hand fell away. "And now you're special and I'm not."

His lips turned down in a sad smile. "That's not what I meant, Tia."

"It's the truth," Tia said. She turned to Veronica, dismissing Victor. "Get dressed. We have to get a move on."

Veronica did as she was told and went to the dressing room, all the while trying to decipher what she had just seen and heard. It was clear that Tia and Victor had a history. It was unclear what kind of history, though. As she took off Victor's precious dress and put her own simple sundress back on, she told herself to keep her nose out of it.

When she reentered the main salon, Tia stood fingering the material of an indigo gown on one of the racks that lined the walls. "I'm ready," she said to get Tia's attention.

Tia didn't turn to her. "Go ahead and ask," she said, still fingering the garment.

"Ask what?"

Tia turned then, and for a brief moment Veronica thought she saw sadness in her eyes. "About me and Victor."

Veronica wanted to know, but she refused to ask. "I don't know what you're talking about."

"And you're not a very good liar. You're going to have to practice more. So ask."

"Did you and Victor used to date?"

Tia shook her head. "Victor wasn't the star he is today when I met him," she said. "So, no, we never dated."

Was Tia saying that her standards had been so high that she wouldn't date anyone who wasn't a star? Veronica wondered if her personal assistant knew how small that perspective made her seem. Of course, she couldn't tell her. They didn't have that kind of relationship. "Oh," she finally said, not knowing what else to say.

"I know what you're thinking," Tia said. "You're thinking that it was my loss because now Victor's a major designer and I'm a lowly personal assistant."

Not exactly, but close enough. "I wasn't thinking that at all."

Tia pursed her lips. "Sure you weren't."

Veronica didn't know how to respond, so she said nothing.

Tia stepped closer to her. "A word to the wise, Veronica. Just because you want to be a star doesn't mean it's going to happen. Just because Legends is doing all of this for you doesn't mean your album is going to be a hit. And if that album is not a hit, you'll be history quicker than this." She snapped her fingers. "And Veronica Y will be over before she even gets started."

Veronica stepped back. Why was Tia saying this to her? And then it hit her. "Were you ever a Legends artist?"

Tia nodded. "I was you two years ago. And look at me now."

A million questions rolled around in Veronica's mind. "What happened?"

"Reality happened. Legends may be one of the best studios in the country, but even they can't guarantee success. A lot of forces have to come together at the right time for

an artist to hit it big. And it's not all about singing ability."
She gave a dry laugh. "Singing ability is the least of it. So if
you really want this career you're being offered, you'd better
step up your game, listen, and follow directions. Regardless
of what Victor tells you about your lovely breasts and his
dresses, remember that Legends is guiding your career. Turn
on them and they'll turn on you. And don't act like a diva
until you earn the title." Tia took a deep breath. "Now, does
that answer your questions?"

"Yes," Veronica lied. In reality, she wanted to ask Tia each
of a million questions that had come to her mind, but she
knew that door was closed. She wondered if there was a way
to open it again.

Chapter 24

I should have told her, Tommy Johns thought for the hundredth time since he'd gotten the call from Morgan Sampson yesterday. *Why didn't I tell her?* he asked himself as he strode from the lower-level parking deck at the Birmingham-Shuttlesworth International Airport toward the meeting rooms on the same level. Until today, he hadn't even known the airport had meeting rooms. Leave it to Morgan to know more about Tommy's hometown airport than Tommy did.

Tommy found room G-5 easily enough. He sucked in a deep breath. *I really should have told Delilah,* he thought one last time before pulling open the door.

Morgan looked up from his seat at the table. When he saw Tommy, he stood to his full six feet. His hair was now grayer, and he was a little thicker around the midsection, but otherwise the years had been good to him. "I wasn't sure you were coming." He reached out his hand.

Tommy took his old friend's hand and gave it a strong shake. The two men had known each other for more than twenty years. Tommy had kept his secret, his and Delilah's, for all that time. "You shouldn't have come, Morgan."

"I know," he said, sitting down, "but this is a conversation we had to have in person."

Tommy took another deep breath. "You can't see her."

"I have to, Tommy," he said, an unfamiliar pleading in his dark brown eyes. Morgan Sampson was a best-selling Grammy-winning and Dove Award–winning gospel producer. He was the talent behind the hottest gospel acts for the last two decades. His face wasn't known to the public, but he was a rock star among gospel artists. And here he was seated in a dingy meeting room at the dinky Birmingham airport begging Tommy for help.

"Delilah's not ready," Tommy said.

"I've waited for three years. How much longer will it take her to get ready?"

"You gave up your rights," Tommy reminded him.

"I didn't have a choice."

Tommy quirked a brow. "We always have a choice, Morgan. You chose to walk away. You chose to give up your parental rights."

Morgan looked away. "I know I did, but there was nothing else I could do. You remember how it was back then. I was riding my first gospel hit, making a name for myself. The scandal would have ended my career, my marriage, and Delilah's marriage. I didn't have a choice. It was what Delilah wanted."

"It was what she said she wanted. Don't forget, she had Rocky breathing down her neck."

"He was breathing down mine too. He made it very clear that the only way he'd forgive her was if I'd walk away and let him raise my daughter as his own. At the time I couldn't decide if he was a saint or a sadist."

"Rocky was neither. He was a man who loved his wife despite the fact that she had cheated on him and gotten herself pregnant by one of his so-called friends."

Morgan flinched at his words. "I was his friend," he said. "I didn't mean for it to happen. She was lonely, and I'm only human."

Tommy understood fully. Rocky hadn't been a very good husband back then. He was on the road most of the time, playing gigs, leaving his family to fend for themselves while he was away. Delilah had been lonely. Even Tommy had seen it. Unlike Morgan, he hadn't taken advantage of her when she was vulnerable. "It's too late for excuses."

Morgan looked toward the windows. "It's too late for a lot of things." He turned back to Tommy. "But it's not too late for others." He took a deep breath. "I want to meet her, to get to know her. She needs to know who I am."

Tommy shook his head in frustration. "Not now," he said again. "Delilah's not ready. You know what's going on with her girls. She has enough on her plate."

"I'm not doing this to hurt Delilah." He met Tommy's eyes. "I'm running out of time, Tommy."

"What do you mean?"

Morgan took another deep breath. "I'm dying, Tommy," he said. "Six months to a year. That's all the doctors give me."

Tommy's growing frustration subsided, replaced by concern for his old friend. Apparently, Morgan's looks didn't tell the full story of his health. "I didn't know. You never said anything."

"I've only known for a couple of months."

"That's more than enough time for you to tell me."

"I didn't have anything to say at the time. I had to do my processing first. And then I had to let Margaret and the kids process it. They know, Tommy. I had to tell them. They deserved to know they had another sister. It would have been cruel to let them find out when my will was read."

"You put her in your will?"

Morgan looked away. "I'm not a bad man, Tommy. I couldn't forget my oldest child, no matter how hard I tried. She's a part of me, and I'm a part of her. I have to see her."

It was Tommy's turn to sigh. "Why don't you talk to Delilah yourself?"

Morgan lifted a brow. "You know the answer to that."

Yes, Tommy did. In addition to signing away his parental rights, Morgan had agreed to never contact Delilah again. And he hadn't. But he'd kept tabs on her and their child. Through Tommy. He should have told Delilah, but he hadn't. He would have to tell her now. Morgan was determined to see his daughter before he died.

"Will you help me out, Tommy? If anyone can talk some sense into Delilah, it's you."

"I'll do what I can."

"You're going to have to do more than that," he said. "I've made plans to see Alisha this weekend at the ASCAP conference."

"It's too soon," Tommy said. "Delilah needs to prepare her.

You can't just show up in her life and tell her you're her biological father. That would be cruel to her and to Delilah."

"I said I was going to see her. I didn't say I was going to tell her who I am to her. I have an opportunity this weekend, and I'm going to take it."

"You're being selfish."

Morgan shrugged. "I know, but I don't have any other choice. Time is running out for me. This is something I have to do while I'm still reasonably healthy."

"I'm sorry about your health, Morgan. I really am."

Morgan nodded. "I know. You've been a good friend to me over the years. Because of you, I know about my daughter. Now I want to know her. Knowing about her is not enough." After a few moments, he added, "I've written a couple of songs for her. I want the opportunity to sing them to her before I die. I need her to know that I loved her and that I never forgot about her. You won't deny a dying man, will you?"

Tommy felt the sincerity of his friend's words, and his heart softened. He guessed that Delilah's would as well. "I'll speak with Delilah, but I can't make any promises. She's emotionally exhausted, but she'll never admit it. I don't know if she's ready for any of this."

Morgan sat back in his chair. "Life works like that sometimes," he said. "Do you think I was ready for the hand God dealt me?" He shook his head. "But I got ready. That's the beauty of it. He really doesn't give us more than we can bear. I believe that for me, I believe it for Delilah, and I believe it for my daughter."

"You've got a lot of believing going on."

Morgan chuckled. "Believing is easy," he said. "Waiting to see that belief come to fruition is the hard part. I know. Do you think it was easy for Margaret and the kids to hear about my illness and then hear about my secret daughter? No, it wasn't. It was hard, but they finally came around. I'm not sure they've forgiven me, and I don't know if they ever will, but they still love me. That's all I can ask. Their love is all I need."

"You don't want their forgiveness?" Tommy asked, finding it hard to believe he didn't.

"I want it," Morgan explained, "but not for me. I want them to forgive me so they don't carry that weight around with them. Unforgiveness will be a cancer to their spiritual body as much as this cancer is to my physical body. It will kill them."

Chapter 25

Veronica had to drag herself out of bed on Thursday morning. The glow of life as a budding superstar had been tarnished a bit by the barrage of Veronica Y improvement suggestions. Of course, her always chipper husband was there to encourage her on her journey. Now she and Dexter sat in the waiting room of Jonas Public Relations, waiting to have their lives dissected.

"Mrs. Timmons," the receptionist at the desk called, "Ms. Jonas can see you now."

Veronica grimaced. "It figures I'd have to go first."

Dexter kissed her cheek. "That's because you're the star."

She frowned at him as she got up. "Right." She headed toward the door the receptionist opened for her. Before she entered, she turned to her husband and said, "Pray for me." His laughter was the last thing she heard before the door closed behind her.

She followed the receptionist down a short hallway to an office. An older woman with grayish hair, probably in her early fifties, met her at the door. "You must be Veronica," she said, extending her hand. "I'm Margaret Jonas. Come on in and make yourself comfortable."

Veronica followed the older woman into her office.

"Why don't we sit over here?" Ms. Jonas pointed to the round table with four chairs in the far corner of the office. "We'll be more comfortable."

Veronica followed Ms. Jonas to the table and took a seat across from her. "I'm sure Tia told you what to expect," the older woman said. When she nodded, Ms. Jonas said, "Good. Then we can get started." She flipped over a sheet of paper on the pad in front of her. "As you know, Legends is in the process of conducting extensive background checks on you and your husband."

"I thought they'd already done that," Veronica said.

"Not fully," Ms. Jonas explained. "A thorough check can take months. My job is to take what they find and what you and Dexter share with me today and determine the best way to address it in the media. So the first thing I need to know is whether there is anything in your background that can be used to embarrass you or your family."

"Not that I know of," Veronica said.

"No scandals, no abortions, no adultery, no stealing, no cheating?"

Veronica shook her head. "You'd have to meet my mother and sisters. Believe me, my family is too boring for scandals."

The older woman gave her a grim smile. "Or they're very good at keeping them hidden."

"I guess that's possible," Veronica said, though she couldn't imagine her mom or her sisters with any type of scandal in their lives.

"If there's something there, our investigators will sniff it out. All we know now is that you know nothing about any scandals. We can work with that. If anything does turn up, we can always portray you as shocked and disappointed because you didn't know." Ms. Jonas flipped the sheet over. "Now I have to ask about your husband and your marriage. Any adultery, cheating of any kind, reported or unreported domestic violence, separations, divorce filings, ex-spouses, hidden children, anything? In other words, how solid is your marriage?"

"My marriage is very solid," Veronica said. "Dexter and I argue as most couples do, but nothing that we don't get over in a matter of days."

Ms. Jonas put down her pencil. "Look, Veronica, it's important for you to be honest with me. I'm not here to judge you. I'm here to help you, but I can only help if you tell me the truth. Everybody has something in their life they wish the world didn't know or that makes them feel a bit of shame."

"Well, there is one thing," Veronica said, feeling as though she were about to betray her husband. "Dexter was up for tenure last year at his university, and he didn't get it. That's been a sore spot with him and with me."

"Do you feel he was treated unfairly?"

Veronica nodded. "I felt he deserved tenure. He works hard and he does good work."

Ms. Jonas jotted on her pad. "Did they give any reasons for his denial?"

"None. They never do. And that's not fair."

Ms. Jonas nodded. "So your husband is out of a job?"

"Actually, he's working on a book."

Ms. Jonas looked up at her and smiled. "Now, that's a good answer and good spin. Instead of focusing on your husband being unemployed as a result of being denied tenure, we'll focus on the opportunities he's pursuing. Can you tell me a little about this book? Of course I'll ask him, but I want to get your take on it as well."

"He's chronicling my career with Legends. You know, small-town girl makes good. That sort of thing."

"Oh," Ms. Jonas said. "I was hoping it was something independent of you."

"It won't be his first book," Veronica said, feeling a need to defend Dexter. "He's written several. I'm sure that's one of the reasons Legends wants him to write the book."

"That's all good," Ms. Jonas said, jotting on her pad again. "But it will go over better in the media if his new career is not so closely tied to yours. We don't want him perceived as a kept man, or worse, as a leech trying to make a name for himself off his wife's popularity. Either of those portrayals will make both of you look weak. I'll have to talk to Mr. Washington about it."

Veronica didn't agree with Ms. Jonas's assessment of how she and Dexter would look to the public, but the more she thought about it she had to concede the woman could be right. Even though she never thought of Dexter as a kept man or a leech and never would, she could see how others would. Sad to say, but she had thought that and worse of some of the lesser-known husbands and significant others of successful female artists. But Dexter wasn't like them. Until now, he'd had a job and supported them.

"Didn't you used to be in a group?" Ms. Jonas asked, interrupting Veronica's thoughts about Dexter.

"Yes, with my two sisters. The group was Delilah's Daughters. We were runners-up in the *Sing for America* competition."

Ms. Jonas nodded. "I remember now. I saw your family on television. I thought you were good. I'm sorry you lost."

"Thanks," Veronica said.

"But you really didn't lose much, did you?" Ms. Jonas asked, tapping her pen on her pad. "You're here with a deal with Legends. Where are your two sisters?"

Veronica rubbed her palms down her thighs. "They're at home in Birmingham."

"Home? What are they doing? Are they still singing?"

Veronica wanted to stand, felt she needed to move around. "My older sister, Roxanne, is an entertainer for a major cruise line. She travels a lot. My younger sister recently quit her job as a jingle writer for a top advertising firm and is focusing on her career as a songwriter."

"How do they feel about you being here?"

Veronica took a deep breath. "May I have some water?" she asked.

Ms. Jonas smiled at her. "Of course," she said. She got up, went to the wet bar in the corner of the room opposite the table where they sat, and brought back a bottle of water. "Here you go."

Veronica accepted the water and quickly took a few sips.

"Feel better?" Ms. Jonas asked.

Veronica nodded. "Much. Thanks for the water."

"Remember when I asked you about any scandals in your past?"

Veronica nodded, taking another swallow of water.

"Well, this breakup with your sisters could be considered a scandal. The media could try to present you as a fame-seeking diva willing to desert her musical family for a shot at fame."

"That's not the way it was," Veronica said, getting up from her seat. "I tried very hard to talk Legends into taking all of us, but they only wanted me."

"I know," Ms. Jonas said. "But I also know that you and your sisters were offered another contract by a smaller label. You turned that one down to take this one by yourself. How would you explain that to the media?"

Veronica picked up her bottle and took another swallow of water. "I don't know," she said.

"And that's all right, because figuring out the appropriate response is my job. Are your sisters supportive of your new career?"

Veronica shook her head. "They didn't want me to leave the group."

"That's understandable. It'll take them some time to get over their hurt at being left behind, but they'll come around. Close families always come around, and I get the impression yours was a very close family."

Veronica sat back down, taking comfort in the words Ms. Jonas spoke. She wanted to reconcile with her sisters. The contract buy-out money had been offered as a peace offering, but it hadn't been received the way she'd wanted. In fact, she thought the offer had served only to widen the breach between them. She cleared her throat. "You should know that I plan to use part of my Legends advance to buy myself out of that other contract with my sisters."

"So you're paying them off?"

"Certainly not," Veronica said. "But that's how they saw the offer."

Ms. Jonas stopped writing and looked up at her. "I'm not judging you, Veronica. You're trying to make things right with your sisters. You're treating them like business associates by buying yourself out of the contract, which is good business practice. We can work with that."

"Finally, some good news," Veronica said dryly.

Ms. Jonas chuckled. "Don't worry. Your case is an easy one, so far. It would help us a lot if we could get some promo shots of your family reconciled, happy and smiling, sometime soon. If that doesn't happen, we'll have to go another route. But let's think positive for now."

Veronica nodded, feeling safe in the hands of Ms. Jonas.

"Can you think of anything else you need to tell me?"

"Not a thing," Veronica said. What more did the woman want? She'd already opened up a vein by talking about her family. She had nothing more to give today.

Chapter 26

A *kept man. A leech.* Dexter couldn't get the words out of his mind. The voice of that PR woman rang in his ears even as he sat through the Friday morning retreat sessions given by the Legends publishing team. People would think he was a kept man or a leech if he didn't establish an identity apart from Veronica, she'd said. And the book about Veronica was not enough to alter that perception. *What will be enough?* he wondered as one of the speakers yammered on about the art of writing celebrity books.

The perceptions described by the PR woman had caught Dexter by surprise. He had never looked at himself in the way Ms. Jonas said others would, and he was sure Veronica hadn't either. Well, she hadn't until Ms. Jonas had suggested it to her, and even though Veronica hadn't mentioned it, Dexter was sure the older woman had done so. Both he and Veronica had a lot on their minds last night, so much that they had gone to bed without their usual recap of the day, each hugging one side of the bed, keeping their bodies and minds apart.

"It's time for lunch, man," the brother who had been sitting to the left of him said.

"Oh," Dexter said, embarrassed to have been caught not paying attention.

"Don't worry about it," the guy said. "That was a pretty boring speaker." The guy extended his hand. "I'm Alex Barrow," he said. "I'm doing a book on DJ Ray."

Dexter shook his hand. If this guy was writing about DJ Ray, the hottest rapper of the moment, he was someone Dexter wanted to know. "Dexter Timmons. I'm doing a book on Veronica Y."

"I've heard about her. I hear they're pulling out all the stops for her first album. I wish I had it like that. Do you think she's sleeping with Washington? I hear he's a real ladies' man."

Dexter's jaw tightened. "I know she isn't."

"Don't take it personal, man," he said. "These artists will do about anything for a contract, and the A&R reps know it, so they take advantage. That's the way it works in this business. Too bad you can't put that in the book. If you did, Legends would never let it be published."

Dexter decided against telling Alex he was Veronica's husband. He would definitely be one to think along the same lines as Ms. Jonas. "Are you saying Legends censors their authors?"

"I'm saying Legends wants their artists and their label presented in a positive light. Affairs between new artists and established A&R reps don't fit the image they want presented to the public."

Dexter followed Alex to the hotel restaurant. "You seem to know your way around this place," he said.

"I've done several books for Legends, so I've attended several of these retreats. They always hold them here. I think they own the building."

After a waiter seated them at a table near the wall of windows with a view of the Atlanta skyline, Dexter asked, "How long have you been writing?"

Alex chuckled. "You won't believe this, but the first book I wrote was a celebrity book on my wife, who was a new Legends artist at the time. Her career didn't make it, and neither did our marriage. Washington loved the book, though, and gave me a shot at another celebrity effort. That time the star made it and so did the book. Since then I've done five more books for him." The waiter came then and took their orders. When he was gone, Alex asked, "So how did you end up here?"

Dexter thought about lying but decided against it. "Veronica Y is my wife."

Alex sucked in his breath. "I've really put my foot in it, haven't I? I'm sorry, man. I had no idea."

"No need to apologize," Dexter said. "I appreciate the honesty. I can guarantee you, though, that my wife has not slept with Mr. Washington. She didn't even meet him until a few weeks ago. She was on that show *Sing for America*. She and her sisters came in second place. They performed as Delilah's Daughters."

"Hey, I remember them. They were good." Alex winked. "And good-looking too."

Dexter chuckled. "I'll take that as a compliment. My wife and her sisters are very attractive women. We just got to town on Sunday, and this week has been an eye-opening introduction to what our new life is going to be. The business ain't no joke."

"You're telling me," Alex said. "Are you up for it?"

"I thought I was," Dexter said. "But some things are coming at me that I didn't expect. I'm trying to figure out how to deal with them."

"I know what you mean," Alex said, "because I've been where you are. You have two things that you have to keep in check: your ego and your wife's demands. You've got to keep your ego in check when you're out in public. Your wife is the star, and the focus is going to be on her. You've got to accept that and be okay with it."

"Easier said than done," Dexter said, thinking of his reaction to the fans Veronica acquired during the *Sing for America* competition.

"Practice," Alex said. "And pray. And get ready to be called Mr. Y."

"Ouch," Dexter said.

"I feel you, but that's your life if your wife makes it big." Alex took a swallow of the sparkling water he'd ordered. "Once you get your ego in check, you have to keep your wife's demands in check. She can be a diva in public, as long as she doesn't disrespect you, but at home she needs to be your wife. You've got to be the man in your home, brother, even if she does bring in most of the money."

Dexter hadn't really thought about how the money and who was making it would affect his marriage. He was used to Veronica deferring to him and had assumed things would continue that way. But Alex had a point. Once Veronica hit it big, she might try to bring that diva attitude into their home. He'd have to be on the watch for any of that so he could nip it in the bud. "You paint a pretty bleak picture, man."

"Just remember who you are. Keep your identity and don't let anybody try to tell you who or what you are. You have to know that for yourself."

Dexter shook his head. "I don't have identity problems." At least, he hadn't before that meeting with Ms. Jonas.

"Then you haven't spoken with Ms. Jonas or else she's changed her spiel. I was fine until I spoke with her. Things went downhill fast from there. She had me looking at myself differently and thinking that my wife was looking at me differently. Before I knew it, my marriage was over."

The waiter came with their food. When he left the table, Dexter said, "I met with Ms. Jonas today, so I know what you mean."

After taking a bite of his hamburger, Alex said, "Then I see why you couldn't concentrate on those sessions. That old woman can mess a brother up really bad. Don't let her do it to you. Trust your wife. Support her. And forget what other people may be saying about you or your marriage. Believe me, if I could get a do-over, I'd take it. Jann and I had a good marriage."

"What's Jann doing now?" Dexter asked.

"She went back home to North Carolina. Said Atlanta wasn't for her. She was right. Legends almost killed her spirit, but she's got it back now. She's remarried with a couple of kids, singing in the choir every Sunday, and as happy as can be."

"Why didn't you go back with her?"

Alex opened his arms wide. "Because I love it here, man. I love being a part of the action, even if it's behind the scenes. I like knowing the real stories behind the artists." He tapped a finger to his temple. "My retirement book is up here. I know Legends will fight my publishing it, but I believe I've found a way around them. I'm just waiting on the right time."

Dexter chuckled. "I can't believe you're telling me this, man. How do you know I won't take it back to Mr. Washington?"

Now it was Alex's turn to chuckle. "Because deep down you know Mr. Washington doesn't care about you or your wife. When he looks at her, he sees dollar signs. When he looks at you, he sees somebody he has to put up with in order to keep his moneymaker happy. Why would you give him the heads-up on anything I'm doing?"

"Good point," Dexter said, concluding he'd made a good contact in Alex. He decided to make good use of it. "I want my wife and me to be successful in this business. The two people who seem to have the most input on that are Charles Washington and Tia Martin. What can you tell me about them that may give us some leverage down the road, if we need it?"

Chapter 27

*Y*ou should have come with me, Roxanne," Alisha said into her cell phone. She sat on a concrete wall outside the conference center at the Los Angeles Music Pavilion. "It's been phenomenal." She pressed the Home key on her phone so she could see the time. "Look, I've got to run. I've got a mentoring session in ten minutes. You'll never guess who I'm meeting with."

"Don't make me guess," Roxanne said. "Tell me."

Alisha laughed. "I'm not telling you," she said. "You'll have to wait until this evening. After the mentoring session, I'm going out with a group of folks I met here. It'll be late when I get in, but I'll be sure to call and let you know how everything went."

"Alisha, don't you dare hang up this phone without telling me who you're meeting with."

Alisha kept laughing. "Bye-bye, sis. I'll talk to you tonight."

"Alisha—"

Grinning, Alisha pressed the Off button. Then she picked

up her book bag and headed toward room 215, where she was scheduled to meet with the mentor. Roxanne would be amused to know that Alisha herself didn't even know who the mentor was. ASCAP was funny that way. If you wanted a mentor, you had to complete an application packet. This packet was distributed to several potential mentors, who selected mentees from among the applicants. Alisha knew she was very fortunate to have been picked. She pressed her hand down the front of her dark blue two-piece suit. Her advertising wardrobe was paying off big now. She knew she looked every bit the part of the professional. Taking a deep breath, she pulled open the door. She froze in her steps when she saw who was seated at the table. *It can't be*, she told herself. *It can't be.*

A big smile on his face, the man stood and extended his hand. "I'm Morgan Sampson," he said. "And you must be Alisha Monroe."

Alisha heard the words, but she couldn't really make sense of them. This couldn't be Morgan Sampson, not *the* Morgan Sampson. There had to be some mistake.

A smile still on his face, he said, "Are you all right?"

Those words seem to unfreeze Alisha's feet. "I'm sorry," she said, walking fast to reach him so she could shake his outstretched hand. "Yes, I'm Alisha Monroe. It's so great to meet you, Mr. Sampson. I know all of your work." Alisha kept shaking his hand. "I can't believe you're really here. I can't believe I'm really here."

Morgan Sampson laughed a deep laugh from down in his belly. "Believe it," he said. "Now sit down so we can get to know each other. I've read your application, of course, but why don't you tell me a little about yourself and your interest in songwriting."

Mr. Sampson's warm smile made Alisha feel comfortable, so she began to talk. She told him about her parents, her sisters, and how her love of music developed.

"You've been writing since you were a child?"

She bobbed her head up and down. "My parents encouraged all of us. I've always been the writer. My sister Roxanne is the singer. And Veronica is the dancer and entertainer."

He nodded. "Go on with your story. I didn't mean to interrupt."

Alisha proceeded to tell him about the origins of Delilah's Daughters, the impact of their father's death on the group, and the *Sing for America* contest.

"Delilah's Daughters should have won that contest," he said. "You and your sisters have something special."

"I wish the voters had seen it."

Mr. Sampson waved off her comment. "Annie Jones wasn't bad, and she'll have a decent career because her fans will buy her first couple of albums. After that, she'll fade because her ceiling is low. The ceiling for you and your sisters was high. Why did you split up?"

"My sister Veronica got an offer she couldn't resist from Legends."

"Don't take it personally. Charles Washington looks for a certain type of artist. I'm not surprised he didn't offer the group a contract. Gospel groups aren't his cup of tea. I can see him branding your sister as a pop-gospel artist with the emphasis on pop. Delilah's Daughters was very much gospel-pop, with the emphasis on gospel. That was the power and strength of the group. You and your other sister aren't giving up on the group, are you?"

Despite the conversations she'd had with Roxanne and her mother about relaunching the group with her mother as a member, Alisha had refused to invest all of her energy in the project. There was too much risk for failure and disappointment. A few words from Mr. Sampson had changed all of that. No way was she giving up on the group. Not after Morgan Sampson himself told her they were special. "We're not giving up, Mr. Sampson, but we needed some direction, and I think you're giving it to us."

He smiled. "I'm happy to know that I'm helping. The purpose of these mentoring sessions is to provide insight from someone who's been in the business a fairly long time and who has attained a certain amount of success. I'm not always right, but my instincts are good. I can spot talent, and you and your sisters have it. I could see that from the show."

"I can't believe you watched us."

"I'll be honest," he said. "Don't be embarrassed. My son DVR-ed you and made me watch it."

Alisha laughed. "I'm not embarrassed," she said. "I think I owe your son a dinner or my firstborn child. I'm not quite sure which one."

"You have a wonderful sense of humor, Alisha. That will also help you in this business. The only thing you can take seriously is your music. Everything else has to be viewed through a lens that can see the humor and ridiculousness in everything around the music. If you do that, you won't get caught up in the drama that ensnares so many young artists."

"I'll remember that," Alisha said.

"Did you write any of the songs you sang on the show?"

She nodded. "We only got to perform a couple of my original songs over the length of the competition. We mostly did stylized arrangements of existing songs."

"And you did those arrangements?"

She nodded.

"Pretty impressive," he said. "Those arrangements showcased the talents of you and your sisters in a unique and provocative way. They show that you know what the heart and soul of the group is. It takes some groups years to find their heart and soul. Some never find it. You've found yours, and that's what sets you apart."

"Thank you," Alisha said, because she couldn't think of anything else. Morgan Sampson had complimented her on her arrangements. She felt lightheaded. She hoped she didn't pass out and embarrass herself and him.

"Now, do you have any questions for me?" Mr. Sampson asked.

Alisha had a zillion questions, but she couldn't think of one right now. Before she could make one up, Mr. Sampson reached in his jacket pocket, pulled out a gold case, opened it, and slid a business card across the table to her. "That card has all my numbers on it. If you think of a question, give me a call. If I don't answer, leave a message and I'll get back to you."

Alisha studied the card. She really couldn't see herself calling Mr. Sampson up out of the blue. "Thank you," she said. That was all she could come up with right then.

"I'm serious," he said, as if sensing her uncertainty. "I want to see and hear great things from you and your sisters. Are you working on a demo?"

"As soon as I get back we get started," she said.

"You're working with Magic City Studios?"

She nodded. "Mr. Johns offered Delilah's Daughters a contract, but he had to withdraw it when Veronica left. So right now we're trying to put a new Delilah's Daughters in front of him and see what he thinks. We're hoping he offers the new group a contract."

"Tommy is a good man. He'll give you good advice, I'm sure. But I'm serious about you contacting me if you have any questions or if you want to bounce something off me. And I want to hear that demo, so make sure I get a copy."

Mr. Sampson's graciousness overwhelmed Alisha. "I don't know what to say," she said. "'Thank you' isn't enough. I can't believe you're extending yourself this way to me and Delilah's Daughters."

"Don't think about it. Somebody helped me when I got started. It's the least I can do."

Alisha thought it was much more than that. "My mom and sisters are going to lose their minds when I tell them about this session."

Mr. Sampson laughed. "Let's hope they don't go that far."

Chapter 28

Veronica sat with Tia on a leather couch in one of Club Dance Atlanta's VIP rooms on Friday evening. She rocked her shoulders to the beat that thumped in the celebrated midtown club.

"You look like you're having fun," Tia said to her.

"I'm itching to get out on the floor," Veronica said, now popping her fingers. "I hope Dexter gets here soon."

"You know you don't have to wait for Dexter to hit the dance floor," Tia said. "There are plenty of men here who'd gladly be your partner."

"Not an option, and neither is dancing solo," Veronica said. If she were at one of her hangouts in Birmingham or Tuscaloosa, she'd be on the floor by herself in a minute. It wouldn't matter there because everybody knew her and knew she loved to dance. In this new city, she wasn't sure what message a woman dancing alone would send, especially in the hot pink Victor Meggan mini she was sporting.

Max, their waiter, walked over to them. "You ladies are popular tonight," he said. "Two more drinks for you."

Tia took one and smiled in the direction of the man who had sent it. Veronica smiled as well, but she passed on the drink. "Do yourself and me a favor, Max," Veronica said. "If I get any more drink offers, please turn them down for me."

"Will do," Max said. "How about you, Tia?"

Tia shook her head. "No way. I don't want to miss out on my Mr. Right or Mr. Right Now." She tipped her glass toward Veronica. "She already has hers."

Veronica chuckled. "If my Mr. Right doesn't hurry and get here, I may have to go with a Mr. Right Now myself."

Tia leaned close to her. "That 50 Cent wannabe over there looks like he wants to be your Mr. Right Now. He's been staring at you all evening. All it would take is a signal from you."

"No way," Veronica said. "Besides, it's not me these guys are interested in. It's this dress."

Tia fingered the lace of the bodice of the black bustier. "I can't believe Victor sent one of his designs over for you to wear tonight. You definitely made a strong impression on him."

"I couldn't believe it either," Veronica said. "But his generosity made for a great ending to a not so great day."

Tia took a handful of nuts from the bowl on the table in front of them and tossed them in her mouth. "What was wrong with your day? I thought everything went well."

Veronica searched Tia's face for any trace of sarcasm. When she found none, she said, "The producers seemed to think my voice lacks personality. I have no signature style. I translated that to mean my voice is boring."

Tia rolled her eyes. "Oh, please," she said. "Don't get it

twisted, Ms. Diva. They did say your voice lacked definition, but they also said definition can be learned. Producers would much rather work with someone who has voice training but no defined style over someone who has defined their vocal style and is unwilling to change it. Believe me, they're licking their lips thinking about what they can do with you. They're like painters before a blank canvas."

Veronica rubbed her finger down her glass of iced tea. "Thank you," she said. "I think—"

Before she could finish, Max returned to the table. "There are three guys over there who are dying to meet you and take a photo," he said to Veronica, pointing to three buppie-looking guys at the bar. They looked fresh from the nine-to-five in some downtown office. She'd guess they were lawyers or bankers. "Apparently, they saw you on *Sing for America*. Is it okay for them to come over?"

"Definitely," Tia said to Max. Then she said to Veronica, "This is now business, and those are fans. You always meet fans, so get your best smile on."

After getting the go-ahead from Max, the three men headed toward the table. They quickly introduced themselves as the Thompson brothers—Calvin, Edward, and Judd. When they finished, Tia excused herself, suggesting that the brothers keep Veronica company until she got back.

After the men were seated, Judd said, "I have to tell you that we fell in love with Delilah's Daughters when you were on *Sing for America*."

"We never missed a show," Calvin said.

"And we think you were robbed," Edward said. "No way that country girl should have beat you."

Veronica gave the three men a genuine smile. "Thank you for your support. We had a great time on the show. I'll have to tell my sisters about you."

"Give a special hello to Roxanne for me," Judd said. "I loved you all, but there was something about her that got to me." He pressed his hand across his heart. "She sang herself straight into my heart."

His brothers laughed. "And then he was sad all week until he got a chance to see her again the next week," Edward said. "He did everything in his power to get tickets to that finals show, hoping he'd meet her, but he couldn't make it happen."

"I don't deny it," Judd said. "But I wasn't the only brother with a crush. Let's just say you and Alisha had your admirers as well."

"Alisha was my girl," Calvin said. Then Calvin and Judd both looked at Edward.

"Now I'm embarrassed," Edward said. "It's okay for them to talk about their crushes since your sisters aren't here. I'm beginning to wish I wasn't here."

Veronica reached out and covered one of Edward's hands with one of hers. "There's nothing to be embarrassed about. As an artist, it's always nice to know you've made a connection with the audience."

"You made a connection, all right," Judd said. He slapped Edward on the shoulder. "Old boy here cried like a baby when he found out you were married."

Veronica couldn't help but laugh at the glare Edward shot his brothers. "Stop teasing him," she said to Calvin and Judd. "You three remind me of me and my sisters. We give each other a hard time just like you do, but it's all done in love."

"Well, don't be surprised if you read an article in tomorrow's paper about a man giving his two brothers a beat-down for embarrassing him in front of a beautiful woman," Edward said.

"Thank you," Veronica said. "You're too kind."

"Can we get a picture or two with you, Veronica?" Judd asked.

"Of course," she said.

"What if you take one with each of us? Will that be okay?"

"Great," she said. Then she patted the space next to her. "Who's going to be first?"

Edward stepped up. He settled next to her on the couch. "Is it okay if I put my arm on the couch behind you? I promise not to touch you."

Veronica chuckled. "You're too sweet," she said, cuddling close to him.

Judd took the picture with his camera phone. Then they rotated until pictures of all three had been taken with her.

Just as they finished, Tia returned with a camera guy in tow. "I'm Veronica's personal assistant," she told the men. "Would you be willing to take a few promo pictures with Veronica? She's a new artist at Legends, and we need pictures for her press portfolio. You'll have to sign releases for us to use the pictures."

The men quickly agreed. As Tia directed them from one shot to the next, Veronica found herself enjoying the company of the brothers and their quirky sense of humor. They had her laughing the whole time. After they shot the last staged photo, Veronica gave each brother a hug, which was also captured on film. "Thank you so much," she told them.

"No need to thank us," Edward said. "It was our pleasure. We'll never forget this night. Thanks for putting up with us."

As the men shuffled off, Tia said, "Good job. You even looked like you enjoyed it."

"I did enjoy it," Veronica said, tapping her feet to the music. Her time with the brothers had only made her more eager to dance. "They're nice men."

"Whatever," Tia said. "Why didn't you ask one of them to dance? I don't know what's holding Dexter up."

"Neither do I," Veronica said, getting up. "I do want to dance before the evening is over. Let me go make Edward's night." She winked at Tia and walked to the bar where the men had gathered and tapped Edward on the shoulder. When he turned, she said, "Dance with me? It seems my husband has stood me up."

His two brothers laughed. "He doesn't dance."

Edward stood and took her hand. "I do now."

Veronica laughed her way to the dance floor. Edward didn't talk much as he seemed to be concentrating on his moves. "Your brothers were wrong," she said to him. "You can dance."

He laughed. "It doesn't come natural. I can tell you that."

She threw back her head and laughed again. And that's when she saw Dexter. He stood at the corner of the bar staring at her. And he didn't look happy.

Dedra Knighton

Chapter 29

D exter nursed his drink and watched his wife. She'd finally seen him after he'd watched her flirt with three men, follow them back to the bar, and then end up on the dance floor laughing her head off with one of them.

"Don't even think about it."

Dexter looked back and saw Tia standing behind him. "What are you talking about?"

She took the stool next to his and waved to the bartender for another drink. "You'd better get your mind in the game, Dexter. This is the life you and Veronica have chosen. She's no longer yours. She belongs to Legends now, and if things go according to plan, she'll belong to the world. There's a cost to fame, no matter what you've been led to believe."

"You don't have to preach to me," Dexter told her. "I know the deal."

"Then act like it," she said, picking up her glass. "Lift your drink to your wife and smile at her so she doesn't feel compelled to end the dance early to come soothe your bruised ego. This is business, not some high school boyfriend-girlfriend stuff. Grow up."

Though Dexter wanted to throw a few of the juicy tidbits Alex had given him about Tia in her face, he restrained himself, deciding to save his knowledge for another day. He pursed his lips and lifted his glass to his wife as he'd been told.

"Now that's a good boy," Tia said. "You keep doing that and your marriage may survive her career."

"What are you talking about, Tia? What would you know about marriage or surviving a career?"

Tia put down her glass. "I figured Veronica would tell you about me," she said. "Look, I'm not ashamed of my past. I went for the gold ring. I didn't get it, but I went for it. And if I get another shot, I'm going to go for it again."

He wanted to ask if that was why she was sleeping with Charles Washington, but again, he decided to save that chip for later. He'd let Tia keep thinking she had the upper hand for now. When the time came, he'd use all the information Alex had given him. Until then, he would play things her way. "I'm not hating on you," he said.

"Good. Then maybe I won't have to tell Mr. Washington about your jealousy issues."

He studied his drink. "Is that a threat?"

She sipped her drink. "It's a promise. Legends won't allow anybody to stand in the way of their plans for Veronica. Not me. And definitely not you. You're either with the program totally or you're out. There's no middle ground. You'd best remember that."

So this is the way it's going to be, Dexter thought. No more pretenses about concern for me and my career. This was all about Veronica. "I'm 100 percent behind my wife," he said. "Her success is my success."

"Just don't forget that fact," Tia said. "Look, I don't mean to come down hard on you. In fact, I'd like for us to work together in the best interest of Veronica's career."

He eyed her. "What do you mean?"

Leaning close to him, Tia said, "I know you have a lot of influence with her. If she's skeptical about an approach Legends wants to take with her, it'd be good to know that you'll be on our side working to get her to see it our way. If you would agree to do that, it would make everybody's life easier."

"I'll always look out for my wife's interests," he said, pretending not to have understood her request for him to sell out Veronica.

"I want you to think in terms of Legends' interests," she clarified.

He stirred his drink with a straw. "Aren't they the same?"

She nodded. "But sometimes your wife is not going to see it that way. Take the 'boob job' issue. It's in her best interest to get one, but she doesn't see it that way. We need her on board with it. You can help get her on board."

"And why would I push her to do something she's dead set against? What's in it for me?"

Tia smiled at him. "Ah," she said. "Now we get to the bottom line. What do you want?"

He returned her smile. "Let me think about it."

Chapter 30

When Veronica left Sunday morning service at Victory Center Community Church, a megachurch that catered to Atlanta's elite, she wanted to pull away and spend some time in prayer and meditation. Unfortunately, her schedule didn't include any such downtime. Tia had hired a car service to take them directly from church to Charles Washington's summer house on Myrtle Beach for a luncheon meeting.

Veronica spotted their car and driver as soon as she exited the church. The driver opened the back door of the black sedan as she and Dexter reached the car. She slid in first, with her husband following. Tia joined them a couple of minutes later.

"How'd you like Victory Center and Pastor Finley?" Tia asked as the car pulled away from the church and started on the five-hour drive.

"I liked it," Dexter said. He nudged Veronica's shoulder. "Pastor Finley had Veronica tearing up a couple of times."

Veronica beat back the groan that bubbled up in her at Dexter's insensitivity. "The sermon touched me. What can I say?"

Dexter hugged her. "I was teasing, babe. It was a good sermon. The pastor confirmed what I've been saying all along: now is our time."

"Pastor Finley is like that," Tia said. "His messages are always relevant."

Veronica sank back in the corner of her seat and let Tia and Dexter's conversation swirl around her. She agreed with both of them on the day's message. The sermon, "Everything in Its Time," had been timely for where she was in her life. She couldn't help but feel God had planned the message just for her.

Everything in its time. The sermon confirmed for her that leaving Delilah's Daughters had been the right thing to do—for her, for her mom, and for her sisters. They'd been so close and relied on each other for so long that they needed to trust God and step out into the unfamiliar. Her mom and sisters might not see it that way yet, but the sermon confirmed that they would. She hoped it would be soon because she missed them terribly. In the meantime, she'd have to move forward in faith along this new path God had put before her.

Everything in its time. She knew she was on the right path, but she didn't know quite how to navigate the path. If she listened to Tia and Dexter, she'd do everything anybody at

Legends asked her to do without raising a question or offering any resistance. Was that what God wanted for her? She didn't think so. But she didn't know where to draw the line. Should she agree to the weave and nix the boob job? Or should she nix both? Or agree to both? Should she agree to being branded a pop-gospel artist rather than a gospel-pop artist, or did it really even matter?

Everything in its time. Was she making these decisions too difficult? Her father had always likened walking along God's path to driving on the highway. There was the main roadway, the path God wanted us to follow, and on either side there were the shoulders, the sin that we should avoid at all costs. The key to following God was to stay on the road and off the shoulders. So what was the road and what were the shoulders in her life now? She sighed deeply.

"What are you sighing about?" Tia asked. "I thought you were asleep."

"Just thinking," Veronica said.

"Well, don't think too hard," Tia told her. "This meeting with Mr. Washington is very important. The thing that needs to be foremost in your mind is how much you want the career that Legends is offering you."

Veronica sat up. "Why are you always questioning whether I want this? I want it," she said, knowing her frustration sounded in her voice. "I wouldn't be here if I didn't want it."

Dexter put a hand on her knee. "Calm down. Tia didn't mean anything by her comments."

She pushed Dexter's hand away. "Why do you have to speak for Tia? She's sitting right here."

"I didn't mean anything by it," Tia said. "I'm only doing my job."

Veronica rolled her eyes. She couldn't help it. "Then let's make a deal. Unless you see me do or say something that specifically indicates that I don't want to be here, let's drop that question and any related ones. I'm here. I'm in the game. Case closed."

"Okay, diva," Tia said. "Just don't get to Myrtle Beach and start telling Mr. Washington what you will and will not do. You'll find yourself back in Birmingham so quick you won't even believe you were ever here."

Veronica took a deep breath. "I'm not an idiot, Tia, so you don't have to repeat everything you tell me fifty times. I signed with Legends because I believed they could help me achieve the career I wanted. Why would I work against them now?"

"That's the question I keep asking," Tia said.

"Well, don't ask it anymore," Veronica said. "This is my career, not a redo of yours. Don't get me wrong. I appreciate your advice and the special insight you have because of what you've experienced, but you're my personal assistant, not my boss. We need to get our boundaries clear."

"Tia's only trying to help," Dexter said.

Veronica cut a glare at him. "Just once," she said to her husband, "I wish you'd side with me instead of Tia."

Dexter was about to respond, but Tia started laughing.

"What's so funny?" Veronica asked.

"It's only been a week and you've officially turned into a diva."

Veronica had no idea what Tia was talking about, but if standing up for herself was being a diva, then she guessed she was a diva. She didn't really care what Tia thought because the morning's sermon had given her some clarity. God had put her on this road, and she would stay on it. She'd do what Legends wanted of her as long as it didn't send her off the road and onto the shoulders.

Chapter 31

S ince receiving the checks from Veronica in the mail the day before, Delilah couldn't get her mind off her middle daughter. She'd started praying for Veronica during morning church service, and she was still praying for her now as she prepared dinner. She wanted the best for all her girls, so she would never agree with Veronica's decision to sign with Legends, but she still loved her. *Lord, keep her safe, physically and spiritually.*

As she pulled a pan of cornbread out of the oven, she heard the front door open and Alisha call out, "I'm home."

"I'm in the kitchen," Delilah called back as she cut the cornbread into squares and placed the squares on a platter. "Welcome back," she said to her youngest daughter when she entered the kitchen. "How was the conference?"

"Fantastic," Alisha said, kissing her mother's cheek. "Hey, what are you cooking? It smells good in here."

Delilah slapped Alisha's hand when she reached for a cornbread square.

Alisha laughed. "I'm hungry, Momma, I've had a long day." She picked up a cornbread square, broke it into two pieces, and popped one of the pieces into her mouth. "This is delicious," she said. "It's so warm. All I need is some butter."

"No, you don't," Delilah said. "Dinner will be ready in a few minutes. You'll live until then."

Alisha leaned back and rested against the counter next to the sink. "If I faint from hunger, Momma, it'll be your fault."

Delilah chuckled. The things Alisha came up with. "I'm sure you'll live, sweetheart," she said. "Now tell me about your conference."

"It was wonderful, Momma," Alisha said. "I signed up for this mentor program, and you'll never guess who chose me as his mentee. I couldn't believe it myself. I still can't believe it. You'll never guess."

Delilah's heart filled with joy at Alisha's childlike excitement. After everything that had gone on with the contest and Veronica leaving, she realized how much her youngest child needed something for herself. She was disappointed in herself as a mother because she hadn't recognized the need sooner. She rested a palm on her daughter's cheek. "It's good to see you so happy, Alisha." Dropping her hand, she added, "Now tell me who your mentor is."

Alisha hopped up on the counter, shaking her head. "You'll have to guess, but you'll never guess."

Delilah laughed. "If I'll never guess, why are you making me guess?" She went to the refrigerator and pulled out a bowl of potato salad, Alisha's favorite. "Tell me," Delilah said, "or I won't feed you."

"I'll fight you for that potato salad," Alisha said, hopping down off the counter. She picked up a spoon. "I'll tell you," she said, "but I need a test taste to ready myself."

Laughing, Delilah pushed the bowl toward Alisha. "Tell me while you scoop."

Alisha dug her spoon into the bowl of potato salad. With a big scoop on her spoon, she closed her eyes. "Morgan Sampson chose to be my mentor." Then she put the spoon in her mouth. After she swallowed, she opened her eyes. "Morgan Sampson chose me," she repeated. "I still can't believe it."

Delilah couldn't believe it either. She didn't want to believe it.

"He said he saw Delilah's Daughters on TV and thought we should have won," Alisha continued. She proceeded to tell Delilah about her conversation with Mr. Sampson.

Delilah busied herself with clearing the stove while she listened to Alisha's excited chatter, relieved that no immediate feedback was required from her. She needed the time to compose herself. "It sounds like you're happy with Mr. Sampson."

"Happy? Momma, happy doesn't come close." She stood and spread her arms. "I'm ecstatic. Morgan Sampson gave me his stamp of approval. He thinks I have what it takes to make it in this business. I still can't believe it. I hope this is not a dream. If it is, I don't want to wake up."

Alisha's pure joy forced Delilah to put her concerns on hold. If meeting Morgan made Alisha this happy, then Delilah would be happy too. For now. She reached out and pinched her daughter's cheek.

"Ouch," Alisha said, rubbing her cheek. "Why did you do that?"

Delilah laughed. "So you'll know what happened was not a dream."

Alisha laughed, and then she kissed her mother. "You're the best, Momma. You really are. I love you so much. I'm so grateful for what you and Daddy did for us with Delilah's Daughters and all. I'm so grateful for that contest even though we lost. If we hadn't been on, Mr. Sampson probably wouldn't have chosen me to mentor."

Delilah tried to keep a straight face. The contest might have played a role in Morgan's decision to become Alisha's mentor, but she was sure it wasn't the most important factor. "Mr. Sampson knows talent when he sees it."

"That's an understatement, given his track record. He's worked with the biggest stars in gospel music. And I told him all about our plans to rebrand Delilah's Daughters with you as a member. He was all for that idea."

I'll bet he was, Delilah thought with a tinge of sarcasm. "Will you help me get these serving bowls and trays to the dining room?" she said.

"Will do." Alisha picked up the bread platter and the potato salad bowl. "It's just the two of us?"

Delilah added ice to a pitcher of tea. "Roxanne was supposed to be here, but she accepted a schedule change, so now she won't get in until Wednesday. She told me to tell you that she's going to want the lowdown on the conference."

"I'll give it to her," Alisha said, heading out of the kitchen. "I hope she'll be as encouraged as I am when she hears what Mr. Sampson had to say. We both have been due for some good news, and we've finally gotten some. You know, this may be crazy, but a part of me was hoping that Veronica would be here too. I'd like to share our good news with her."

Delilah walked into the dining room behind her daughter. "It's not crazy," she said. "You've been thinking about Veronica too?" When Alisha nodded, she said, "That makes two of us. The checks she promised to send arrived in the mail yesterday. She's been on my mind since they came. I've been praying for her."

Alisha put the platter and bowl on the table. "I need the money, but I'm not sure how I feel about taking the check now. The meeting with Mr. Sampson opened my eyes and my heart in a lot of ways. I think I was unfair to Veronica. Maybe we all were."

"We all could have handled the situation differently, me included," Delilah said.

"I'm surprised you haven't called her by now," Alisha said.

"Believe me, I've thought about it. In fact, I've picked up the phone a couple of times to do just that."

"Why haven't you?"

Delilah pulled out a dining room chair and took a seat. "It's such a difficult situation for all of us," she said. "I want to call and find out what she's doing, but I'm not ready to give her the encouragement she needs to see her new commitment through. If I can't encourage her, I'm only going to hurt her, and I don't want to do that."

She said grace as soon as Alisha was seated in the chair across from her.

"I called her during my layover in the Atlanta airport today," Alisha said, popping another cornbread square into her mouth. "You know, when Veronica took the Legends contract and Magic City withdrew the other one, I was a bit lost. Now that I have some direction and feel positive about where my career is going, I can be happy for Veronica. I called to tell her that, and I wanted her to be happy about our plans for restarting Delilah's Daughters. I miss her, Momma. I think I even miss Dexter."

Delilah spooned some potato salad onto her plate. "I understand, darling. What you're feeling is only natural. How is Veronica doing?"

Alisha shrugged. "I don't know. I didn't get to speak with her, so I left a message. She hasn't called back, though. I'm not sure what that means. Maybe she's still upset with us? What if those checks are her last communication with us?"

"Don't read so much into it. I'm sure she has a full schedule. She probably didn't return your call because she's busy."

"Too busy for family? That's not very encouraging, especially since she seems to have time for clubbing."

"What are you talking about?" Delilah asked.

Alisha dabbed at her mouth and then got up from the table. "Hold on a minute." When she returned to the room, she had a newspaper in her hand. "Look what I picked up at the Atlanta airport during my layover." She opened the Sunday edition of the *Atlanta Journal-Constitution* to the front page of the entertainment section and held it out for Delilah to see.

"That's Veronica," Delilah said, leaning close to get a good look at the picture of her daughter flanked by three handsome young men. The background suggested they were in a nightclub.

"It's her and the three Thompson brothers," Alisha said.

Delilah looked over at her youngest daughter. "Thompson brothers? Who are they?"

Alisha sat back down. "Apparently, their family owns one of the largest real estate companies in the Southeast. They own a lot of commercial properties in cities like Atlanta and Charlotte, but they made a killing with the beachfront property they scooped up along the Atlantic coast." She inclined her head toward the picture. "That picture was taken at a midtown Atlanta nightclub on Saturday night. Anything the brothers do is big news in Atlanta. This was a coup for Veronica and her handlers. Some people would kill for this kind of exposure. Read the caption."

"Real estate moguls welcome rising Legends superstar, Veronica Y, to the Atlanta club scene," Delilah read. "Ms. Y might be familiar to *Sing for America* fans. She was one of three sisters comprising the second-place group, Delilah's Daughters. Veronica Y seems to be flying solo these days."

"So, she's not that busy," Alisha said. "Maybe we should try calling her again?"

Delilah studied her middle daughter's face. She looked happy and safe, like she was thriving in her new world. "Let's not push it. You've already called. She'll call back when she's ready." She pushed the newspaper aside.

"But—"

"That picture tells us that she's fine. We'll have to accept that for now. Besides, that's enough about Veronica for now. What else did Mr. Sampson say about the group?"

Alisha shrugged. "That was about it. He did encourage us to get in the studio and get the demo done. Mr. Tommy will help us out with that, won't he?"

"He'll welcome the chance to do it."

"Then you'll set up a meeting with him?"

Delilah already had plans to meet with Tommy. They had a lot to discuss. "I'm meeting with him first thing Monday morning. I'll put the meeting on his schedule then."

"Great," Alisha said. "We need to get started sooner rather than later. I'm free anytime, but it'll have to be after Roxanne gets back. I think we all should be there."

Though Delilah had a mounting concern about Morgan's involvement, she was happy to see her daughter's excitement return. "That conference lit a fire under you, didn't it?"

Alisha nodded. "I don't feel left out anymore," she explained. "I feel I have purpose and possibilities ahead of me. When Legends chose Veronica and not me and Roxanne, I felt that we were lacking something. After speaking with Mr. Sampson, I realized that we were just not what Legends was looking for. It wasn't about a lack in either of us. The group was not a good match for what Legends wanted to do. It was as simple as that."

"Exactly," Delilah said. "That's all I was trying to get you girls to see. Bigger doesn't always mean better. Just because a door is open doesn't mean you should go through it. Unfortunately, I failed to make Veronica realize that."

Alisha met her mom's eyes. "Is it possible, Momma, that Veronica chose the path for her? Maybe it wasn't the path for the three of us. Maybe God always meant for the three of us—you, me, and Roxanne—to sing together. If Veronica hadn't left, you never would have agreed to join the group, and we wouldn't be on this new path."

Chapter 32

*V*eronica couldn't muster very much excitement at the tour Tia was giving her and Dexter of Charles Washington's Myrtle Beach estate. The A&R rep's flight had been delayed in Chicago due to weather, so the three of them had eaten and were now exploring the grounds of the estate. At least, that's what they were supposed to be doing, but all Veronica could think about was her sisters and her mom. That sermon had only made her miss them more.

Dexter nudged her in the side. "Earth to Veronica," he said.

"Stop nudging me," she snapped.

Tia propped her hands on her hips. "This is what I was talking about in the car. What's this attitude about all of a sudden? You ought to be grateful to be here."

Veronica knew Tia was right, but that didn't mean she liked hearing what the woman had to say. "Let's not go there again, Tia."

Tia shook her head. "Hey, I'm doing my job. You need to do yours."

"Don't you understand English?" Veronica asked.

"I understand Diva when I hear it. And it's much too soon for you to even start thinking like a diva." Tia snapped her fingers. "Right now, you are nothing but a plan on a piece of paper. You better watch yourself. Papers can get lost."

"Maybe that was your experience," Veronica said, wanting to land a blow on the almighty Tia. "You may have flamed out before you started, but that doesn't mean I will."

Tia leaned toward Veronica. "You—"

Dexter cut her off when he stepped between the two women. "Both of you need to calm down. I'm pretty sure Mr. Washington wouldn't be pleased to see you two going at it."

"You've got that right," Tia said. "Mr. Washington hired both of us to do a job, and he wants that job done."

"I'm doing my part," Veronica said to Tia. "But it seems to me that you don't understand your role. You work for me."

Tia lifted her chin. "I work for Legends," she said. "We both work for Legends. You'd better get that clear in that little diva-pea-brain of yours."

"That's enough, Tia," Dexter said, taking up for Veronica finally. "I'm sure your job doesn't require you to insult the talent. That's not professional."

Tia looked from Dexter to Veronica and back again. "You know what? I'm done with this tour. You two can stand here like lumps on a log until Mr. Washington arrives. They don't pay me enough to put up with you."

"She has some nerve," Veronica said as she watched Tia stalk back to the house.

Dexter put a hand on her shoulder. "What's going on with you?" he asked.

"Nothing," she said, knowing Dexter wouldn't understand how much she missed her mother and sisters.

"Come on," he coaxed, pulling her close. "You can tell me. You've been off-kilter since we left the church. Tell me what's going on."

Veronica sighed. "I miss my family."

Dexter pulled back a little. "I thought I was your family."

Veronica leaned into his chest so she wouldn't have to look into his eyes. "You know what I mean," she said. "I miss my mom and my sisters. I should be sharing this experience with them."

Dexter leaned back so he could look down at her. "That was Plan A, but Plan A didn't work out. Now we're on Plan B. And it's a pretty darn good Plan B, if you ask me."

"I know," Veronica said. "And I am grateful, but I still miss them. It's been more than two weeks since I've spoken with them. I can't believe they haven't called, not even to say they received the checks. Heck, I still can't believe they didn't come to my going-away party."

"Want to know what I think?" Dexter asked.

She nodded.

"I think you're being selfish. You want your sisters to be happy for you, to share this experience with you, but that's not possible right now. In some ways, you left them high and dry, Veronica, regardless of the checks you sent. You went for a chance to achieve your dreams. Unfortunately, when you chose to take your shot, you took away theirs. That has to be hard for them."

Veronica wiped at the tears that puddled in her eyes. "I know you're right, but I still miss them."

"Give them some time," he said. "They'll call when they're ready."

"But—" Veronica began.

"Mr. Washington is here," Tia called. "He wants you to meet him in his study."

Dexter looked down at her. "You ready?"

She nodded and put her hand in his. "Let's go."

"Just Veronica," Tia clarified, with a smirk on her face. "You can wait here, Dexter. We can continue our tour after I get Veronica to the study."

Veronica felt her husband's body stiffen and knew he didn't like being left out. His full, but fake, smile covered his disappointment well. Tia probably bought it, but Veronica knew better. "It'll be all right," she said to him. "I'll tell you everything he says."

Dexter nodded and let go of her hand. "Knock him dead," he said.

She took his offered words of comfort with a smile. "I'll try." Then she turned to Tia. "Lead the way."

Veronica followed Tia down a long marble breezeway to a set of brass double doors. Tia pulled both doors open, and Veronica followed her in. Charles Washington was seated behind a huge gold-edged glass desk. He stood when they entered. "Welcome, Veronica," he said. "I'm sorry I was late. I hope you enjoyed lunch and that Tia made your wait interesting."

"Lunch was delicious," she said. "And you know Tia, she's always on the job."

"I never doubted her for a minute." Mr. Washington looked at Tia. "Why don't you leave us alone so that Veronica can update me on the first week of her journey to stardom? We'll join you and Dexter on the east terrace when we're done."

Tia nodded, and was gone.

"Have a seat," Washington said, pointing to the chair in front of his desk.

Veronica did as she was told. Then she waited while he made his way back around the massive desk and into his own chair.

After he sat, he leaned back and steepled his fingers across his nose. "So how has the week been?"

Veronica said the first words that came to her mind. "Exhausting, exhilarating."

Washington chuckled. "And frustrating?"

She shook her head. "Not really. Tia prepared me well for what I was going to face, so I was ready for it."

He lifted a brow. "So none of it was off-putting?"

She pushed the thought of the suggested breast implants from her mind. "Not really."

"Not even the recommendation for the breast augmentation?"

Veronica took a deep breath. "What do my breasts have to do with my singing? Beyoncé doesn't have big breasts. Neither does CeCe Winans."

He dropped his fingers from his face. "So you see yourself in the same league as Beyoncé and CeCe?"

Veronica squirmed in her chair. "Not really. I'm just saying that they didn't have to go to such extremes."

He leaned toward her. "Let me give you a piece of advice, Veronica, based on my tenure in the music business."

She nodded, but she also held her breath, anxiously anticipating what he was going to say.

"Never compare yourself to established artists. The comparisons are never good ones. You're trying to get to where they are. In order to do that, you're going to have to do more than they did and work harder than they did. Things don't get easier in this business. They get harder. You're trying to build an audience, so you first have to get their attention. And getting their attention takes more than a voice. It takes a brand. That's what Legends wants to make for you—a brand. And a brand has a voice and a look. Veronica Y has to be special. Legends only deals in special. So you're either going to put yourself in our hands, trusting that we're doing what's best for you and your brand, or you're going to fight us. There's no middle ground. I thought I made that clear before you signed the contract. Have you changed your mind?"

"No," Veronica said, "I haven't changed my mind. I just—"

Washington lifted his hand, effectively cutting her off. "No ifs, ands, or buts. You're either in or out. Which is it?"

"I'm in," Veronica said, but her heart really wasn't in her answer. She hoped her broad smile hid her uncertainty.

Chapter 33

*T*he Sunday night late show ended around midnight, but Roxanne didn't make it to Empress Deck until around two in the morning. After an especially good show, she liked to wind down with the cast. Tonight had been a very good show. She'd been anxious about coming back to the ship after losing the *Sing for America* contest, but the cast had welcomed her back with an honest show of disappointment that Delilah's Daughters hadn't won. Their warm reception had reminded her how fortunate she was to be able to return to the ship and continue the work she loved. She didn't plan on being with the cruise line forever, but for now it provided a safe haven of steady work. While she, Alisha, and her mother had tossed around the idea of relaunching Delilah's Daughters, with her mother taking Veronica's place, Roxanne knew the idea was a long shot. Their best chance of success was with Veronica in the group, but that was no longer an option.

Roxanne grew depressed every time she thought of Veronica and her Legends contract. It stung that her younger sister was enjoying the success that she always believed would be hers. It stung even more because she knew she had more talent than Veronica. Sleep hadn't come easy for her since her less-talented sister had gotten that Legends contract. It really wasn't fair.

By the time she reached Gavin's stateroom, she had worked herself up and needed to be calmed down. She needed Gavin to tell her how great she was and how her time was coming. Their relationship had its problems—namely, he was married—but she could always count on his encouragement and support when it came to her career. She needed that encouragement and support tonight.

She pulled the key card out of her purse and slid it in the door. She'd expected him to greet her as soon as she opened the door, so she was surprised when he didn't. "Gavin," she called out, "it's me."

She stopped in her tracks when she fully entered the stateroom and saw Gavin seated on the suite's orange leather couch next to a thin, blond woman who she could only guess was his wife.

"Now the fun can begin," the woman said. She turned to Gavin. "Don't be rude, darling. Introduce us."

Gavin met Roxanne's eyes, and she read the apology in them. "Roxanne, this is my wife, Darla. Darla, this is Roxanne."

Darla twisted a lock of Gavin's blond hair. "You can do better than that, Gavin. You told her who I am to you, but you didn't tell me who she is to you."

Gavin met Roxanne's eyes again. "She's a friend," he said. "A very good friend."

Darla laughed a dry laugh, clearly not believing her husband.

Roxanne knew she should turn and leave the stateroom, but it was as though her feet were glued to the floor. "Yes, we're friends," she stammered out.

"Friends, huh?" Darla said. "I'd say friends with benefits is a better description."

"That's enough, Darla," Gavin said, glaring at his wife. "You've had your fun. Now leave us alone."

Darla lifted a brow. "Why should I leave?" she asked. "I'm the wife. In all the movies I've seen, the mistress is the one to leave."

Gavin bit down on his lower lip. "You've gotten what you wanted," he said through clenched teeth. "Now go back to our suite. I'll join you shortly."

Darla laughed. "I'm sure you will." She stood and brushed her hands down her cashmere slacks. "Don't take all night," she said to Gavin. When she reached Roxanne, she said, "I hope you didn't think this thing between you and my husband had any future. You look smarter than the other ladies he's had, and he's had several. Gavin's what I call a serial adulterer." She fingered the pearls around her neck. "But he's *my* serial adulterer, and I intend to keep him. Next time you want a married man, you shouldn't aim so high. Pick someone in your league, socially and culturally. You stepped way above your station with Gavin." With those words, Darla brushed past Roxanne and out of the stateroom.

Roxanne released a deep breath that seemed to shake her out of her stupor. She looked at Gavin, but couldn't find any words to speak. "What am I doing here? I'm leaving," she said, turning toward the door.

Gavin jumped up from the couch, grabbed her shoulders, and turned her around. "You can't leave," he said. "We have to talk."

"What's left to say, Gavin? I think your wife said it all."

Gavin sighed. "I didn't want this to happen, but Darla is a drama queen, and she had to turn this into a theatrical performance with her as the star."

Roxanne shot a glare at him. "From what she said, I gather she's very familiar with her role."

Gavin pulled her to him. "I'm so sorry," he whispered. "I'm so sorry. I didn't mean for it to end like this."

Roxanne wanted to laugh, but the pain and shame were too deep. She had no room to rant or rave. She'd known for a long time that Gavin was married. That she hadn't stopped seeing him as soon as she found out was on her. She had no one to blame. Not Gavin. Not his wife.

"Look, Gavin," she said, stepping away from him. "You don't owe me a thing, not even an apology. I'm a grown woman, and I'm responsible for my actions. There was never any future for us. I think we both knew that from the beginning. I do thank you, though, for helping me land this job. I'll always be grateful to you for that."

Gavin stuffed his hands in the pockets of his trousers. "Please sit," he said. "We need to talk about you, me, and the cruise line."

Roxanne's heartbeat raced. "I don't want to sit," she said. "Tell me what you have to say, and I'll be on my way."

He met her eyes and then looked past her right ear. "Darla doesn't want us working together."

Roxanne folded her arms across her chest. "Well, you'd better quit, because I'm staying put. I like working here."

Gavin took his hands out of his pockets and put them on her forearms. "You're not understanding me," he said. "The guy who hired you is Darla's uncle. He has already prepared your separation papers."

Roxanne did sit then. If she hadn't, she was sure she would have fallen flat on her face. "What are you saying?"

Gavin sat next to her. "I'm sorry," he said. "I'm so sorry, but tonight was your last performance for the cruise line."

"You can't do this to me," she said. *This can't be happening to me,* she thought. "The cruise line can't do this to me. Why do I have to go and you get to stay?"

Gavin could only shrug. "It's a family thing," he said. "You understand family."

Roxanne could only stare at him. She wanted to rage at him, hit him, but the only anger she felt was directed at herself. She had been in two family competitions in less than a month and had come out on the losing end in both. What did she really know about family? "I signed a contract," she said, trying to find some leverage that would allow her to keep her job. "The cruise line has to honor it."

"It has a morals clause. They've invoked it."

Roxanne refused to roll over for Gavin as she had rolled over for Veronica. She stood and looked down at him. "I'm going to fight for my job, Gavin. You and your wife will have to deal with it."

"You'll lose," Gavin said as she opened the door to leave. "You've already lost."

She slammed the door shut behind her.

Chapter 34

"Sit down, Delilah," Tommy told her as she paced back and forth in front of his office windows on Monday morning. "You're working yourself up over something you can't control."

"He had no right to contact her, Tommy. No right at all."

"He's her father."

Delilah stopped pacing and stared at him. "Rocky is her father."

"In all ways but one."

"In all the ways that matter. Sperm does not a father make."

"Don't be crude."

She shot him a glare. "The truth is the light. I'm only speaking the truth."

Tommy got up, walked to her, and pulled her into his arms. She leaned into him, willingly accepting the comfort he offered. "How did he find her at the conference? It's more than a coincidence. Do you think he has someone checking up on us?"

"Come over here and sit down," Tommy said, guiding her to the couch. "I have to tell you something that I know you don't want to hear."

Delilah sat as she was directed. "You're scaring me, Tommy. Tell me already."

"I was the one who told him Alisha was going to be at ASCAP."

Delilah blinked twice, fast. "What? How?"

Tommy took her hand. "He calls every now and then wanting to know how she's doing, so I tell him."

Delilah eased her hand out of his. "How long has this been going on?"

"Years," he said.

Her eyes widened. "And you never thought to tell me?"

Tommy shrugged. "I knew that knowing would hurt you, and I didn't see a reason to hurt you needlessly."

"Needlessly," she repeated, her voice rising.

"Yes, needlessly. All he wanted was to know how she was doing. He never once considered breaking the agreement he had with you and Rocky. He just wanted to know."

"He had no right."

"I felt sorry for him. I know how it feels to love someone from a distance. There's a hole there, Delilah. You don't know that feeling. I do. Morgan does. I had to help him, but I wouldn't have done it if I thought it would bring harm to you or your family."

"It seems you were wrong," she spat out, wanting to hold on to her anger. His words about loving from a distance made that difficult, though, since she knew he was talking about himself and the secret love he had carried for her while she'd been married to Rocky. "Why is he bothering her now? He has a wife and kids. Surely, he's not trying to bring her into his family, so what does he want?"

Tommy reached for her hands again. "He's dying, Delilah."

"Dying." She sank back against the couch. "Morgan's dying? I don't believe it. He's making it up to gain your sympathy. He knows he's wrong for going back on his word, and he wants you to feel sorry for him."

Tommy shook his head. "It's true. The doctors give him less than a year. He wants to do right by Alisha before he goes. He's already told his wife and children about her and about what he wants to do. He didn't want her or them to find out when his will was read."

"Will?" she said, still trying to get her mind to grasp the idea that Morgan was dying. "Alisha's in his will?"

Tommy nodded. "He's treating her like a daughter in his will because that's how he thinks of her."

None of this makes sense, Delilah thought. "But he doesn't even know her."

"It doesn't matter. She's his blood. Besides, he wants to get to know her in the time he has left."

Delilah felt as though someone had thrown a bucket of ice on her. All she felt was cold. And empty. How could she be angry at a man who was dying? How could she accuse Tommy of betraying her when she knew that was not his intention? "You should have told me, Tommy. I shouldn't have had to find out this way."

"I know," he said. "I know. I just couldn't think of a way to tell you that you would understand and accept."

"You should have tried."

He sighed. "I know. And I'm sorry I didn't." They sat silently for a few moments. Then he asked, "What are you going to do?"

Delilah closed her eyes. "I only have two choices. I let him tell her, or I tell her first."

"He won't tell her," Tommy said. "He knows that's your decision. If all you'll let him be while he's alive is her mentor, he'll take that. He won't like it, but he'll take it."

"Then after he's dead Alisha will learn that he was her father and that I never told her."

"That's about it."

Delilah sighed. "I have to tell her and her sisters." She rubbed her hands down her face. "How can I make them understand?"

"You trust your love for them and their love for you."

Delilah squeezed her eyes shut to block out the tears. "That's easy for you to say."

He didn't respond, only held her closer.

"I should probably talk to Morgan first so that we can get on the same page."

He still didn't say anything.

"The girls are not going to understand," she told him.

"You don't give them enough credit. They're grown women. They know life is not always pretty."

"Not pretty is one thing, but to learn your mother had an adulterous affair and brought home another man's baby, well, that's major." She closed her eyes again. "Rocky is going to look like a saint and I'm going to look like Jezebel."

Tommy squeezed her shoulders. "It won't be that bad."

Delilah tried to take comfort in Tommy's words, but deep

down inside she knew he was wrong. Her girls, all three of them, were going to be devastated by this news. And Rocky's sacrifice would have been for naught. "I'm so sorry, Rocky."

"What did you say?"

She didn't realize she had spoken her thoughts. "I was thinking about Rocky. He didn't want the girls to know. He especially didn't want Alisha to know. He feared she would doubt his love for her. The only good thing about all this is that Rocky is not here to see it. It would break his heart to see another man claim his daughter."

"Rocky loved Alisha like she was his."

"She *was* his," Delilah said. "In his heart, she was his. I'm still amazed that he forgave me, really forgave me. That forgiveness was the best gift he ever gave me. That and his obvious love for Alisha. It would have broken my heart if he had held any animosity toward her because of me. But he didn't see me and Morgan when he looked at her. He saw her as the second chance for our marriage. Rocky and I didn't love each other perfectly, but we did love each other."

"I know you did."

She sighed. "I don't know if I have the strength to do what needs to be done."

"That's all right," Tommy said. "I'll be strong for you. You don't have to do this alone, Delilah. I'll be with you every step of the way."

She looked up into eyes that shone with love for her. "When this is over, I'm going to be angry with you."

"Why?"

"For keeping secrets. For talking with Morgan behind my back. For not telling me he was going to see Alisha at ASCAP.

You have a lot to answer for, and I'm not going to give you a pass, but it'll have to wait."

"Why is that?"

She curled into his side. "Because now I need you to hold me while I cry for the innocence of my children and the pain I'm about to inflict on them."

He pressed his lips against her head as her tears fell unheeded.

Chapter 35

"So why are you and Washington shutting me out?" Dexter asked Tia on Monday morning after a car had picked up Veronica to take her to see the plastic surgeon about breast augmentation surgery. He'd wanted to go with her for support, and Veronica had wanted him there for the same reason. Tia had other plans.

Tia lowered her coffee cup from her lips and placed it on the counter of the kitchen bar. "Get real, Dexter, nobody's shutting you out. Your little wife had a doctor's appointment. Besides, you're supposed to be working on a book. Shouldn't you be getting started?"

"That's exactly my point," he said, after taking a sip of coffee. "How am I supposed to chronicle Veronica Y's rise to stardom if I'm not allowed in meetings or on trips?"

Tia tapped her finger against her cheek. "I knew it. You've got your nose out of joint because Mr. Washington wanted to meet with Veronica alone on Sunday night. That's it, isn't it?"

It was, but Dexter refused to admit it. "No, that's not it. I just want to do this book justice. Give the readers the real picture of what the business is like."

She stared at him as if he had two heads. "You don't get it, do you?" she asked.

"Get what?"

Tia tilted her head to the side. "Are you sure you and your wife didn't just fall off the turnip truck or something? How far away from civilization is Birmingham exactly?"

"There's no need to be insulting or condescending," he shot back. "Veronica's right about one thing. You do overstep at times. I guess sleeping with the boss makes you bold."

Tia's lips curved into a sly smile. "What? Do you expect me to deny it? Please. I'm a grown woman. I can do whatever I want."

Dexter studied her. Her practiced nonreaction told him that he had chosen the right moment to use this tidbit Alex had given him. "What do you get out of it—sleeping with Washington?"

Tia tossed her hair back over her shoulder. "I enjoy it," she said. "Charles is a great lover."

Dexter wasn't fooled by her nonchalance. He knew his words were getting to her. "Were you sleeping with him when he canceled your contract, or did this start afterwards?"

Bam! Those words knocked the smile off her face.

"That's none of your business," she said, sliding off her stool. "And I advise you to keep what you know to yourself. Charles doesn't like gossip, especially when it's about him."

"That ship has sailed," Dexter said. "How do you think I found out?"

"Who told you?" she demanded.

Dexter got up from his stool and faced her. No way was he giving her a name. "I can't divulge my sources. Professional integrity and all that."

Her smiled returned. "You're out of your league, Dexter. You'd best focus on keeping your wife on track and getting that book written. That's your job. And let me be straight up with you: the former is more important than the latter."

Tia had already made it clear that the book didn't mean much to Legends. It was only a bone they had tossed him to sweeten the deal for Veronica. Dexter was determined to make the most of his opportunity, though. Alex had the right idea: use them before they use you. "So we've come full circle. I'm going to need access if I'm going to do this book the right way."

She moved to stand close to him, her nose almost touching his. "Look, let me put it out there for you. If you're not invited to an event, that event shouldn't be in the book. Do you really think we want the public to know we strongly encouraged Veronica to get a boob job? Do you think Charles wanted his Sunday conversation with Veronica to one day show up in a book? In case you haven't figured it out, the answer to both those questions is a resounding NO!"

The buzzing of Veronica's telephone, which she had forgotten in her haste that morning, got the attention of both of them. Dexter walked over to the counter near the refrigerator and looked at the caller ID on the phone. He turned back to Tia without picking it up.

"Who was it?" she asked.

"Veronica's mother," he answered.

A slow smile formed on Tia's face. "Smart man. It's best

she not have contact with them for a while. She doesn't need the distraction. Maybe you're doing your job, after all."

When the phone gave the beep it normally gave after a voice mail had been received, Dexter picked up the phone.

"What are you doing?" Tia asked.

He looked over at her. "Duh. I'm erasing the message."

"Duh," she repeated. "Don't you think you should listen to it first?"

Dexter shot her a glare. Then he played the message.

"This is Mom, Veronica. The checks arrived on Saturday. Thanks for sending them so soon. I know you're busy, but call us when you get some time. I'd really like to talk to you."

Dexter looked at Tia. "Satisfied now?"

When she nodded, Dexter deleted the voice mail and also deleted Delilah's number from the recent calls list.

"Good boy," Tia said. "There may be hope for you yet."

"I'm not an idiot, Tia," he said. "And I'm not a pushover. We're going to have problems if you don't start treating me and Veronica with a little respect."

Tia walked over to him. This time she stood so close that he could hear her heartbeat. "Are you sure respect is all you want, Dexter?"

He took a step back. "I'm a married man."

She chuckled. "So?"

Dexter wasn't surprised by her response. Not after Alex had told him how she'd seduced him and broken his wife's heart, effectively ending their marriage. He didn't want that end for himself. He loved Veronica. "What kind of game are you playing?"

"I don't play games," Tia said. "I live my life, and I do it on my terms. What about you? Are you going to be content to be Veronica Y's leech of a husband, or do you want more?"

He took the blow of her words for the payback he knew them to be. "Okay, now we're even."

She smiled and stepped back from him. "Don't start something that you can't finish, Dexter. And if you don't know the rules of the game, don't engage an opponent. You'll lose every time." She checked her watch. "I've got things to do and people to see. I'll leave you here to do whatever it is that you writers do when you're alone at your computer."

Chapter 36

On Thursday, after her return from the ASCAP conference, Alisha followed her mother into the office of Tommy Johns, president of Magic City Studios. She'd been excited that Mr. Tommy had agreed to meet with them on such short notice. It wasn't a problem for her that her mother's relationship with the man probably influenced his decision to open up his schedule for them. No, the only thing bothering her that afternoon was Roxanne's absence. Her sister had been scheduled to get in on Wednesday, but she hadn't arrived until this morning, and she'd looked as though she'd been in an emotional battle and lost. She'd tried to tell them that her problems were physical in nature, but Alisha didn't believe her for one minute. She might not have a lot of experience with men herself, but she knew heartache when she saw it. Her guess was that something had gone badly wrong between Roxanne and her secret man. Alisha would get to the bottom of the matter soon. Neither Roxanne nor her mother, nor she herself, could afford the distraction. There was too much on the line.

"Thanks for seeing us, Mr. Tommy," Alisha said.

He gave Delilah a quick embrace, and then he offered his hand to Alisha. "It's good to see you, young lady." He glanced at Delilah. "I know your mother has told you about our relationship, and I want to thank you for your understanding."

"There's nothing to understand, Mr. Tommy. All of us want Momma to be happy, and you make her happy. You're good for her." She glanced at her mother. "And it seems you're good for Delilah's Daughters too."

Tommy met her eyes. "I want you to know that it's easy for me to separate business and pleasure. My interest in Delilah's Daughters was based totally on your talent. I'll admit that my relationship with your mother—and your father too, rest his soul—brought your talent to my attention, but it was your talent that led me to offer you a contract. It's important to me that you understand this. I'm very sorry things didn't work out for Magic City and Delilah's Daughters. We could have made a special kind of magic together."

Alisha nodded. "Thanks for saying that, Mr. Tommy. It's always encouraging when somebody believes in your talent."

Tommy lifted a brow in Delilah's direction. "Your mother tells me I'm not the only one who believes in your talent."

Alisha smiled. "So she told you about Morgan Sampson."

He nodded. "That's big news."

"I thought so," Alisha said. "I'm honored he sees something in me and in the group, but I'm not quite sure how to make the best use of his support."

Tommy leaned forward, resting his hand on the desk. "Tell me what he said."

Alisha did as he requested. Then she said, "I hope he wasn't just being nice."

Tommy laughed. "I know Morgan. He wasn't just being nice. There are a lot of ways to be nice. If you didn't have the talent, being nice would have been to be honest and direct with you and tell you so. No, Morgan wasn't being nice; he was giving you his honest appraisal and truly opening up his experience and knowledge for your use. He sees something in you."

"Your confirmation means a lot, Mr. Tommy," she said, finally allowing herself to fully accept Morgan Sampson's appraisal as sincere. "So what do we do next? I don't want us to miss out on this opportunity."

Tommy sat back and steepled his fingers across his nose. "The first thing you need is a demo that we can send to Morgan. Do you have a song in mind?"

Alisha swallowed hard. "I have a couple," she said.

Tommy smiled. "That's even better. Magic City will help you cut the demo, but Delilah's Daughters would be better off letting Morgan handle things from there, if he's willing."

"I pray he'll love the demo," Alisha said.

Tommy chuckled. "Pour your heart and soul into it, and I'm sure he will."

"You make it sound easy," she said.

He shook his head. "You know it's not easy, but when you love it the way you, your sister, and your mom do, it's good work—hard work, yes, but also good work. You're going to work until you're bone-weary, but you'll wake up every morning refreshed and ready to keep working. That's how it is for all true musicians. It's hard work, but it's work you have to do and work you love doing."

Tommy's words told Alisha they were kindred spirits who would work well together. "So when do we get started?"

He steepled his fingers across his nose again, and Alisha held her breath while she waited for what he would say. He looked from mother to daughter. "You've taken the first couple of steps already. Adding your mother to the group was a brilliant idea. I've often wondered why she hasn't made more use of that beautiful voice of hers."

"She's been busy doing other things, like raising a family," Delilah said, apparently not appreciating being discussed as if she were not there. It was unlike her to remain so quiet, but Alisha appreciated her mother letting her take the lead during the meeting.

Tommy glanced over at Delilah and smiled. "Nice of you to chime in," he said. Then he turned back to Alisha. "I think you've hit on something here that could be really big."

Alisha gave a sigh of relief.

"You two girls and your mother as a gospel group is perfect. It's such a great idea that I'm disappointed I didn't think of it myself." Looking from her mother to Alisha, he added, "There is one thing to keep in mind, though. To work in gospel, not only do you need songs and a sound, you also need a testimony, a story about your lives that you can share with your listeners and fans. In the pop and R&B world, it's fairly common and fairly easy to fabricate backgrounds. That won't work in gospel. That market requires a level of transparency that other markets don't."

"We haven't really thought about that," Alisha said, already seeing the value Mr. Tommy brought. She glanced at her mother. "We tell our stories in the songs, don't we, Momma?"

"That's good," Tommy said, not waiting for Delilah to answer, "but the three of you also have to be ready for the criticism of your lives and lifestyles that is going to come from both the church and secular communities. When you sing about God's love, the public expects you to be living a godly lifestyle, where they define what that means. Living under that kind of scrutiny can be tough."

"We were brought up singing in church, so we're ready for the scrutiny. We don't have anything to hide." She glanced at her mother again. "Do we, Momma?"

Delilah shot a quick glance at Tommy. "No, we don't," she said. "We were under a lot of scrutiny during *Sing for America*. We can handle it."

Tommy nodded in Delilah's direction. "Don't forget that on *Sing for America* Delilah's Daughters modified themselves a bit. You moved from your natural gospel-pop blend to more of a pop-gospel sound. We can talk more about the different markets for the two at a later time. Now the next step is the actual demo. The quicker we can get it to Morgan, the better. It's good to strike while the iron is hot, as they say. It would be great if we could have it ready by the time of Gospelfest. That way, we could get some listener reaction before sending it to Morgan."

The timeline was short, a little more than four months, but

Alisha thought they could do it. She looked at her mom for assurance. When the older woman nodded her confirmation, Alisha said, "We're serious about moving forward with these ideas, Mr. Tommy. I've quit my job so I can write full-time, and Roxanne can arrange time away from work when we need to be in the studio. I'm certain we can have a demo by Gospelfest."

Tommy sat back in his chair. "That means you and I will start spending a great deal of time together, young lady. I want to work closely with you on your arrangements once you're ready to share what you have. Once we nail down the music, cutting the demo will be a piece of cake. When do you want to get started?"

"Now, today," Alisha said, knowing her emotions were running too high for her to even think about focusing on something other than the demo.

Tommy laughed. "Next week is soon enough. You, your mom, and your sister should celebrate before the hard work starts. You won't get another break until after the demo drops. Your mom and sister will have a bit of time until we get ready for them in the studio, but your work starts next week."

"I'm ready, Mr. Tommy," Alisha said.

Tommy stood and extended his hand to her. "I can see that you are. Welcome to Magic City Records, Alisha. We're going to make a beautiful demo together."

Chapter 37

Veronica sat in a hospital gown on a table waiting for the plastic surgeon to give her the results of the series of tests she had taken in preparation for her upcoming breast augmentation surgery. A part of her hoped the doctor had uncovered some health condition that made her a bad candidate for the surgery.

"Now that's some crazy thinking," Veronica said aloud.

What she needed now was a good, nurturing conversation with her mother. How she missed talking to her! And if she hadn't forgotten her cell phone this morning, she'd have called her by now. She was done with waiting for her mother or one of her sisters to call. Too much time had passed already.

The door opened and the surgeon entered. "Hello, Veronica," she said, pulling up a rolling stool to sit close to the table. "How are things going?"

"That's what I'm waiting for you to tell me," Veronica said, with a smile.

The doctor smiled back. "I guess you're right." She flipped through the chart of papers she had in her hands. "We've kept you pretty busy this morning."

"I don't have a problem with your being thorough. I'd rather be safe than sorry."

The doctor looked up at her. "Well, I have good news for you. There's nothing in your medical history or in the results of the tests you've taken today to suggest that the surgery will be a problem for you. In fact, you're a great candidate. There are no indications you'll have anything but a successful surgery and recovery." She glanced down at the paperwork again. "I see here that you're in training for the Peachtree Road Race."

Veronica nodded, trying to hide her disappointment that there was no medical reason for her to pass on the surgery.

"Well, we'll want to hold off on the surgery until after the race. We're not going to want you to engage in any strenuous upper-body exercise for a few weeks after the procedure. Other than that, from a physical standpoint, you're good to go."

"Sounds good," Veronica said, taking a bit of comfort in the reprieve that the road race gave her.

The doctor lifted a brow. "As I said, I don't have any health concerns about you and the surgery, but I do have some reservations based on the results of the psychological testing. Why do you want to have this surgery, Veronica?"

Veronica tried to remember the answers she'd written on the test form. "The handlers from the record company think I need it to enhance my image. As a new artist, I need all the edge I can get."

The doctor put down her clipboard. "But how do you personally feel about it?"

Veronica wasn't sure how to respond. She knew Legends had set up this appointment, so she wondered how much confidentiality the doctor would maintain. After all, Legends was paying the bill.

As if understanding her concerns, the doctor said, "Legends sends me several patients a year, but I don't share patient records with them without patient approval. What is said between you and me remains between you and me. So tell me what your reservations are, and I may be able to help you."

Veronica looked at the older woman, debating how honest to be with her. Then she lifted her shoulders in a slight shrug. "I've never seen myself as a plastic surgery person. I've always been satisfied with my looks, so the idea of enhancements doesn't sit well with me. I can't really explain it any better than that. I'm doing this because the record company says I need to do it. If the decision were mine alone, I wouldn't do it."

"Well, you're wrong about one thing," the doctor said. "The decision is yours. I can't ethically operate on you if I feel you're being coerced in any way."

"They're not coercing me," Veronica said, trying to clean up her previous statement. She feared she'd been too honest. "The final decision is mine."

"But you think that if you don't do it, it will negatively affect your relationship with the label?"

And my relationship with my husband, she thought. "I guess you could say that."

"Well, that's what I call coercion," the doctor said. "You need to be mentally and physically ready for this surgery. Today, you're not mentally ready."

"Yes, I am," Veronica said. "It's just jitters."

The doctor didn't look convinced. "It's okay to have the jitters, Veronica. I see them quite often in patients. Some women do this surgery for the men in their lives. Other women, like you, do it looking for some career boost. Then other women do it because they want to feel better about themselves. No reason is better than another. My only requirement is that the woman wants to do it and feels it's her choice. That's the way I want you to feel. The good news in your case is that the earliest we can do the surgery is after the race. Why don't we schedule another visit for you a week or so after the race? That gives you some time to consider what you really want. How does that sound?"

"It sounds good to me, but what will you tell the folks at the record company?" Veronica didn't want to give Tia or the record company any reason to doubt her commitment to her new career.

"Unless you give me permission to discuss your case with folks at the label, which you haven't, the only information they get from me is the bill. If they request any additional information, I'll need your permission to release it." She turned back to the file. "In fact, here's the permission form." She turned the form so Veronica could see it. "Until you sign this, no information leaves this office."

Veronica thought about it for a moment. "It's okay to tell them that we're meeting again after the race and will schedule the surgery then. That's what I'll say if anyone asks."

The doctor bobbed her head. "Good. That's also what I'll say if I'm asked, though I doubt anyone will contact me. The only time they've asked for records in the past has been if there was some indicator that the patient wasn't a good candidate for the surgery. And again, they'd only know that because the patient shared that information."

Veronica smiled, though she was not really 100 percent confident Legends wouldn't get access to her information. "Thanks, doctor," she said. "You've eased my mind about the entire process."

"That's part of my job. This surgery will only be a success if it's what you want. If you disagree with the record company, this may be the time for you to take a stand. But if you think the enhancements will result in some positive benefit to you, have the procedure done with pride. There's nothing to be ashamed about."

Veronica merely nodded. At this point, she was just glad for the short reprieve the race had given her.

Chapter 38

*D*elilah sat on the back porch swing taking in the morning sun. She knew her time was growing short. Tommy had grown impatient with her lack of progress in telling the girls the truth about Morgan and had threatened to tell them himself. While no part of her believed he'd actually do that, his threat made clear how urgent it was for her to do it. *Oh, Rocky, how I wish you were here. Where are the girls going to turn when they find out what I did? They're going to hate me, but they could sympathize with you. They could, and would, turn to you for support and understanding. Now they have nowhere to turn.*

"Momma." She heard Alisha's voice call at the same time she felt her tug on her arm. "Snap out of it."

Delilah shook off her thoughts and turned to her daughter. "What's wrong, Alisha?" she asked.

Alisha dropped down on the floor in front of her. "I should

be asking you that. What were you thinking about? You seemed to be a million miles away."

The door is open, Delilah, a soft voice in her head told her. *Not now,* she responded silently to the voice. "Nothing important," she said to Alisha. "What do you need?"

Alisha sat back on her thighs. "It's Roxanne. Something's wrong with her, Momma. Haven't you noticed how withdrawn she's been? I'm worried about her."

Delilah patted Alisha's knee. She'd been so lost in her own worries that she hadn't paid much attention to Roxanne or Alisha lately. "I know you're worried, sweetheart, but Roxanne is a grown woman. She'll talk when she's ready to talk."

Tears filled Alisha's eyes. "I can't stand to see her like this. She's not interested in the progress Mr. Tommy and I are making on the demo. She doesn't seem to care about the group or anything else."

Delilah put her hands on Alisha's face and wiped her tears. "I know you love your sister, sweetheart, but I can't make her talk, and neither can you. We just have to be there for her when she's ready."

"Something happened on that job that she's not telling us," Alisha said. "It had to be something really bad for Roxanne to quit. She had wanted to win the *Sing for America* contest as much we all had, but after we didn't win, she was glad to be able to go back to the cruise line. Why would she up and quit?"

Delilah had asked herself the same question. She didn't believe the tall tale Roxanne had told about quitting her job, but she hadn't pushed because her oldest daughter's eyes had shown how emotionally raw she was. A push might have done more harm than good. She couldn't help but think the whole thing had something to do with a man. Didn't most women's problems come back to a man? *Mine certainly did,* she thought, as a picture of Morgan flashed in her mind.

"It's been two weeks, Momma," Alisha reminded her. "You've given her enough time to come to us. I think you should go to her. She's probably waiting for you to come to her."

Delilah pulled back from Alisha. "You really think so?"

Alisha wiped her eyes. "I don't know. I just want to see her smile again. It's hard for me to write songs of hope when it seems my sister has none. There has to be something we can do."

"Okay," Delilah said, shaking off her own problems. "I'll talk to her."

"When?" Alisha asked. "She's in her room now. I heard her come in a while ago."

"You're not going to give up until I speak to her, are you?"

Alisha shook her head.

Giving in to her daughter's request, Delilah got up from the back porch swing. "I'll go check on her."

"Thanks, Momma," Alisha said.

Delilah entered the house through the back door and went up the back stairs to the second floor, where all their bedrooms were. Roxanne's door was closed, as it often was these days, so she knocked. "It's me, sweetheart," she said. "May I come in?"

Delilah heard movement behind the door, and then Roxanne said, "Come on in."

Delilah's heart broke to see her twenty-eight-year-old daughter huddled up in her bed the way she had done when she was a child. Delilah sat on the edge of the bed and brushed a lock of her daughter's hair off her forehead. "Tell me what's wrong, sweetheart," she said. "You'll feel better if you get it off your chest."

"It's nothing. I'm fine, Momma."

Delilah shook her head. "You've been telling me and Alisha that for two weeks, but clearly you're not fine. Something's bothering you, and I want to know what it is."

Roxanne covered her face with her hands and began to weep.

Delilah sat closer so she could hold her daughter. "It'll be all right, Roxanne. Whatever it is, it'll be all right."

Roxanne wept harder, and Delilah just held her. When her tears subsided, Roxanne said, "I'm so ashamed."

Delilah tipped her chin up. "The best way to get rid of shame is name the thing that makes you ashamed. So tell me. I love you and I won't judge you."

Roxanne's tears began to fall again.

Delilah rubbed her back. "Tell me, sweetheart," she urged.

Roxanne wiped at her tears with the backs of her hands. "I've been lying to you and Alisha, Momma. I didn't quit my job," she said. "I was fired."

Delilah stopped rubbing Roxanne's back. "I'm surprised to hear that. I thought you were doing so well on your job, especially after the cruise line treated us all to a free cruise. What happened? Why did they fire you?"

Roxanne covered her face. "It was all my fault. I was so stupid. I can't believe how stupid I was."

"I doubt it was all your fault," Delilah said. "Tell me."

Roxanne lowered her hands from her face. "It was my fault. I was dating one of the ship's captains."

Delilah frowned. She knew a man had to be in there somewhere. "Was there a no-fraternization rule? Did he get fired too?"

Roxanne shook her head. "I was the only person fired."

"Well, that doesn't sound right," Delilah said. "Is there any way you can fight it? I would think they'd have to treat both of you the same."

Roxanne began to cry again. "I'm so sorry," she said. "I've shamed myself and the family."

"Please, Roxanne," Delilah said. "A lot of people are losing their jobs, especially in this economy. Besides, it sounds to me like they treated you unfairly if they didn't fire the captain as well."

"He had family contacts," Roxanne said.

"Ahh," Delilah said. "Does his family own the cruise line? If that's the case, it seems to me you have an even stronger reason to fight the dismissal."

Roxanne shook her head. "You don't understand," she said, meeting her mother's eyes. "It's not his family. It's his wife's family."

"Wife?" Delilah repeated, sure she had misheard.

"He was married."

"Married?" Delilah repeated. This time she was sure she had heard correctly, she just couldn't believe it. None of her daughters would date a married man.

"Yes, married," Roxanne said, her eyes red from her tears.

"I'm so sorry, Momma. I'm sorry I let you down, and I'm sorry for being stupid enough to date a married man in the first place. I knew I was wrong. I knew it, but I kept seeing him anyway."

A married man. Delilah still couldn't get her mind around it. "How did this happen, Roxanne? How did you let this happen?"

"I don't know," Roxanne said, with a slight shrug. "It just happened."

Delilah got up from the bed. "Adultery doesn't just happen. You know better, Roxanne. Your father and I brought you up to know better. What were you thinking?"

"I wasn't thinking," she said.

"You surely weren't," Delilah said, turning away from her daughter so she couldn't see the guilt she felt. "You weren't thinking about your family or the man's family. If you had, this never would have happened."

"You said you wouldn't judge me," Roxanne reminded her. "But I knew you would. I knew it."

Delilah turned to her, but found it hard to meet her eyes. "I'm not judging you," she said. How could she? "I'm disappointed. Very disappointed."

"I know," Roxanne said, sniffling now. "And I'm sorry. I don't know what else to say."

Delilah didn't know what else to say either. "Maybe we've said all we need to say for now. We can talk more later. I need some time to digest what you've told me."

Roxanne dried her tears with her bed covers. "I understand," she said. "Please don't tell Alisha. I don't want her to know. I couldn't take both of you being disappointed in me. Not now. I need some time too."

Delilah nodded and left the room. After she pulled the door closed behind her, she leaned back against it. *What have I done, Lord? Veronica leaves the group, and now Roxanne is caught in adultery. Will revealing the secret about Alisha's birth be too much for this family to bear?*

Chapter 39

*D*elilah felt the walls closing in on her. The pressure from the girls and Tommy grew every day. Nothing had improved since her talk with Roxanne. Her eldest daughter was still withdrawn. Alisha had followed her lead and was now buried in work on the demo. A part of Delilah was glad they'd pulled away. It made it easier for her to pull away as well.

Her avoidance strategy would have to end today. She had pushed Tommy to his limit. His lunch invitation today was a command appearance. She owed it to him to stop acting like a child. She knew she needed to tell the girls about Morgan, but she just couldn't muster the courage. Hopefully, Tommy would help her come up with a strategy. She needed all the help she could get.

As she approached the doors to his office, she blotted her lips together so they would be moist and inviting. She was not above using her physical attributes to blunt Tommy's wrath. She'd even taken a little more time with her appearance that morning, choosing a blue sheath since blue was Tommy's favorite color, and accessorizing with the pearl necklace and earring set that he'd given her for her birthday last year. She didn't feel the least bit guilty about her attempt to soften him up. A woman had to do what a woman had to do.

After engaging in their normal pleasantries, Delilah waved off Tommy's secretary, not wanting to be escorted into his office. With a huge smile on her face, she walked through his office doors. "Tommy," she called.

"We're over here, Delilah," he returned.

We, she thought. "I didn't mean to interrupt. Your secretary didn't tell me—"

Delilah's words froze in her throat when she saw Morgan seated on the corner couch.

He stood when he saw her. "It's been a long time, Delilah."

Delilah turned to Tommy without responding to Morgan. "What are you doing, Tommy?" she asked. "Why is he here?"

Tommy walked to her and took her hands in his. "He's here because I invited him. By inviting him, I'm helping you do something that you don't seem to be able to do on your own."

She tried to pull her hands away, but he wouldn't let her. "You had no right," she said.

He squeezed her fingers. "I love you," he said, "and that gives me the right."

His simple declaration of love broke down her defenses. "I'm not ready."

He looked deeply into her eyes, and she knew he was willing her his strength. "I know you're not ready," he said. "How does one get ready for something like this? I don't think you do. It's like taking castor oil: you hold your nose and swallow."

She gave him a weak smile. "Today is castor oil day?"

He nodded. "You don't have to do this alone, Delilah, but you do have to do it." He glanced at his watch. "Alisha is in the studio—"

"Alisha's here?" Delilah said, alarm in her voice. "I'm not ready to tell her, Tommy. Really, I'm not ready."

"It's okay," he said. "You don't have to tell her now. You and Morgan need to talk first. Invite him to dinner. That way, you two can tell her at home tonight."

Delilah swallowed hard. Her heart beat faster at his words, but she knew he was right. It was time. "Will you be there?"

"I'm always there for you, Delilah, always. Don't you ever forget that."

She leaned into him. "I love you," she whispered.

He gave her a tight clasp and then stepped away. "I'm going to meet Alisha in the studio. I'll keep her busy until dinnertime. That'll give you and Morgan time to figure out what you're going to say to her and how."

"You're not going to strategize with us?"

He smiled, and she knew her choice of words was the cause. "Not this time. You and Morgan need to do this together, for Alisha's sake. She needs to know that you two are on the same page and that your only concern is for her. It's been a long time since you and Morgan have seen each other, talked to each other. You need this time to develop some familiarity with each other." He turned back to Morgan. "I'm trusting you with my lady, Morgan," he said. "Don't make me regret it."

"I won't," Morgan said. "I appreciate all you've done for

me, Tommy, now and in the past." Then he said to Delilah, "I didn't mean to break my promise to you and Rocky, Delilah, but cancer has a way of making a man change his mind."

Delilah stepped out of Tommy's embrace and walked over to Morgan. A bit of the warmth she'd felt for him years ago returned, coupled with her sympathy for his condition. "I'm sorry you're sick, Morgan. I always wanted the best for you and your family."

"I know," he said. "And I wanted the same for you and Rocky. And Alisha. But you have to know that I never forgot about her, Delilah. We did the right thing back then; I'm sure of it. But I never forgot my little girl."

His words pierced Delilah's heart, and she broke down in tears. She expected Tommy's arms to enclose around her, but she was wrong. As Morgan pulled her into his embrace, she saw Tommy ease toward the door and out of the room. In that moment, she realized again the depth of his love for her. He wanted her to do the right thing, and he knew Morgan would help her to do it.

She and Morgan stood close. She felt his tears, and she knew he felt hers. Tommy had made the right decision to bring them together again after all these years. The circle was now complete.

When she composed herself, she pulled back. "Well, I didn't expect that," she said. "Did you?"

He tilted his head. "I didn't know what to expect. I'm serious, Delilah. I never meant to come back and disrupt your life or Alisha's."

"I know," she said, taking a seat and waving him back to

his. "Were we naive to think we could keep this secret from Alisha forever?"

"I don't know," he said. "I only know that when I found out I was dying, I had to let her know that I always loved her. You and Rocky did a great job with her, Delilah. She's a wonderful young woman and a talented artist."

"Music is in her genes," she said. "There's no getting around that."

"It may be wrong of me," he said, "but I'm glad she's a writer like me."

"It's something Rocky and I never discussed, but we both saw that part of you in her. It was never a burden to us, though. She was still our Alisha, Rocky's Alisha. It's going to break her heart to know that Rocky wasn't her father, to know that we lied to her all these years."

"Maybe not," Morgan said. "She strikes me as a mature young woman. Of course, it'll be hard news for her to hear, but I have to believe that she'll come around in time."

"How much time?" she asked softly.

"The doctors are saying months. I just want it to be enough for Alisha to get to know me and open the door for her to have a relationship with her brother and her other sister. I'm believing God will give me enough time for that."

Delilah reached out and squeezed his hand. "He will," she said. "But first we have to tell our little girl that we've lied to her all her life."

Chapter 40

Alisha was giddy as she helped her mother clear the dessert plates. "I can't believe Morgan Sampson is in our house, that he ate dinner with us. This is unbelievable. I wish Roxanne was here. She needs to meet him. This could be exactly what she needs to lift her blues and get her excited again about the demo and Delilah's Daughters. What did she say when you talked to her? You've been pretty tight-lipped about it."

Delilah only wished that what Alisha said were true. But she knew her daughter's joy and excitement over Morgan's presence in their home would be short-lived. It was probably best that Roxanne wasn't here. Alisha deserved to hear the news first. "Roxanne needs her privacy. She'll tell you what's going on with her when she's ready."

"What happened? Did she do something stupid and get fired? I bet that's what it is. I knew Roxanne would never quit that job. What did she do?" Alisha asked.

"That's a conversation for you and her to have. I'm sure

she'll tell you when she's ready. Until then, you have to give her time."

Alisha opened the door to the dishwasher and began placing the dishes inside. "Well, I'm going to get to the bottom of this. There is no reason for Roxanne to be down in the mouth about some job, especially when we have this awesome opportunity with Morgan Sampson. You know, she should have been more excited about the news than she was. It's perfect timing for her as well. I'm going to kill that girl. Just wait until she gets home."

Delilah shook her head, meeting her daughter's eyes. "Not this time, Alisha. Let her come to you. Sometimes people have their reasons for keeping secrets. You have to love them enough to leave them alone until they're ready to share."

"What is it, Momma?" Alisha asked, turning away from the dishwasher. "Now you've got me worried. Roxanne's not sick or anything, is she?"

Delilah placed coffee cups and saucers on the serving tray with the coffee pot. "No, nothing like that. It's something that she specifically asked me not to share with you because she wants to do it herself. You have to trust that she knows what she's doing."

"Okay," Alisha said, "but I don't like it. There's no reason for Roxanne to keep a secret from me. She should know that."

"She does," Delilah said. "Just give her time." She took a deep breath. "Now we'd better get back to our guests."

Tommy and Morgan were still seated at the dinner table when the women returned. "More coffee?" Delilah asked, placing the serving tray on the table.

Both men shook their heads.

"I can't eat or drink another thing," Morgan said. "It was a great dinner, Delilah."

"It sure was," Tommy added.

"Thank you both," Delilah said.

"We're glad to have you here, Mr. Sampson," Alisha said, taking her seat. "I know I've told you before, but you've been such an encouragement to us. I can't wait for you to hear our demo."

"And I can't wait to hear it," Morgan said. "I didn't tell you this before," he said, "but I knew your father, Rocky. We were friends back in the day."

Alisha's eyes widened in surprise. "I didn't know that," she said. She turned to her mother. "Isn't that something? Talk about a small world."

"It's smaller than you think," Delilah added. "I knew Morgan back in the day as well."

"What?" Alisha sank back in her chair. "You never let on that you knew Mr. Sampson. Did you think he wouldn't remember you? Is that why you didn't tell me?" Without giving her mother time to answer, she turned to Morgan. "When did you figure out I was Rocky's daughter? Did you know when you saw Delilah's Daughters on television?"

Morgan nodded. "Yes, I knew then."

"Well, I'm glad you didn't tell me when we first met. I'm sure I would have thought you were just being nice to me, to us, because of my dad."

"Not that," Morgan said.

Delilah cleared her throat. "Alisha, there is no easy way to tell you this, so I'm just going to come right out and tell you.

Your father and Morgan were good friends years ago before you were born. Back then, your dad's music kept him on the road more than at home. Morgan was good enough to step in to help out when your dad was away. He was a good friend to both me and your dad."

"I don't understand," Alisha said, looking from her mom to Morgan and back to her mom. "You were good friends? What happened? Why did you pretend you didn't know each other? Why the secrecy?"

Delilah took a deep breath. "Before you were born, we promised your father we would never see each other again. And we kept that promise."

"I still don't understand," Alisha said. "Why would Dad not want you and Mr. Sampson to see each other again?"

Instead of answering, Delilah looked first at Tommy and then at Morgan for help.

"It was because of me," Morgan said. "Your father didn't want me around your mother because of my feelings for her."

Alisha slumped back in her chair. "You were in love with Momma?"

He nodded.

She turned to her mother. "And were you in love with him?"

"I thought I was," Delilah said. "The truth is, I was lonely because your dad was away so much. I had two babies, Roxanne and Veronica, and I was lonely for adult companionship."

"And you found that companionship in Mr. Sampson?"

Delilah nodded. She sensed that Alisha was figuring out what had happened.

Alisha looked from Mr. Sampson to her mother and back again. "Did you two have an affair? Is that why Dad made you promise not to see each other again?"

Delilah wished for another answer, one that wouldn't break her daughter's heart, but she had none. Drawing strength from the forgiveness Rocky had granted to her all those years ago, she slowly nodded her head.

"I loved your mother, Alisha," Morgan said, before Alisha could respond, "and I convinced myself that your dad didn't deserve her. I took advantage of her loneliness."

"And Dad found out?"

"He did," Delilah said. "And he forgave me. Our marriage was stronger than ever. I will never say that the affair made our marriage stronger, but it made both me and Rocky realize how hard we had to work to hold on to and nurture the love and the family we shared. After he forgave me, we never looked back. He never held it against me, never threw it in my face."

Alisha accepted her words with a nod. "That sounds like Dad. He was a good man. All he asked was that you two not see each other again." She turned to Morgan. "Do you feel you're breaking your promise to my dad by being my mentor? Is that why you're here?"

Morgan shook his head. "That's not the reason."

Alisha turned to her mother. "Is it you, Momma? Do you feel guilty because Mr. Sampson is helping us?"

"I feel guilty," Delilah said, "but that's not the reason."

"What is it then?" Alisha asked, her growing frustration obvious in the clenched fingers she rested on the table.

Delilah cleared her throat. "I became pregnant as a result of my affair with Morgan," she said.

"What?" Alisha said, her hands now clenching and unclenching. "You got pregnant? You have a baby out there somewhere? I can't believe this, Momma. It was hard enough to digest that you had an affair, but a baby? How could you do that to Dad? I can't believe this," she repeated. "So what happened to the baby?"

"I had the baby, and Rocky and I raised her along with her two sisters."

Alisha sat for a couple of moments as enlightenment dawned. "You raised the baby?"

Delilah's heart ached for her daughter, but she could only nod.

Alisha stared at Morgan. "It can't be," she said. "You're not my father. Rocky was my father."

"You're right, Alisha," Morgan said. "Rocky was your father in all ways that mattered, but I'm your biological parent."

Alisha began shaking her head left and right. "No, no, no. This can't be true. There has to be some mistake. Rocky is my biological father." She shot pleading eyes to her mother. "Tell him, Momma."

"I'm so sorry, sweetheart," Delilah said. "Rocky never wanted you to know. He couldn't have loved you more had you been his biological daughter. He loved you. You know he loved you."

Alisha couldn't seem to get her mind around what she'd heard. "You and Morgan had an affair," she spat out. "You got pregnant, and I'm the result."

Delilah's heart broke at her daughter's words as she and Morgan could only nod.

"So you've been lying to me all these years?"

Though Delilah expected the condemnation and knew it was deserved, she felt the pain of her daughter's question deeply. "It was the only way, Alisha," she tried to explain. "Rocky and I didn't want there to be any difference in you three girls."

Alisha let out a hysterical laugh. "Is that why the group's name is Delilah's Daughters rather than Rocky's Daughters? Did Dad name us that because I wasn't his real daughter?"

"Don't you ever think that," Delilah said. "It would break Rocky's heart to even think that you doubted his love for you, that you doubted how much he considered you his daughter, that you doubted how much you *were* his daughter."

Alisha turned red eyes to Morgan. "But I'm not Rocky's daughter," she said. "I'm your daughter."

"That's right," Morgan said. "You're my daughter, but you're also Rocky's daughter. I couldn't have stayed away all these years if I thought he didn't love you. You were his daughter in all the ways that mattered."

"So why are you here now after all these years?" she asked, her pain making her words clipped. "Did you suddenly become overwhelmed with guilt?"

Morgan's anguish shone in his eyes. "No," he said simply. "I have cancer and I'm dying. You're named in my will, so you were going to find out who I was to you at some point. I wanted you to find out from me and your mother. I wanted you to understand and to forgive us. I also wanted you to know that you have another sister and a brother."

Alisha squeezed her now-damp eyes shut. "This is too much," she said. "It's too much." She opened her eyes, and they were filled with tears. She looked at her mom and Morgan. "I need to get out for a while, clear my head. This is too much." With those words, Alisha slid out of her chair, grabbed her purse on the table by the door, and headed out.

When Delilah got up to follow her, Tommy pulled her back. "Let her go, Delilah. She needs time."

Chapter 41

*D*elilah sat alone in the dark in her living room, with all manner of negative thoughts going through her mind. Since she had forced Tommy and Morgan to leave, she was left to sit by herself waiting for Alisha to return home. She could only guess at the thoughts that were going through her baby girl's mind. Her only consolation was that Alisha hadn't left in a rage. She'd been upset, but she hadn't been out of her mind with anger. Delilah just wished her daughter would call.

When she saw the lights from a car shine through the windows, she said a quick "Thank you, Lord" and rushed to the door. "Alisha," she called out.

"Sorry," came Roxanne's voice, "it's only me, the wayward daughter."

"Not now, Roxanne," Delilah said, heading back to her perch on a chair in the living room.

"Why are you waiting up for Alisha?" Roxanne asked, following her mother to the living room. "It's been a long time since you've had to do that."

Delilah looked up at her oldest child. "Come and sit with me," she said.

Roxanne did as she was told. "What is it, Momma?" she asked. "Is Alisha all right?"

"She heard some news tonight that was difficult for her to hear and understand."

Roxanne's eyes widened in alarm. "You told her about me, didn't you?" she accused. "I asked you not to tell her, Momma. Why couldn't you do as I asked?"

"The news wasn't about you, Roxanne, so you can calm down. Your secret is still your secret. Alisha is worried about you, though, so you need to tell her what's going on."

"I'll tell her when I'm ready."

Delilah laughed a dry laugh.

"And why is that funny?" Roxanne asked.

"It's not funny, Roxanne," she said. "It's sad."

"I'm going to tell her. Just give me some time. You can do that for me, can't you?"

Delilah looked at her daughter and saw the defiance in her eyes. "You're so much like me," she said. "You always prided yourself on being like Rocky, but you're more like me than you know."

"What?" Roxanne asked, with a sour smile. "Did you have an affair with a married man? Somehow I doubt it."

"I'm not perfect, Roxanne, and neither was your father."

"Did Dad have an affair?"

Delilah shook her head.

"Then what are we talking about?"

"We're talking about me. I had an affair."

"I don't believe it," Roxanne said, shaking her head. "Not you, unless you're talking about you and Mr. Tommy. That's not considered an affair, Momma, since Dad is long dead." She paused for a minute. "Did you have something going with Mr. Tommy before Daddy died? Please tell me you and Mr. Tommy weren't carrying on behind Daddy's back. That would be some foul stuff, Momma. Mr. Tommy was supposed to be Daddy's friend."

"Don't get all wound up," Delilah said. "Tommy and I didn't have an affair. Our relationship is new. There was never anything between us when Rocky was alive."

"Good," Roxanne said. "That would be low, especially given the way you lit into me when I told you about me and Gavin."

Delilah met her daughter's eyes. "I lit into you, as you say, because Rocky and I raised you better. But kids don't always do what they're brought up to do. Boy, do I know that."

"What are you talking about, Momma?"

Delilah closed her eyes briefly against the pain. When she opened them, she said, "I'm talking about me having an affair."

Roxanne settled back in her chair. "When?" she asked, folding her arms across her stomach.

"When you and Veronica were babies, before Alisha was born."

Roxanne began shaking her head left and right, refusing to accept her mother's words. "I don't believe it. Not you."

"Yes, me," Delilah said, wishing it were not so.

Roxanne leaned forward. "Were you and Dad separated?"

Delilah couldn't lie. "I wish I could blame it on that. Your father and I have never been separated. He traveled a lot, but we always considered ourselves married."

"If that's the case, how did you have an affair?"

She met her daughter's eyes again. "You should know how things happen. You don't really plan them. They just happen."

Roxanne held her mother's gaze. "I don't know if I believe things just happen, Momma. In my case, I didn't know the guy was married until after I slept with him. The problem is that I didn't stop sleeping with him after I found out. I still can't believe I didn't."

"Why didn't you?"

Roxanne shrugged. "I don't know," she said. "I guess I felt like I needed him. He was so supportive of my music. I needed that support."

Delilah closed her eyes, remembering the support Morgan had been to her. Support that had quickly turned into something else, something more, something dangerous, something that would change all their lives. "Well, I needed support too, with two babies and your dad gone all the time. I told myself the same thing you told yourself."

"Why are you telling me this now?" Roxanne asked. "If you're trying to make me feel better because of what I did, it's not working."

"No, it's not about you, though I should have been more sympathetic when you told me. How could I berate you when you'd only done what I'd done? To be honest, a lot of my reaction was based in my own guilt."

"It's not your fault, Momma," Roxanne said. "I'm a grown woman, and I made a grown woman's decision. It was the wrong decision, but I made it with my eyes open. I don't blame you, and you shouldn't blame yourself, especially over something that happened more than twenty years ago. Did Dad even know?"

Delilah couldn't believe the acceptance and understanding her oldest child was giving her. In return, she owed her complete honesty. "He knew and he forgave me. He loved me, you know, and I loved him, despite what I did."

Roxanne got up and walked over to her mother. She kneeled down next to her chair and placed her hand on her mother's knee. "That was a long time ago, Momma. Dad forgave you. Why are you bringing it back up? Let it go."

"I wish I could let it go," Delilah said, placing her hand over Roxanne's, "but I can't."

Roxanne sat back on her thighs. "Why can't you?"

Delilah took a deep breath, released it. "Because I did more than have an affair. I became pregnant."

Delilah watched as the color drained from her oldest child's face. "You what?" Roxanne said, as if she couldn't believe what she'd heard.

Delilah wished she had some other story to tell, but she didn't. She simply repeated, "I became pregnant, and I had a baby."

"What are you saying, Momma?" Roxanne asked, her eyes pleading with Delilah to take back what she'd said.

"I'm so sorry to have to tell you this, Roxanne. You don't know how sorry I am, but it's time the truth is out. What I'm saying is that Rocky wasn't Alisha's biological father. I told her tonight."

Delilah watched as Roxanne's mouth opened, but no words came out. She closed it.

"I'm sorry," Delilah repeated.

"Where is she?" Roxanne asked, ignoring the apology. "Where is Alisha?"

"I don't know," Delilah said. "She left, saying she needed some time to think."

Roxanne stood and began pacing in front of the windows. "I don't believe you did this, Momma. Why tell Alisha now, after all these years? What good could it do? Dad went to his grave with the secret. Couldn't you have done the same?"

That was the plan, Delilah thought, but sometimes even the best-laid plans go awry. "It wasn't my secret alone, Roxanne," she said. "It was the biological father's secret as well."

Roxanne rolled her eyes. "So he wanted to tell her? Well, he's more than twenty years too late. Talk about selfish."

"He's dying, and he wanted Alisha to know about him before he died," she said, remembering the anguish in Morgan's eyes when they told Alisha.

"Like I said, how selfish of him," Roxanne repeated.

"Not selfish at all." Delilah needed Roxanne to understand. "He named her in his will, told his wife and kids about her. Alisha was going to find out anyway. He kept his promise to Rocky and never tried to contact her, but he's loved her all these years. He wanted her to know before he died."

Roxanne dropped back down on the couch. "I can't believe this. What is going on with this family?"

Delilah didn't answer, because she wondered the same thing.

"So who is Alisha's biological father?" Roxanne finally asked.

"Morgan Sampson."

Roxanne's mouth dropped open again. "The gospel music producer she met at the ASCAP conference? The man who volunteered to be her mentor?"

Delilah nodded. "One and the same."

Roxanne began shaking her head. "You never let on that you even knew him. I don't know, Momma. You're a better liar than I would have thought. I'm not sure how I feel knowing you are."

Even though Delilah knew she deserved the harsh judgment, her daughter's words cut her deeply. "Just don't repeat my mistakes, Roxanne. Feel how you want about me, but don't do what I did."

Roxanne began to laugh.

"What on earth are you laughing about?" Delilah asked. "I find nothing funny in this entire situation."

Roxanne stopped laughing and wiped at the tears that had formed in her eyes. "You telling me not to repeat your mistakes is hilarious, Momma."

"I don't see anything funny about it. I'm trying to save you some heartache. Be glad your relationship ended when it did. You could have ended up pregnant by a married man. Thank God, you didn't."

Chapter 42

Roxanne had taken her mother's place in the dark living room waiting for Alisha to return. Her mother's confession had provided her a prime opportunity to share the real reason she was still withdrawn from the family: she was pregnant. She knew she should have told her mother about it tonight, but she couldn't do it. The situation with Alisha weighed heavily on her mother, and she didn't want to add to it. What would her mother do when she learned Roxanne had indeed followed in her footsteps and gotten herself pregnant by a married man? In a couple of days, after things with Alisha were cleared up, Roxanne would tell her. Her mother needed to recover first from the major emotional hit she'd taken when she'd told Alisha the truth about her biological father.

Roxanne wasn't sure how she felt about the situation. Though telling Alisha the truth had taken its toll on Delilah, the knowledge of her mother's past had lifted a burden from Roxanne's shoulders. Showing her mother some compassion had allowed her to show that same compassion to herself. She felt better than she'd felt since the night Gavin's wife confronted her.

And she had clarity about what she was going to do next. She pressed her hands across her still-flat stomach. She wanted to do what her mom had done—what was best for her baby. When she'd first found out she was pregnant, she'd thought it was a cruel joke God was playing on her. How else could she explain finding out she was pregnant immediately after her married lover had dumped her? She went through some dark days as she considered all her options, including abortion. When she'd returned home tonight, she still hadn't been sure what her next move should be. After hearing her mother's story, she was now confident in her next actions. She would do what was best for her baby, regardless of the cost to herself.

When headlights from the driveway flashed through the windows, Roxanne knew Alisha had returned. She kept her seat until she heard her sister enter the house. "Alisha, I'm in here," she called out.

"I hope you're not waiting up for me," Alisha said, after she entered the living room.

"You look like you've been through a tornado," Roxanne said, taking in her sister's pale skin and barren eyes.

Alisha dropped down on the couch. "I have. Did Momma tell you?"

Roxanne nodded. "How are you doing?"

"I don't know how I'm doing," Alisha said. "I'm hurt, I'm angry, I'm confused. I can't hold a coherent thought in my head. The only thing that's clear to me is that Rocky wasn't my father. And that hurts. It hurts more than anything else."

Roxanne leaned forward. "Rocky *was* your father, Alisha," she said, with great admiration for her father. Her dad's actions gave her renewed faith in the goodness of people. It comforted her to know that he forgave her mother, because that meant he would forgive her as well. "Don't ever doubt that. He chose to be your father. He chose to love you. And he did. You've never doubted his love before, so don't start now. It would break his heart if you did. You know it would."

Alisha wiped at her eyes. "I wish he were here. I wish he had been the one to tell me. That makes no sense, does it?"

"If it makes sense to you, it makes sense. Right now, you're all that matters. It's your life. Momma and Daddy wanted you to feel safe and loved, and they made sure you were. Don't forget that."

Alisha lifted damp eyes to her sister. "But they lied to me all these years. Did she tell you I have another sister and a brother? I can't believe it. And Morgan Sampson is my father. How can I believe anything he said about my talent or Delilah's Daughters? He had his own agenda. Everybody has an agenda. First Veronica. Now Momma, Daddy, and Morgan. Is anything real? Does anybody tell the truth?"

"We all make mistakes, Alisha," Roxanne said, thinking of the major ones she'd made recently. "Life gets messy sometimes."

Alisha cocked her head to the side. "You're taking this well. You know this means that Momma cheated on Dad, don't you? You don't get pregnant talking on the phone."

Roxanne folded her arms across her stomach. "I know

how pregnancy happens, Alisha," she said. "I'm as surprised as you, but I'm cutting Momma some slack. She's human. She made a mistake."

Alisha snorted. "Forgetting to pay the cable bill is a mistake. Sleeping with somebody who's not your husband is a bit more than a mistake, I think. What Momma did to Dad was foul. Lying to me all these years was foul. I don't even know who Momma is anymore. This doesn't seem like the woman I've known and loved all my life. That woman couldn't do these things. Not the mother I loved."

"You're being too harsh on her, Alisha."

"I can't believe you're taking up for her," Alisha shot back. "The high and mighty Delilah was an adulterer. How's that for being a role model?"

Alisha's words hurt. Even though she was referring to their mother, Roxanne knew her sister's disdain would be directed toward her as well if she knew about Gavin and the pregnancy. "I've made my share of mistakes too," Roxanne said, "so I can't be harsh with her. Then I'd have to be harsh with myself. To be honest, I don't have the energy."

"Well, you're a better woman than I am. I don't know if I'll ever be able to look at Momma the same way. How can I?"

"It's called forgiveness, Alisha. You've heard of it before, haven't you?"

Alisha cast a quick glance at her sister. "I wonder how quick you'd be to forgive if you were in my shoes? How would you feel if you found out Rocky wasn't your biological father?"

"Okay," Roxanne said, "you have a right to be upset, I'll give you that."

"Thanks," Alisha said dryly.

"Come on, Alisha, I'm trying to understand both you and Momma."

Alisha dropped down in a chair. "Well, I'm done trying to understand Momma for the night. I wish I could forget everything that happened today." She sighed. "I can't do that, but I can change the subject. Let's talk about you. Are you going to tell me why you've been so gloomy lately?"

Roxanne looked at her sister, unsure how much to tell her. "I don't know if you can handle it."

Alisha chuckled, but no humor was in it. "I can handle it. After today, I can handle anything."

Roxanne took a deep breath, choosing to believe her sister's words. "You were right about me having a male friend on the ship."

Alisha rolled her eyes. "Tell me something I don't know."

"I don't think you knew he was married."

Alisha gave her sister a hard glare. "What?"

"He was married," Roxanne repeated. "His wife confronted me on my last cruise. Her family owns the cruise line, so I'm out of a job. I didn't quit, I was fired."

Alisha continued to stare at her. "Please tell me you're joking."

Roxanne shook her head, pressing her hand across her stomach. "It's no joking matter."

Alisha began to laugh, a deep belly laugh.

"What's so funny?" Roxanne asked.

"Us. Delilah's Daughters, the budding gospel group. We're funny."

"I'm not getting it," Roxanne said.

"Mr. Tommy said something the other day before he agreed to work with us on the demo. He said if we were going to do gospel, our lives had to be open books. That folks listening to our music would expect our lives to reflect some kind of relationship with God. It seems we've failed on that front and failed miserably. I can see it now. Me, you, and Momma on the cover of *Gospel Today* airing all our dirty laundry and talking about how Christians aren't perfect."

Roxanne felt her sister's words as a punch to her midsection. "That's cruel, Alisha, and it's beneath you."

"It's the truth, Roxanne," she said, with no hint of mirth in her voice. "How can we put ourselves forth as a gospel group right now given the shambles that our personal lives are in? It's soon going to be common knowledge that Morgan Sampson is my real father, that Momma committed adultery, and that you followed in her footsteps."

"That's enough, Alisha. I get that you're upset with us."

Alisha got up from the couch. "I'm more than upset. I'm disgusted to even be a part of this family. Veronica turned out to be the smart one. She got out before all the crap hit the fan. I think I'll follow her lead."

Roxanne got up and followed Alisha to the stairs. "What are you talking about?"

"I need to get away," Alisha said, turning back to look at Roxanne. "I need some time to myself to figure out what I'm going to do next. Delilah's Daughters is done. Morgan Sampson is done. I don't have a father. I don't have a family. I don't have a job. I don't have anything. I've got to figure out my future. A future for one."

Chapter 43

$\mathcal{V}$eronica found the quiet and empty townhouse welcoming after a long afternoon in the gym. She loved Dexter, but these days loving him from a distance was easier. The pressure of being Veronica Y was starting to weigh on her. She needed some place and some time where she could just be Veronica. A trip to Birmingham to see her mom and sisters would do the trick, she was sure, but there would be hell to pay from Legends and from Dexter if she even brought up the idea of leaving Atlanta.

She went to the refrigerator and pulled out a bottle of cold water. After removing the cap, she took a long swallow and sat down at the counter. There was her cell phone, where she'd left it this morning. She was beginning to make a habit of forgetting to take it with her. She didn't want to think of it as her way of getting away from Legends, but that had to be it. Tia and Dexter were the folks who called her most. If only her sisters or her mother were calling her. That would make her remember to keep her phone with her.

She picked up the phone and flipped it open. Of course, she had a voice-mail message. And she knew it had to be from Dexter or Tia. Who else could it be? She pressed the button to play the message anyway.

> *Hey, Veronica, this is Alisha. I'm getting the feeling that you're ignoring my messages, so I won't leave another one. I figure you'll call when you're ready. You know, we're a really screwed-up family.*

Veronica stood holding the phone, wondering what Alisha meant by leaving her messages, when Dexter arrived home.

"Hey, babe," he said. "Did you have a good day?"

Closing her phone, she said, "I got a strange voice-mail message from Alisha. She said she's been leaving me messages and I've been ignoring them. I don't know what she's talking about. I haven't gotten any messages from her."

"Head games," Dexter said. "She's trying to make you feel guilty. Ignore her."

Veronica didn't agree. "Alisha's not like that, Dexter. She was disappointed in my decision to leave the group, but she was more supportive than Momma and Roxanne."

Dexter looked away, not meeting her eyes. "I wouldn't worry about it. If she called once, she'll call again."

"Look at me, Dexter," she said, curious about his reaction. When he turned to her, she read the guilt in his eyes. "What have you done?"

Still not looking at her, he said, "I haven't done anything."

She moved to stand in front of him. "Look at me," she said. When he did, she said, "This is me, Dexter. What have you done? What do you know about Alisha leaving me messages? Has she called before?"

"Maybe," he said, meeting her eyes for a short moment before looking away. "I don't really remember."

She dropped down on the stool at the bar in the kitchen. "Oh, Dexter, please tell me you haven't been deleting messages from my phone. It's beneath you."

He looked down at her. "I'm just watching out for you. You don't need any guilt trips from your mom or your sisters."

She peered up at him. "So you deleted my messages?"

He shrugged. "It's not that big a deal."

She forced herself to remain calm, though she wanted to rail against him. "It's a big deal to me. Why would you do something like that?"

He sat down next to her. "Because you don't need the distraction. Legends has invested big money in you, in us. You need to stay focused."

She began shaking her head. *How could Dexter have done this to her?* "Look," she said to this man who was her husband, the man who was supposed to be on her side, "we've got to separate our marriage from this business. Maybe it wasn't such a good idea for you to take on a Legends project. I need you to be my husband. I get enough managing from Tia and the others. I don't need it at home. Can you understand what I'm saying?"

He looked away. "I only want what's best for us."

She turned his head so he faced her. With her hands on his cheeks and her eyes boring into his, she asked, "And what do you think that is?"

He put his hands atop hers. "You becoming a major pop

star and me becoming a best-selling author. It's what we've always wanted, and we're so close to having it. We can't drop the ball now."

She let her hands fall away from his face. "And to you dropping the ball is me talking to my family?"

He looked away again. "Given the way we left, yes."

She stood. "Well, I think you're wrong. I think we've handled this entire situation wrong. I never should have left Birmingham without talking to my mom at least. Family is important to me, Dexter. I thought you understood that."

"I do," he said.

She sighed. "Not if you're okay erasing messages from my sister. Just how many did you erase?"

"A couple," he murmured.

She lifted her arms in frustration. "Dexter!"

"One from your mom and one from Alisha. That's all."

She bit down on her lower lip to keep from screaming at him. "When did they call?"

"Your mom called the day you went to the plastic surgeon, and Alisha called a few days before."

Veronica's heart grew full at the thought of how much those calls would have meant to her. "You can't do that anymore, Dexter. You can't keep me from my mother and sisters. I don't care what Legends says. I want the success that you want, but not at any cost. I want success, but I'm not willing to sell myself for it."

"And you think I am?"

She wasn't sure. "I hope you're not. I hope the man I married is made of sturdier stuff than that, but there are days I wonder. I've said it before and I'll say it again. I need you to be my husband, not a Legends handler. That's the only way this marriage is going to work."

"Hey, hey," he said, reaching out to bring her close to him. When she stood between his open legs, he pulled her close and said, "Now you're taking it too far. Of course, our marriage is going to work. I love you. You have to know that everything I do is out of love for you."

"It doesn't feel like love, Dexter," she said, stepping out of his embrace, "not all the time. It feels like manipulation. Love is not manipulative."

"I'm sorry," he said, pulling her back to him. "I'm sorry. I won't do it again."

She settled against him, removing the physical barriers between them, though the emotional ones remained. "It's going to take more than words. You're going to have to show me that our marriage is more important to you than this Legends deal. I need you to hear me when I complain and not tune me out. Like with this breast augmentation. This is a real issue for me, and you simply disregard it and tell me to get on board with the plan. I expect those words from a Legends handler, but I expect a bit more understanding, sympathy, and support from my husband. I need a husband; I don't need another handler. I don't know how much clearer I can be."

"You're clear," he said, squeezing her close. "And I want to be clear. I love you, Veronica. I love you. If you walk away from this Legends deal, I'll still love you."

She pulled away so she could look into his eyes. "I wish I

believed that," she said. "I want to believe it, but I'm just not sure. Not anymore, especially not after learning you deleted those messages."

"I'm sorry," he said. "How many ways do I have to say it?"

"I don't know." She stepped out of his embrace fully and picked up her phone. "I'm going upstairs so I can have some privacy when I talk to my mom and sisters."

"Give them my regards," she heard him call after her.

She didn't acknowledge his words because she doubted their sincerity.

Chapter 44

Alisha drove around for what seemed like hours because she couldn't figure out where to go. She didn't feel up for the explanations any of her few girlfriends would want, so she didn't bother contacting them. She soon found herself parked in front of Jeff's apartment building. She wasn't quite sure how had she ended up here, but it felt right. She could trust Jeff. He wouldn't poke and prod for information. He'd merely take what she had to offer and not ask for more, which was exactly what she needed for the night.

When she reached his apartment, it took her a moment to gather herself before she rang the bell. She held her breath while she waited for him to open the door. When he did, the question in his eyes almost made her laugh.

"Alisha?" he said, as if not believing it was her.

"Every day," she said. "May I come in?"

"Of course," he said, as if remembering his manners. He pulled the door fully open so she could enter. "What brings you by?" he asked, picking up newspapers and scattered clothes from the burgundy leather couch in his great room. "I wasn't expecting company."

"I'm sorry for coming by uninvited," she said. "But I couldn't stay home, and I couldn't think of any other place to go."

He turned and met her eyes. "I don't know whether to be insulted or complimented. Which should I be?"

She dropped down on the couch. "I know it wasn't an insult, but I'm not sure it was a compliment. It depends on how you see me as a houseguest."

He sat down next to her. "What's wrong, Alisha?" he asked.

The kindness in his voice was almost her undoing. "Everything is wrong. Everything in my life, that is. I don't know how things got so screwed up."

"Do you want to talk about it?" he asked gently.

"I don't know where to start."

"How about the beginning? That's always the easiest."

Alisha didn't think she'd be able to share everything that happened, but Jeff's kind eyes gave her the encouragement she needed. When she was finished with her story, she was both tired and rejuvenated, which made no sense. "Wow," she said, a bit embarrassed she'd shared so much. "You got more than you bargained for, didn't you?"

Jeff shook his head. "I'm honored that you shared it with me. That's some story."

"You're telling me."

He rubbed his hand down her arm in what felt like a show of support. "I always knew there was something special about you," he said.

Her lips turned down in a frown. "Because I came from a screwed-up family?"

He shook his head. "That you came from a family where you were so well loved."

She looked up at him. "How'd you get that from what I told you?"

He smiled at her. "Your biological father loved you even though he never really knew you. He's had you in his heart all these years. His putting you in his will and telling his family about you are proof of that love."

Alisha wanted to believe him. "How can I be sure? What if it's only guilt?"

He shook his head. "Nah. Putting you in the will would have taken care of the guilt. He could have died and had you find out then, after he was gone. He didn't take the coward's way out, though. He wanted to embrace you, to bring you into his family as his daughter. He's claiming you, Alisha, for all the world to see, despite the cost to him, his family, and his reputation. I say that's love."

She considered Jeff's words. "I hadn't really thought about it that way," she said, a bit of awe in her voice at Jeff's insight. "Have you always been this smart?"

He gave her a bashful grin. "It's easy to see into other folks' hearts. It's my own heart that gives me trouble."

"You have a big heart, Jeff. I've known that since I met you. And everybody at work knows it as well."

"So I'm Jeff with the big heart, huh? Doesn't sound very masculine or attractive."

She shook her head. "I'm serious," she said. "In some ways, you remind me of my dad. I mean Rocky. I guess that's why I ended up on your doorstep. I really wanted my dad today, and you're the closest I could get to him."

He pressed his hand across his heart. "Oh no, things are going from bad to worse. Now you see me as a father figure. That's not exactly the impression I wanted to give, though I do take it as a compliment. Your dad, Rocky, was a great guy, a great guy who loved you more than his pride. I don't know a lot of men who would have done what your dad did. He chose love over vengeance, over everything. He loved your mother and he loved you. And he understood forgiveness. He's given you something to live up to. If he could forgive your mother, you owe it to him to try to forgive her too. Don't make his forgiveness and his love something given in vain. I'm sure he wouldn't want you to carry around unforgiveness in your heart."

She thought Jeff might be right. "Easier said than done."

"Do you think it was hard for your dad?"

She shrugged her shoulders. "I don't know, but I don't see how it could have been easy. He loved my mother, and she betrayed him, with one of his friends no less. How could forgiving that have been easy?"

"Your dad wasn't perfect, Alisha. I'm not saying that he did anything to deserve his wife cheating on him, but he did spend a lot of time on the road. He sounds like he may have had his priorities out of whack early in his marriage, like he put his music before his family. Maybe, just maybe, you were his constant and loving reminder of the importance of family. You've always talked about how invested he was in Delilah's Daughters, that he always wanted the group to be about family. Maybe he could forgive because he saw what he could lose if he didn't."

"That's a lot of maybes."

"I know," Jeff said, "but they sound right, don't they?"

Alisha yawned. "I don't know, but you've certainly given me something to think about."

"Well, now it seems you're thinking about sleep. Did you bring any clothes?"

She shook her head. "I sorta left in a rush."

He got up. "No problem. I think I can find something for you."

It occurred to Alisha that she could be overstepping her boundaries. "Look, Jeff, I don't think it would be right for me to wear your girlfriend's clothes. I'm sure she wouldn't like it."

"There is no girlfriend," he said. "I was thinking along the lines of one of my T-shirts. It should work as a sleep shirt for you."

For some reason, the thought of wearing his T-shirt made her heartbeat speed up. "Don't go to any trouble. I can stretch out right here on the couch in my clothes."

He shook his head. "Nobody sleeps on this couch but me. The bed you can have, but not this couch."

"I'm not going to put you out of your bed," she said.

"You're not putting me out, I'm letting you in. Now don't turn your nose up at my hospitality. You've had a long day, and you need a good night's sleep. You're probably going to have an even longer day tomorrow."

"Thanks," she said. "Words don't seem enough for what you're doing for me, but they're all I have right now. Maybe one day I can return the favor."

He winked. "Count on it."

Chapter 45

*V*eronica couldn't get yesterday's phone conversation with Alisha out of her mind. After she'd apologized to her sister for not returning her call—she didn't have the heart to tell her that Dexter had deleted the messages—they'd had a fairly long but disturbing phone call. Alisha was all upset with something Momma had done, but Veronica hadn't been able to get Alisha to tell her what the something was. All Alisha would say was that "Momma will have to tell you herself." Alisha also told her that Roxanne had lost her job on the cruise ship, but again, she was vague on the details. What was clear from Alisha was that all was not well in the Monroe household. While Veronica was having her share of trouble in Atlanta, it never occurred to her that her mom and sisters might be dealing with issues of their own that had nothing to do with her contract with Legends. She'd been pretty shortsighted and self-centered in her thinking.

"Okay, Miss Diva," Tia said, interrupting her thoughts. "I

heard your vocal lessons were a mess today, that your head wasn't in the game."

Veronica had to remind herself that Tia wasn't a school yard bully, even though she often sounded like one. "Don't you ever knock?"

"I saw Dexter outside washing your car. He told me to come on in, so I did. Now what about the vocal lessons this morning? Your coach called as soon as you left."

"I had a lot on my mind," Veronica said. She'd apologized to the coach, but apparently that hadn't been enough to keep him from tattling on her.

"Legends isn't paying you to have a lot on your mind. In case you don't remember, they're paying you to have only one thing on your mind—your recording career. Nothing is more important."

Veronica disagreed, but didn't see the point in saying so to Tia. The woman would never understand. "I hear you, Tia. You're like a broken record, playing the same song over and over."

"Some people need repetition to learn. Apparently, you're one of them. I'm as tired of having this conversation with you as you are."

"I'd never have known it."

Tia sighed. "Look, Veronica, if something is bothering you, talk to me about it. Maybe I can help."

Veronica wanted to laugh in Tia's face. Never would she trust this woman with her personal problems. Tia would have her business in the street before she could say boo. "I appreciate the offer, but I can handle it."

"Are you and Dexter having trouble?" Tia asked, lowering her voice, as though Dexter might walk in and hear them talking about him. "I know how men in this business can be. Some want to control you even when you're the one making all the money. Others want to bask in the glory of your success. Others are secretly afraid you're going to leave them, so they hold on too tightly, become smothering. Which one is Dexter?"

Veronica thought holding on too tight and being too controlling described Dexter, but she wasn't about to tell that to two-faced Tia, who'd probably run straight to Dexter and tell him that she was complaining about him. She wouldn't put it past the woman to try to interfere in her marriage. "Look, Dexter and I are fine. Everything's fine."

"Well, if it's not Dexter, it has to be your family. Has something happened to your mother? Your sisters? Tell me. I want to help."

Veronica studied Tia. "Do you really want to help me, Tia? I mean *help* me, not manipulate me to do what you want me to do?"

Tia laughed. "My job is to make sure you toe the line and follow the script that Legends has for you, but I also know everybody has their breaking point. Tell me what you need and I'll see what I can do."

Veronica sighed. Against her better judgment, she decided to confide in Tia. "I need a couple of days to go to Birmingham so I can spend some time with my family."

Tia rolled her eyes. "You're having trouble focusing because you're homesick? Is that it? You're missing your momma?"

Veronica folded her arms across her chest. "I should have known you didn't want to help. Why did I even believe you? Forget it," she said. "I don't need your permission anyway."

Tia laid a hand on her arm. "Look, Veronica, don't do anything stupid. Your calendar is packed from now until your album drops. There's no time in your schedule for a visit to Birmingham. You've known that since day one. Nothing has changed."

A lot has changed, Veronica thought. *Before, I didn't know that Dexter hadn't invited my momma and sisters to my going-away party—now I do. Before, I didn't know that Momma and my sisters had been trying to get in touch with me—now I do. Before, I didn't know that Roxanne was depressed because she had lost her job with the cruise ship—now I do. And I didn't know that Alisha had left home because of some blowup between her and Momma—but now I do.*

While Veronica didn't know the details behind any of the events, thanks to her phone conversation with Alisha yesterday, she knew enough to know she needed to go home. Her family needed her, and Lord knows she needed them.

"Have you spoken to Dexter about this trip?" Tia asked.

"Not yet, but he'll support me on it." *He'd better,* she thought to herself. If he didn't, she'd leave him in Atlanta and go without him. "He's my husband, and he wants what's best for me."

"Whatever you say," Tia said. Then she looked at her watch. "Look, I've got to run. I think my work here is done anyway."

"Yes, it is," Veronica agreed.

"Don't do anything stupid like leave town without permission, Veronica. I'm telling you right now that Mr. Washington won't like it."

Veronica didn't really care what Mr. Washington liked at this point. She knew what she had to do. "See you later, Tia," she said, dismissing her assistant. "I have things to do too."

Veronica didn't wait for Tia to leave. She headed upstairs while the woman was still standing in the kitchen. She had to pack and get on the road if she wanted to be in Birmingham before it got dark.

Chapter 46

Veronica stood on her mother's porch feeling like a returning prodigal. Since she was pretty sure no fatted calf would be rolled out to celebrate her return, she had stopped by the bakery and picked up a cherry cheesecake. Food worked for women as well as men, or so she hoped. She rang the bell. And waited.

She was surprised when Roxanne, not her mother, opened the door. Roxanne blinked twice, as if unsure who she was. "Veronica?"

"Please, girl, you know it's me. Let me in before this cheesecake melts."

Roxanne propped one hand on a hip. "It had better be cherry."

Veronica smiled. Things were going to be all right. "I wouldn't have the nerve to bring any other kind."

Roxanne gave her a broad, welcoming smile. "Come on in, sistergirl. That cheesecake is calling my name."

"Where's Momma?" Veronica asked as she followed Roxanne into the kitchen.

"Mr. Tommy took her to lunch."

"Mr. Tommy?"

Roxanne looked back at her over her shoulder. "You didn't know? I guess you'd left by the time she told us. Anyway, Momma and Mr. Tommy are an item. They've been seeing each other for a while, but they've only recently make it public."

"I had no idea."

"We didn't either, but it's all good. He cares about her, and she cares about him. She's happy, so I'm happy for her."

"I am too," Veronica said. "Daddy's been gone for a while. Momma needs somebody in her life."

Roxanne pulled down two dessert plates from the cabinet and took two forks and a knife from the silverware drawer.

Veronica put the cheesecake box on the table and opened it. She took the knife Roxanne handed to her and cut two pieces, putting each one on a dessert plate.

"That looks delicious," Roxanne said, taking one of the dessert plates. She quickly stabbed her fork into her slice and chunked a piece into her mouth. "It *is* delicious," she said, after the first bite. "Good choice, sis."

"It's a peace offering," Veronica said, in all seriousness.

"I know," Roxanne said, "but it wasn't necessary."

"Yes, it was. I left under bad terms."

Roxanne shrugged. "You did what you had to do. We all make choices."

"That's not what you said when I left."

"Well, let's just say I've grown up a lot since then. It's been a short time, but a lot has changed."

"I've had my share of growing pains too," Veronica said.

"So life in Atlanta hasn't been perfect?"

Veronica shook her head. "Hardly. In some ways, it's been all we'd dreamed it would be. The first week I was there, all I wanted was for you and Alisha to be there sharing the experience with me. I thought about you all the time. I still do. I miss you both and Momma too."

"You sound surprised that you miss us."

"I guess I was," Veronica said. "It's not like I'm alone. I have Dexter, and Legends keeps me busy 24/7. But even with all of that, I've missed you all more than you can know. It's true about success being sweeter when it's shared with the ones you love and who love you. That's the downside to Legends. There's not a lot of love going around. Mostly just orders."

"How does that old song go—you have to pay the price to be the boss? Are you saying the cost is too high?"

Veronica shrugged. "I really don't know. That's what I'm trying to find out. Like I said, I enjoy some parts of it, but other parts I could do without."

"Isn't that true for everything in life? You have to take the good with the bad. Nothing is ever going to be 100 percent perfect. Not in this life, anyway. You just have to figure out if you can live with the imperfection."

"When did you get so smart?"

"I've had my ups and downs too."

Veronica nodded. "Alisha told me about your job."

"Alisha? When did you talk to her?"

"She called me a couple of days ago. She told me bits and

pieces of what's been going on in the family and let me know I needed to come home."

"Well, well. I wonder why she called you. Neither Momma nor I have heard from her since she left."

"Why did she leave, Roxanne? She mentioned some disagreement between her and Momma, but she wasn't very clear. She merely said Momma would have to explain."

Roxanne nodded. "She's right. It's best if Momma tells you. She should be home soon."

Veronica fought back the anxiety brought on by the unknown before it overtook her. "I've waited this long. I guess a couple more hours won't hurt. So what about you? What happened with Dreamland?"

"You don't want to know."

"Yes, I do," Veronica said. "I know how much that job meant to you. It's understandable that you'd be a bit depressed about losing it, especially right on the heels of losing out on *Sing for America* and then losing the Magic City deal because of me. I'm sorry, Roxanne. I really am. I never meant for anybody to get hurt."

"I was hurt," Roxanne said, "but I was also jealous. To be honest, I probably would have made the same choice you made if I'd been offered a Legends contract. But I wasn't, and that stung. I'm the oldest sister, and I've always seen myself as the leader. When Legends offered you that contract, I felt as though you were taking what was mine."

Veronica hated that she was the cause of her sister's pain. "I don't know what to say except I'm sorry."

"There's nothing for you to be sorry about. That's my issue. I have good things in my life now to balance out the losses."

Veronica grinned. "Sounds like you're talking about a man."

"Better than that," Roxanne said. She stared closely at her sister, as if debating how much to tell her. "I'm pregnant."

Veronica's eyes widened. "Pregnant? Well, Alisha didn't tell me that."

"She couldn't tell you because she doesn't know. Neither does Momma. You're the first person I've told."

Veronica sat back in her chair. "Why haven't you told them?"

Roxanne sighed. "Other than the obvious reason that I am not married?"

Veronica smiled. "There is that, but you aren't the first Christian woman to jump the gun before jumping the broom. Who is the lucky guy, by the way?"

Roxanne looked away. "You don't know him. He's a guy from the ship."

Veronica hadn't missed the pain in her sister's eyes. "Do you love him? Are you going to get married? Is he happy about the baby?"

Roxanne laughed at the barrage of questions. "No, no, and he doesn't know."

"Why haven't you told him?"

"We broke up."

"Wow. Your decision or his?"

Roxanne met her sister's eyes. "His wife's."

Veronica swallowed. "Oh."

"Yes, oh. Momma and Alisha didn't respond too well to the wife part, so I thought I'd best hold off on telling them the pregnancy part. It's going to break Momma's heart and send Alisha into even more of a tailspin than she's in already."

"You don't know that," Veronica said. "You told me, and I'm handling it well."

Roxanne smiled. "But you came home looking for forgiveness yourself. Given your situation, I figured you'd be compassionate about mine."

Veronica reached for her sister's hand. "I'm glad you felt comfortable telling me, but you're going to have to tell Momma and Alisha."

"I know," Roxanne said, "and I will. I just need to find the right time."

"And the father? Are you going to tell him?"

Roxanne met her sister's eyes. "I don't think I have much of a choice. He deserves to know."

"How do you think he'll respond?"

Roxanne sighed. "I have no idea. He ended our relationship pretty easily when his wife found out, and he didn't stand up for me with the cruise line at all. Did I mention that his wife's family owns the cruise line?"

Veronica chuckled. "When you step in it, you really step in it, don't you?"

"It seems that way, doesn't it?" Roxanne said, smiling. "This has been some welcome home for you, hasn't it?"

Veronica reached for her hand again. "It's all good. I guess it's true what they say—every family has its drama."

Roxanne grunted. "You don't know the half of it."

Chapter 47

$\mathcal{D}$elilah returned home with her spirits a bit uplifted, but as she strode to her bedroom the feeling of despair she'd felt since Alisha had left the house swept over her. She wished her daughter would call or make some kind of contact. When she opened her bedroom door and flicked on the light, she took a step back at the sight of a body in her bed. "Roxanne?" she called, rushing toward the bed. "What's wrong?"

Delilah stopped short when she realized that Veronica, not Roxanne, was in her bed.

"Veronica?"

Her daughter wiped sleep from her eyes. "It's me, Momma," she said.

"What are you doing here?" Delilah asked, sitting next to her.

Veronica gave a wobbly smile. "I missed you," she said. Then she fell into her mother's embrace. "I'm so sorry, Momma."

"There's nothing to be sorry about," Delilah said, rubbing her daughter's back. "You're here, that's all that matters."

Veronica pulled back. "No, I need to apologize," she said. "I was wrong to leave Birmingham the way I did, without saying good-bye to you, Roxanne, and Alisha. I don't know what I was thinking."

Delilah was glad to hear those words. "It did sting a bit when we found out about your going-away party."

Veronica looked away. "I'm sorry about that too," she said. "It wasn't my doing."

Delilah lifted a brow. "Dexter?"

Veronica nodded as she turned back to her mother. "I don't know what's gotten into him, Momma. Things have been different since the night Delilah's Daughters lost the contest and we learned about the Legends offer. Can you believe he actually told me that he'd invited you to the celebration but you turned him down?"

Delilah could believe it, but she knew saying so would give neither her nor Veronica any satisfaction. "He was doing what he thought was right," she said. "Unfortunately, sometimes good intentions have disastrous results."

"It's a disaster, all right, a disaster for our marriage. Dexter is more concerned about the career of Veronica Y than he is about his wife. I don't like it."

Delilah patted her hand. "I understand where you're coming from," she said, "but don't be too hard on Dexter. We all make mistakes. Big ones."

It was Veronica's turn to lift a brow. "Is this really you, Momma, taking up for Dexter?"

Thinking about her own mistakes, Delilah said, "Maybe I've been too hard on him. He's your husband, and all he's wanted is your time and attention. If I had embraced him more, maybe he wouldn't have felt threatened by our relationship."

"That's no excuse for what he's done," Veronica said. "Did you know he deleted voice-mail messages from you and Alisha? I never got your messages, Momma," she said. "I would have called you back. I did call Alisha."

Delilah's heart raced. "When did you speak to Alisha?"

"Day before yesterday," Veronica said. "I got her second message. That's how I found out what Dexter was doing. After I had it out with him, I called her."

"How is she?"

Veronica cocked her head to the side. "I'm not sure, Momma," she said. "Something tells me you have a better idea than I do. Alisha was very mysterious on the phone. All I could really get out of her was that I needed to come home."

Delilah squeezed her daughter's hand. "I'm glad you're here."

"And I'm glad to be here, but I need to know what's going on with you and Alisha."

"I'm surprised she didn't tell you herself," Delilah said.

"Believe me, I tried to pry it out of her, but she wouldn't budge. I couldn't get Roxanne to tell me either."

"You've seen Roxanne?"

Veronica nodded. "She was here when I got here. I think I won her over with cherry cheesecake."

Delilah smiled. "You came home in full surrender mode, didn't you?"

Veronica pulled her mom into a second embrace. "I'm lost without you all, Momma. I have no idea what I was thinking. Maybe you were right all along. Maybe the Legends deal wasn't right for me, for us."

It was Delilah's turn to shake her head. "I don't know about that," she said. "A lot has happened since that decision was made that has me reconsidering my position."

"I can't believe us, Momma. Are we ever going to get on the same page about this Legends deal?"

Delilah chuckled. "You have a point," she said. "Recently, I've been forced to take a hard look at what motivates me, and I haven't liked everything I've discovered."

"Are you talking about me and Legends, or you and Alisha?"

"Both," she said.

"You're stalling, Momma," Veronica said. "You still haven't told me what happened with you and Alisha."

Delilah looked down at her hands. "It's a difficult story to tell," she said.

"Now you're scaring me," Veronica said. "Tell me before I have a heart attack or something."

Delilah took a deep breath. "I had to give Alisha some news that your father and I had hoped she'd never have to know." She paused and took a deep breath. "I had to tell her that Rocky was not her biological father."

Veronica's eyes widened. "What? What do you mean Dad wasn't her biological father? Are you saying Alisha was adopted? That can't be."

Delilah began shaking her head. She held tighter to Veronica's hands. "Alisha's not adopted," she said. "I'm her biological mother, but Rocky wasn't her biological father."

Veronica's mouth dropped open. Then she closed it. Then she opened it again. "What are you trying to tell me?"

"That another man is Alisha's father. That I had an affair and Alisha was the result."

Veronica pulled her hands out of her mother's. "This can't be true," she said. "You and Daddy had the perfect marriage."

"There's no such thing as a perfect marriage, Veronica."

"I still can't believe it. How could you do this to Daddy, to us? How could you?"

"I was young and foolish," Delilah said. "And that's not an excuse."

"Daddy is not Alisha's father," Veronica repeated. "No wonder she left."

"You're wrong about one thing, Veronica," Delilah said. "Rocky was and is Alisha's father, in all the ways that matter."

Veronica shook her head. "It's not that simple, Momma," she said. "I'll bet Alisha was devastated. Why did you even tell her? It was so long ago. She never needed to know. None of us did. This is one time when lying might have been the best option."

Delilah hated that her past actions had led her daughter to this type of warped thinking. "Her biological father is dying, and he wanted to meet her before he dies."

"Whew," Veronica said.

"That's about how I felt."

"What about Alisha? Where is she?"

"I don't know," Delilah said. "You're the only one she's spoken to. Roxanne and I haven't heard from her."

"She must be feeling all alone, if I'm the one she turned to."

"Have you tried calling her since you've been back?"

Veronica nodded. "She's not answering her phone."

"Maybe she needs some time to get her thoughts together."

Veronica shook her head. "I might have agreed with you at one time, Momma, but not now. Alisha needs her family, now more than ever. Pulling away from the ones you love, and the ones who love you, is never the right thing to do, no matter the situation."

Delilah didn't want to make Veronica's declaration all about her, but she had to ask: "So you're not angry with me?"

Veronica shrugged. "I don't know how I feel. I'm torn up inside. There's me and Legends. There's Roxanne and her married lover. And now you, Alisha, and her biological father. It's too much to process."

"So Roxanne told you?"

"She did," Veronica said. "She told me everything."

"Like mother, like daughter," Delilah said glumly.

"More than you know, Momma," Veronica said.

Delilah lifted her eyes to meet those of her middle daughter. "What do you mean?"

Holding her gaze, Veronica said, "Roxanne's pregnant."

Chapter 48

Alisha awoke the next morning in Jeff's bed, wearing his T-shirt. She'd made the right choice in coming to him. He was just what she needed. As if hearing her thoughts, he rapped on the bedroom door and said, "Time for breakfast."

She glanced at his nightstand for the clock, which read seven o'clock. "It's too early," she called out. "Go back to bed."

"No way," he said. "You'd better cover yourself because I'm coming in."

She giggled. "I'm covered," she said. "Come on in."

She sat up in bed when he entered the room with a tray table in his hands.

"What's this?" she said as he walked toward her. "Breakfast in bed. Is this for me?"

He placed the tray table across her legs. "Not just for you, greedy. For me too."

She reached for a piece of toast. "You didn't have to go to all this trouble," she said, taking in the omelet, bacon, waffles, and juice that rounded out the breakfast fare.

"Easy for you to say," he said, taking a strip of bacon from the tray. "Manly men like me need our sustenance."

She giggled. "You're silly," she said.

"I may be silly, but it worked." He reached out and touched her face. "I love seeing you happy. You didn't look happy last night."

Alisha felt something different in Jeff's touch this morning and saw something different in his eyes. "Well, I have you to thank."

He dropped his hand from her face, and the look she thought she saw in his face was gone. "You're more than welcome," he said.

She leaned her head to the side. "Does that include me staying here another night?"

"You can stay here forever," he said, that look returning to his eyes again.

She gave an uneasy laugh. "Another night should do it. I don't want to run out my welcome."

"My door is always open to you," he said. "You're welcome to stay as long as you need. I'm here for you, Alisha. I've always been here for you."

Something about Jeff's words touched Alisha's core, and she knew he meant them. "I know," she said.

"Do you really?"

She met his eyes, saw for the first time what she suspected was love in them. Overwhelmed at the knowledge, she murmured, "I know."

He studied her for a moment, and then he leaned across the tray toward her. His eyes were open as were hers. She saw the question in his, which she answered by closing her eyes and parting her lips. His kiss was soft, sweet, and welcoming. But it wasn't enough. She leaned toward him, wanting to get closer, but the tray table was in the way. Jeff grunted as he pulled away from her slightly and deftly moved the tray to the floor beside the bed. When he came back to her, she welcomed him with open arms.

What had begun as a kiss quickly became much more. This was what she needed, she thought. She needed someone who cared only about her, and she knew Jeff was that person. She could admit to herself now that she'd always known he had feelings for her that went beyond friendship. There was safety in knowing that he was always there for her, would always be there, and would never hurt her.

She deepened the kiss and sank back in the bed, pulling him down with her. She knew what was about to happen, and she knew she wanted it to happen. She needed this. "Please," she said.

"I know," he said, deepening the kiss.

She relaxed as he rested himself against her. "Please," she said again.

He pulled back and looked into her eyes. "I love you," he said.

She saw the truth of his words in his eyes, a truth so bright that she was forced to close her eyes against it.

"I love you," he repeated.

She opened her eyes. "I know," she said simply. "I've always known."

He nodded. "Is that the real reason you came to me last night?"

Though she hadn't realized it at the time, she knew he was

right. But it wasn't something she wanted to discuss now. She'd done too much thinking lately. Now she only wanted to feel. "Do we have to talk about this now?"

He pulled away from her. "Yes."

"No," she said, reaching to pull him back to her.

Holding himself apart from her, he said, "I want you more than you know, but not like this."

"Like this?"

"Not when you're stinging from the pain of your mother's revelation. When, and if, we come together, I'm selfish enough to want it to be all about us." He pulled away and sat up fully. "I've waited this long for you," he said. "I can wait a little longer."

"You don't have to wait," she implored. "I don't want you to wait."

"I know you don't," he said. "Right now, you need somebody, and I'm here. I don't want to be your guy of the moment. I want to be your guy for all time. I can't settle for less."

His words touched her heart. "You're turning me down?" she said.

He shook his head. "I'm just not allowing you to use me and what I feel for you to escape from the pain of your current situation. I want more from you than that. I'm not willing to risk the future for this moment."

"What if this moment is the beginning of our future? I care about you too, Jeff. You have to know that."

"I know you care about me, but I love you. There's a difference."

She couldn't respond, because she knew he was right.

"What are you going to do?" he asked.

"I guess I should get dressed and eat my breakfast since you've turned me down."

He reached for the tray on the floor and placed it back on the bed in the space between them. "I'm not talking about that. What are you going to do about your mother and your biological father? You can't continue to avoid them."

She snorted. "Just watch me." She sat up next to him and pressed a kiss on his cheek. "Last chance."

He rested his hand on her cheek. "No, it's not," he said. "I won't let it be."

She sat back and reached for a piece of bacon. "You seem pretty sure of yourself."

He grinned at her. "I have every reason to be. I have you in my bed, in my T-shirt, eating my food, and offering yourself to me."

She punched him in the shoulder. "You'd better take your chance while you have it, buddy."

He folded her hand in his. "I want to be what you want, Alisha, not a substitute."

"You're not a substitute," she said. "I'm not that shallow."

"You're not shallow, you're in pain. You're a little lost now, and I'm very familiar. But that's not enough reason for us to fall into bed together. Nothing good and lasting can come of it."

"I don't know if I agree with you," she said.

"Look at what happened between your mother and your biological father."

She shot her eyes up at him. "It's not the same."

He squeezed her fingers. "Maybe not, but it's close. Your mother turned to Morgan when she was missing your father, who was her foundation. You're turning to me when you're missing your foundation."

She couldn't deny the truth in his words, but she didn't appreciate the comparison. "If you're right, you're not playing the part of Morgan very well. Apparently, he took my mom up on her offer."

"I know how he felt," Jeff said. "It's not easy for me to turn you down, when you're the only thing, the only woman, I've wanted since I first met you. We would probably be making love right now had we not had the conversation we had last night. We can't start something by making the same mistakes that led you to come to me in the first place."

"You're overthinking this," she said.

"I don't think so," he said. "I'm thinking long-term. You're trying to avoid the present."

"Ouch," she said.

He pressed his hand against her cheek. "I'm not trying to hurt you."

She gave a slight smile. "I know."

"What are you going to do?" he asked again.

She shrugged. "I guess staying here with you all day is not an option?"

He smiled. "My door will be open for you after you take care of what's in front of you."

"Promise?"

"Always."

---

Chapter 49

*D*exter slammed his cell phone shut at the sound of Veronica's voice mail. He refused to leave another message. His wife was behaving like a spoiled brat. A spoiled, undisciplined brat. She needed to be here, in Atlanta, working with her coaches instead of back home in Birmingham trying to mend her family ties.

Why wasn't he enough family for her? he wondered. She was more than enough for him; she was exactly what he wanted and needed in a family. Why did she need more?

When the doorbell sounded, he didn't have to guess who it was. He went to it and pulled it open. "Good morning, Tia," he said, before she could speak.

She brushed past him and into the townhouse. "I don't see what's so good about it." When he closed the door and turned to her, she asked, "Where's your wayward wife? She missed her appointment this morning. Please don't tell me she went to Birmingham."

Dexter dropped down on the leather couch. "Then I won't tell you."

"No, she didn't," Tia said.

"Yes, she did."

She began pacing in front of him. "And you didn't stop her?"

"She's a grown woman. I can't stop her from doing what she wants to do."

She stopped in front of him. "Then why are you even here? Why do we even need you if you can't do something as simple as keep your wife in line? I don't think either of you understand what's at stake here. I thought you wanted the life and the lifestyle that Legends could offer?"

"We do," Dexter said. "Of course, we do."

Tia started pacing again. "You're not acting like it," she said. "Neither of you."

"I'm doing what I can."

"It's not enough. Did she really have to go back to Birmingham?"

"She went, didn't she?"

She stopped in front of him again. "The crap is going to hit the fan when Charles finds out."

Dexter thought Tia was blowing the situation way out of proportion. "She'll be back in a day or two. Can't you hold off on telling him until then?"

Tia lifted a brow. "Are you sure she'll be back?"

"I'm positive," Dexter said, hoping he was right. He wasn't sure what his wife would do. There was a lot going on with her, much of which he didn't understand.

"I don't know if I believe you," she said. "You weren't able to keep her from going in the first place."

"She needed some space," he said. "You crowded her, pushed too hard. We both did. I didn't realize how much the separation from her family would affect her. That was a major miscalculation on my part."

Tia snorted. "That's an understatement. What happened? Did she find out that you'd been deleting her messages?"

"That's beside the point."

Tia shook her head. "No, that *is* the point. Maybe you're right. Keeping her from her mother and sisters was the wrong way to go. Maybe we should have worked on getting them to support her."

"Mr. Washington didn't seem interested in placating Veronica's family. In fact, he seemed to want her to distance herself from them and the group."

Tia rolled her eyes. "That's Charles, but he's been wrong before."

"Can you get him to see that?"

Tia sat down on the couch next to him. "I can't go to Charles without a plan. The first thing I need to do is reschedule Veronica's appointments for this week. It's better to reschedule than for her to just not show up."

"You can do that?"

She nodded. "I can, but it's not the best route. We can make it work, though."

"Why didn't you just reschedule when Veronica told you she needed to go home?"

Tia lifted a brow. "Why didn't you ask me to reschedule?" When he didn't answer, she said, "You don't have to answer. I know why you didn't ask. For the same reason I didn't offer.

We're both trying to make a good impression on Mr. Washington. I want him to see that I can take care of Veronica, and you want him to see that you can be an asset to her. Well, her up and leaving the way she did doesn't make either of us look good. We have to work together, Dexter, if we're going to get what we want. I've asked you this before and I'll ask again. Are you on board with me? Can we work together to get Veronica Y launched?"

Dexter knew enough about Tia to be suspicious of her motives. "Why should I work with you and against my wife?"

Tia shook her head. "You really are thick-headed. Nobody is working against Veronica. We're trying to make her into a star. What's so awful about that?"

"Nothing," Dexter said. "Nothing at all. It's just your tactics. They're too heavy-handed for her. She's not used to being dictated to."

"She's being paid too handsomely to use the dictatorship analogy. Her actions are best characterized as diva-ish."

Dexter knew his wife better than to think she was acting the diva. No, she was simply missing her family. "The only way this is going to work is to get Veronica's mother and sisters on board. Are you willing to work with me to make that happen?"

"Duh. I've already said I was. I can handle Mr. Washington and the appointments here. You have to be the one to get Veronica back to Atlanta. You have two days. I can't hold it down here any longer than that. You get her back here, and we'll deal with her family. Hell, they can all move in here with you and Veronica for all I care. I just need them on board with Veronica Y. Is that a task you can accomplish?"

Dexter wasn't sure, but he would definitely give it a try. "I'm heading to Birmingham as soon as you leave. I'll have Veronica back here in two days. Count on it."

Chapter 50

*D*elilah sat in a suite in the Westin Hotel in downtown Birmingham with Morgan, a man who represented a past she wanted to forget, and Tommy, the man who represented the future she wanted to experience, all the while thinking about Rocky, the man who had held her heart for almost all of her adult life. Even now she missed him.

"Well, Alisha's contacted Veronica," Tommy said, "so that's a good sign. I'm sure she's fine."

Delilah knew that Tommy was trying to reassure her, and she didn't have the heart to tell him it wasn't working. "I wish I could talk to her. Maybe I could do a better job of explaining how things happened."

Tommy pressed his hand against hers. "I'm not sure there's anything you can say to her, Delilah. She has to make sense of this on her own and in her own way."

"He's right," Morgan said. "We have to give her the time and space she needs to come to grips with what we've told her. We've basically turned her life upside down. Maybe it was wrong of me to want her to know."

Delilah didn't think this was the time for recriminations. "Even though I didn't want to go through this, don't want to go through it even now, it's the right thing to do. We probably should have told her before Rocky died, so he could have shared his perspective with her. But it's too late for that now."

"I still can't help but feel my selfishness has led us here," Morgan said. "Alisha's life. The lives of my other two kids. My wife. I've been a one-man wrecking crew, wrecking lives left and right."

"I'm with Delilah on this, Morgan. Alisha deserved to know, and so did your family. Rocky and Delilah raised Alisha well. She'll get past this and be a better woman because of it. I really believe that."

"From your mouth to God's ears," Delilah said. "You've already been through this once with your wife and kids, Morgan. How did they take the news?"

Morgan closed his eyes. "It was tough on them. I told my wife, Margaret, first. I owed her that much. The cancer that is killing me actually saved my hide with her. It hurt her to learn of the adultery and the child, made her question the foundation of our relationship."

"But she got past it?" Delilah said.

"Thanks to the cancer," he said, with a sad laugh. "She's angry with me, but I'm dying and she loves me, so she doesn't want our last days together to be tarnished with harsh feelings. My condition forced her to speed up the forgiveness process, which thankfully, she did."

"She sounds like a wonderful woman," Delilah said. "We both lucked out in the spouse department."

Morgan nodded. "More like we were blessed beyond what we deserved."

"Amen to that," Delilah said. "What about your kids?"

"Margaret and I told them together," he said. "I think having her there and having them know she supported me helped them to accept the news. Paige, the oldest, took it hardest. It was hard for her to hear that I shared my heart and my love with another daughter. Again, the cancer helped her get quickly to the forgiveness part of the process. It's not fair really. The disease that is killing me is making my last days much easier."

"That's another blessing," Tommy said. "Don't overlook it."

"I'm not," Morgan said. Then he chuckled. "My boy, Morgan Jr., was disappointed in me for keeping Alisha a secret for so long. He's the person who brought the *Sing for America* contest and Delilah's Daughters to my attention. He can't wait to meet her and her sisters. I'm so proud of the man he's grown to be."

"Sounds like you and Margaret raised a couple of good kids," Delilah said.

"Thanks," he said. "You didn't do too bad yourself."

Delilah looked at Tommy. "I'm not so sure. My family is falling apart all around me, and I don't seem to be able to do anything to stop it. It seems that I'm the cause of it all. Veronica ran off to Atlanta because I didn't agree with the Legends deal, Alisha has run off to who knows where because of the lie I told, and poor Roxanne is following much too closely in my footsteps. She's probably paying the biggest price. All three of them are looking at me very differently these days. If I was ever on a pedestal in their eyes, those days are long gone."

"They'll come around," Tommy reassured her. "They know you love them, and that whatever you did, you did out of that love. They'll see that."

"If my tribe did, so will yours," Morgan said. "Yours just may take a while since you're not dying from cancer."

"Stop saying that, Morgan," Delilah said. "You're not dying, you're living the life you have to the fullest. Nobody knows when their last day will be. Me or, God forbid, Tommy could go before you. We never know."

"She's right, Morgan."

"I hear you," he said. When his cell phone rang, he reached into his pocket and pulled it out. He looked at it, and then he said, "It's Alisha."

"Alisha," Delilah said, "let me speak to her."

Tommy reached for Delilah's hand to keep her from taking the phone away from Morgan. "No," he said. "She's calling Morgan. Let her talk to him. She has to do this her way, Delilah."

She nodded as Morgan answered the phone. "Hello, Alisha," he said. "I'm glad you called. We've been worried about you."

It took all of Delilah's will and self-control not to snatch the phone from his hand so she could speak with her daughter.

"I'm in room 415 at the Westin," Morgan was saying. "You can come directly to the room when you get here, or I can meet you somewhere. Whatever you want."

Delilah breathed a sigh of relief. Alisha was coming here, so she would get to see her child soon.

"Okay," Morgan said. "I'll see you in about an hour." Then he hung up.

"What did she say?" Delilah asked.

"She wants to come over and talk." He shrugged. "She'll be here in about an hour. That's all she said."

"That's a long time to wait," Delilah said. "It's going to seem even longer."

Tommy reached for her hand. "We can't be here when she arrives, Delilah. She wants to speak with Morgan. We have to give them this time."

"But—" Delilah began.

"This is what Alisha needs, Delilah," Tommy said. "She'll come to you when she's ready. Don't push her."

"He's right, Delilah," Morgan said. "You have to let her come to you. I'll encourage her to do that sooner rather than later. I trusted you and Rocky with her for all of her life. Now I'm asking you to trust me with her for a couple of hours. Can you do that?"

Tears welled in Delilah's eyes. "I don't know. You're asking too much."

"You can do it," Tommy said. "You can do it because you're her mother and you love her. You'll do it because it's best for her."

Chapter 51

Alisha stood with Jeff outside the door of Morgan's suite. She looked up at him. "I don't think I can do this," she said.

He smiled down at her. "I'll be right here if you need me."

"You're sure you don't want to go in with me?"

He tapped her on her nose. "I wish I could go in *for* you, but I can't. This is something you have to do for yourself."

She nodded. Then she took a deep breath and knocked on the door. Morgan opened it as Jeff headed for the elevator. "Hi," she said.

"Hi," he said back. "Come on in."

Alisha took in the suite. It was impressive. She'd almost forgotten that this man, her biological father, was *the* Morgan Sampson. Of course, he'd be in a suite. He could certainly afford one.

"Do you want something to eat or drink?" he asked. "I took the liberty of having room service bring up some lunch."

She shook her head. "I'm not hungry."

"Thirsty?"

"Water is fine."

He nodded. "Thanks."

"For what?" she asked.

He chuckled. "For giving me something to do to work off this nervous energy."

His confession made her relax a bit. "You're nervous too?"

"Of course I am. This is one of the most important moments in my life, and I don't want to blow it."

She didn't know what to say, so she didn't respond. She looked around the suite. "This is a really nice room," she said, feeling even more tongue-tied than she'd been when she first met him at the ASCAP conference.

He handed her a glass of water. "I've spent so much time in hotels that they all look the same." He nodded toward the couch. "Take a seat."

She took a sip of water as she did what he asked. "So you've traveled a lot," she said, searching for something to talk about.

"I've done my share," he said. "I only stay in hotels when working. When I'm vacationing, I much prefer leasing a house or condo. Hotels remind me too much of work."

Alisha nodded. His mention of home made her think of his family. "You said you had a son and daughter."

He leaned forward and pulled his wallet out of his pants pocket. "Both are younger than you, of course. Paige is twenty-four, just graduated from Stanford, in business, and Morgan Jr. is twenty-two. He fancies himself a producer like his old man."

Alicia scanned the wallet-sized pictures, looking for some

hint of herself in them. Seeing none, she searched Morgan's face for the same. "He looks like you," she said. "She doesn't."

He closed his wallet, smiling as he did so. "Like you, she got her good looks from her mother. You're both lucky in that regard."

Alisha didn't have a suitable response to that comment, so she asked, "What do they think about me?"

He put his wallet back in his pocket. "I'd be lying if I said they welcomed the news. I'm just glad that they've now accepted it."

She lifted a skeptical brow. "I'm not sure I believe you."

He rolled his fingers around the top of his glass. "To be honest, it's been a little easier for Morgan Jr. than for his sister. You and your brother have your love of music in common. Paige is of a different breed. Her interests fall on the business side of the music industry."

It was strange for Alisha to hear him talking about her in the same breath as he spoke of his other children, the children he had raised. "So is Paige worried about her inheritance?"

Morgan laughed. It was a rich laugh. "Let's just say it crossed her mind."

Alisha smiled, appreciating his honesty. "I don't blame her," she said. "You really don't have to include me in your will, Morgan. You don't owe me anything."

He put down his glass and leaned toward her. "I owe you more than I can give you. But you're not in my will because I owe you. You're in my will because you're my child and I love you. My estate belongs as much to you as it does to Paige and Morgan Jr."

The forcefulness and sincerity of his words caught Alisha off-guard. "It doesn't," she said. "You don't even know me. I'm your daughter by biology only. It doesn't have to matter. Rocky was my father. He'll always be my father."

Morgan sat back in his chair. "I know that," he said. "I don't want to take Rocky's place. I know that's impossible. I can't be a father to you because you don't need one, but I can be a mentor, and I can give you a brother and another sister. Those are the things I can do for you. I won't even try to re-place Rocky. I know that would be impossible."

Alisha stared down at her glass of water. Why was he making this so easy for her? Didn't he want anything from her? "And what do you want in return?"

He shrugged. "What I *want* is the impossible, so I won't even go there. What would make me happy would be for you to find some joy in having a brother and sister and maybe some joy in sharing your music with me. That would be enough."

Alisha wasn't sure she could give him that.

"What do you think?" he asked, when she didn't respond.

"I'm not sure," she said, meeting his eyes. She wanted him to see the uncertainty she felt. He'd been honest with her, so she wanted to be honest with him. "This is all so new to me. I still can't quite believe it. It's as though my world has turned sideways. I don't know what to say or how to react."

"That's fine, Alisha," he said. "I won't pressure you."

But you're dying, she thought. "You're sick," she said.

He nodded. "Cancer. I'm fighting it, but the odds aren't good. You need to know that too."

Alisha swallowed. "How long?"

"Long enough for you to take the time you need. My health shouldn't force you to do anything you don't want to do."

She looked at him. *How can it not?* she thought. "So you still want to be my mentor?" she said.

"Of course," he told her. "Everything I told you about your music was true. You're very talented. You can have a long career in this business, if you want it."

Oh, she wanted it all right. She just wasn't sure she could trust his instincts when it came to her. "I'm not sure I believe you," she said. "I keep thinking you're telling me what you think I want to hear because I'm your dau——. . . because you're my biological father."

Morgan chuckled. "After you get to know me, you'll find I'm very straightforward. It would be cruel of me to tell you that you have talent if you didn't. Instead of lying to you, I'd be looking for an easy way to tell you to consider another profession. No, you have the *it* that is necessary for success in the music business."

She didn't say anything, so he added, "I have a suggestion," he said.

She looked up at him. "What is it?"

"Why don't we try this? Why don't we put our biological relationship on the back burner for now and focus on our professional mentor-mentee relationship? That will allow us to get to know each other."

"I can't pretend I don't know who you are."

"And I don't want you to. All I'm asking is that you don't let the biological relationship color the professional one. You were excited to be working with me before you found out who I am to you. Is it possible we can get that back?"

"I don't know," she said, wanting to keep things between them honest. "I'm sorry if that's not what you want to hear."

"Don't be," he said. "We've dropped a lot on you. So where do we go from here?"

"I don't know," she said, wishing she did.

"I've offered my professional suggestion. Now let me offer a personal one. Talk to your mother. You know she loves you. And you have to know how much it hurts her that you aren't speaking with her. The same with your sisters. You need each other now, Alisha, more than ever. If you want to punish someone, punish me, but don't punish them. Delilah cared about me, but she always loved Rocky. I knew that, but it didn't stop me from falling in love with her."

"But she was married, and so were you."

He nodded. "Yes, we were, and we were wrong. But it happened, and we can't take it back. We wouldn't take it back. To take it back would be to not have you, and neither Delilah nor me, nor Rocky would want to give you up. What we did was wrong, but everything about you was right. Your birth gave Rocky and Delilah another chance. My marriage survived because, even though I didn't tell my wife what had happened, I made a promise to myself to be the best husband that I could be. In the process, I fell back in love with my wife."

Alisha thought about the things Morgan was saying and the things Jeff had said last night and earlier this morning. Maybe there was hope for her and Morgan. "Do you really think I have talent?" she asked.

He smiled at her. "Finish that demo and I'll prove it to you."

Chapter 52

*D*exter sat in his car outside Delilah's house, gathering his courage and his wits. He'd need both to face his wife and the in-laws who had never really accepted him. He took a deep breath, got out of the car, walked up to the door, and rang the bell.

Roxanne opened the door. Before he could speak, she said, "What are you doing here?"

Dexter walked past her and into the house. "I'm looking for my wife," he said. "Where is she?"

"You've got some nerve, Dexter," she said. "Why would you want to keep Veronica from her family? I don't get it."

"What are you talking about?" he asked.

She rolled her eyes. "I know about the deleted voice-mail messages and what you told Veronica about our not attending the party you had for her. You didn't even invite us!"

Dexter felt all the disdain he usually felt from Veronica's sisters flowing toward him. "Look, Roxanne," he said, "I'm not going to argue with you. I want to see my wife."

She made a noise that sounded like a snort. "At the rate you're going, she may not be your wife for long."

"That's enough, Roxanne," Veronica said, causing Dexter to turn around and face her. His immediate thought was that she looked completely relaxed and at ease, a complete contrast to the unrest he felt inside. "You're looking for me, Dexter?"

He nodded. "We need to talk."

She folded her arms across her chest. "Okay, talk."

"Not like this," he said. He glanced at Roxanne, and then he said, "We need to talk alone."

Veronica turned to her sister. "Do you mind?"

Roxanne looked from her to Dexter. "I just want to know why he lied. Tell me that and I'll leave."

"Leave now, Roxanne," Veronica said. "This is between me and Dexter."

Mumbling something under her breath, Roxanne left the room.

Dexter sat on the couch. "Your sisters can be rude at times."

"Please, Dexter," Veronica said. "You did lie. It's not rude when someone calls you a liar because you've lied about them or to them."

This conversation wasn't going the way Dexter had planned. "Look, I didn't come here to talk about that. When are you coming back to Atlanta?"

Veronica looked away. "I don't know," she said. "Maybe I'm not coming back."

"What are you saying?" Dexter said, but he was afraid he knew exactly what she meant. "Of course you're coming back. That's where our life is now."

She turned back to him. "I'm not sure it's the life I want anymore."

He came and stood next to her, not liking what he was hearing from her. "You don't mean that. We're living our dream."

"Sometimes it seems more like a nightmare," she murmured.

"You don't mean that either," he said, praying she didn't. "We've had some rough patches, but we didn't expect it to be easy, did we? We knew it was going to take a lot out of us. We can do this. Together, we can do anything."

She looked at him, seeming unmoved by his words. "But I didn't know it would cost me my family."

"It doesn't have to," he said. "We can work through this."

"How, Dexter?" she asked. "Tell me, how do we work through this? Forget Legends and Atlanta. I'm talking about you and me now. Do you realize that you've been lying to me since before we went to Atlanta? That's foul, and it gets more foul each day I think about it. The man I married wouldn't have done what you did. I don't know what's happened to you."

Dexter rubbed his hand across his head, trying not to show his frustration. "Nothing's happened to me," he said. "Maybe you're the one who's changed. Legends is offering you everything you said you wanted. Have you decided it's too much work for you? That it's too hard?"

"You don't get it, do you?" she asked. "Legends is the last thing on my mind. I'm worried about our family, you, me, my sisters, and my mother. That's my family, Dexter. I don't think you see it that way."

"I had hoped we were starting our own family," he said. "You and me."

"But I shouldn't have to give up my momma and sisters in order for us to have a family. Why does our family have to exclude them? I have enough love for you and them. It's not a competition."

It sure feels like one, Dexter thought. "Your mom and sisters don't like me, Veronica. They tolerate me, but they don't like me. They never have. I'm not stupid."

"It goes both ways, Dexter," she said. "You put up so many walls that they can't get to know you. I wish they could see the parts of you that I fell in love with, but you keep those parts hidden behind a stuffy and aloof facade of academic and intellectual superiority. You say my folks don't accept you—well, it goes both ways, because you don't respect them and you've never appreciated their talent."

"I love you," he said, needing to change the subject and remind her of the most important truths between them. "I trust you. I don't trust them."

"And that's a problem for me. They haven't given you any reason to not trust them. You, on the other hand, have given them every reason to not trust you."

"You shouldn't have told them," he said. "That was between you and me. You don't have to tell them everything. That's part of the problem."

She frowned. "There have been too many secrets and lies in this family. I wasn't going to add to them. I want them to love you, but I'm not going to start lying and covering up for you. The things you did were foul, but I know my family. If you seek their forgiveness, they'll give it."

"Forgiveness? Me seek it? What about them? Your mother has never accepted me as a son-in-law. When is that going to happen? And it's apparent your sisters don't think I'm good enough for you. When is that going to change? I came here to convince you to come back to work, to Legends, to Atlanta, but maybe I should be asking you to come back to *me*. Do you fight for me with your family the way you're fighting for them with me?"

Without giving her a chance to respond, he said, "I know the answer. We both know the answer. Maybe the answer is why I'm threatened by your relationship with them. You've made it clear to me how important they are to you, but you haven't been as clear with them about how important I am to you."

"Now you're talking crazy," she said, recalling the numerous times she'd defended him and their relationship to her family. "Of course, I've been clear to them about how important you are to me. I married you, Dexter, despite the reservations of my family. They thought we were rushing into marriage too soon after Daddy's death, but I convinced them that the love between us was real and time wouldn't change it. Now I'm not so sure."

"That makes two of us," he said. Then he stood. "I've checked into the Sheraton. I'll be there for a couple of days before I go back to Atlanta. If you want to see me, you know where to find me."

With those words, Dexter strode to the door. As he stalked to his car, he had the sinking feeling that he had lost a very important argument.

Chapter 53

*D*elilah sat on the swing in Tommy's backyard. "She's not coming," she said to him. "I love you for planning this family picnic, but she's not coming. I know she's not."

Tommy rested his hand on hers. "You don't know that. There's still time."

Delilah leaned close against him. She was more grateful each day for his support. She didn't think she would have made it through the last few weeks without his love and caring.

"Veronica and Roxanne are enjoying themselves," he said. "That's a start."

She looked across the property to where the girls were feeding the horses. "They needed this. It's so relaxing out here. We needed to get away. Thank you again for inviting us."

"Pretty soon you won't need an invitation," he said. "This

will be your home too. Have you thought any more about when that will be?"

She shook her head. "How could I with everything going on?"

"Maybe that's the reason you need to think about it. Everything has been so up in the air lately. Our marriage would be one thing we could finalize."

She peered up at him. "You want to get married in the middle of all this chaos?"

He pressed a kiss on the top of her head. "I'm beginning to think that chaos, as you call it, is really just life and it's always happening. We can't escape it."

Delilah thought he had a point, but she had her concerns. "Right now, I'm not even sure I could get all my girls to attend a wedding," she said. "And I can't have one without all of them there."

"I know," he said. "I just want you to start thinking about a date. We're not getting any younger, you know."

She smiled. "Speak for yourself, old man."

He leaned down and kissed her lips. "I'm not that old."

When he raised head, she told him, "I love you."

"I love you more," he said, "and I can prove it."

"How?" she asked.

"Look behind you."

When Delilah turned, she saw Alisha walking up the path to the gazebo where they sat. "She came," she said. "And she brought a friend."

"Told you."

She kissed him again. "Thank you."

"Hello, Mr. Tommy, Momma," Alisha said when she and

her friend reached them. "This is my friend, Jeff Parker. We used to work together at McKinley and Thomas."

"Nice to meet you, Jeff," Tommy said, extending his hand.

"Welcome, Jeff," Delilah said. "It's a pleasure to meet one of Alisha's friends."

Delilah watched the look Jeff gave her daughter and knew he felt something special for her. She was grateful Alisha had him to lean on during this time of trouble.

When Tommy stood, she asked, "Where are you going?"

"I think you two need some time alone. I'm going to show my new friend Jeff here around the place." He looked at Jeff. "Are you game?"

Jeff glanced at Alisha before answering. "Thank you," he told Tommy. "I'd love to see your property. We saw some horses driving up. Are those yours?"

Tommy nodded. "Are you a horseman?"

Jeff grinned. "I love to ride, but I wouldn't call myself a horseman."

Tommy clapped him on the back as they walked away. "We'll have to change that."

Looking after them, Delilah said, "Tommy sure took to him quick."

"Jeff has that way about him," Alisha said. "I can't explain it."

Delilah studied her daughter, trying to see if what she saw in Jeff's eyes was reflected in her daughter's. "I'm glad you came," she said. "I wasn't sure you would."

Alisha took a seat on the swing across from her mother. "I wasn't sure I would either. Jeff helped me decide."

"He's good for you then."

She met her mother's eyes. "I think so."

Delilah knew this was their time to clear the air between them, but she didn't know where to start.

"I went to see Morgan," Alisha said.

"He told me."

Alisha nodded. "I'm not surprised."

"How did it go?"

"How did he say it went?"

"He thought it went well, but I didn't ask for details. I didn't think it was my business."

Alisha looked away. "All my life I've been one of Rocky's girls. Who am I now?"

"You're still one of Rocky's girls, Alisha. Nothing has changed."

She turned back to her mother. "How can you say that? Everything has changed." She looked across the property to where her sisters now sat on the edge of the pond. "They're my half-sisters," she said. "And I have two other half-siblings. Things may not have changed for you, but they have certainly changed for me."

Delilah wondered if she'd ever be able to say anything right again from Alisha's perspective. "You had to know, Alisha. My only regret is that Rocky and I didn't tell you. That way, he could have reassured you of how much you meant to him. I'm sorry we didn't give you that. I'm sorry I didn't give it to you."

Alisha wiped at her eyes. "I've been thinking about Dad a lot lately. I miss him so much, especially now."

Delilah wanted to pull her daughter into an embrace, but she didn't because of the distance she felt between them. "I miss him too."

Alisha looked up at her. "I know you loved him," she said. "I know you did, so how did this fling between you and Morgan happen? I still can't get my mind around it."

"I can't explain it any better than I already have," Delilah said. "There is no real explanation. Morgan and I were two people who felt they needed each other. When I look back on it now, I understand that I was more to blame than he was."

"Why do you say that? Morgan says he took advantage of you at a time when he knew you were missing Dad."

"That's how I wanted to remember it too," Delilah said, her memory of the past clearer now than it had ever been, "but it's not true. You see, though he never spoke the words, I knew that Morgan was in love with me. It wasn't something we discussed. We both loved Rocky, and neither one of us would ever have done anything to hurt him."

"But you did," Alisha said.

"I know," Delilah said. "Maybe a part of me wanted to hurt your father. I was angry with him for leaving me and your sisters alone so much. I had begun to wonder how much he really wanted a family. I was feeling like extra, unwanted baggage. And there I was with two little girls and practically no husband. Yes, I was angry. And there was Morgan who loved me. And who also loved your father." Delilah closed her eyes. "Believe me when I tell you, nothing would have happened between me and Morgan had I not wanted it to happen. I'm not proud to say it, but it's true."

"Thank you for being honest," Alisha said. "There's been too much dishonesty among us, too many secrets. From Roxanne and her married lover, to Dexter deleting messages and lying to Veronica, to Morgan meeting me at ASCAP without telling me who he was, and to you and Daddy keeping a secret that really shouldn't have been kept. It's too much. I'd rather know the truth than live a lie."

Delilah breathed a deep sigh. "Does that mean you're ready to forgive me?"

Alisha shrugged. "Jeff said something that made me think about it. He said that since Daddy forgave you, then I should too. He said if I didn't, I'd make Daddy's forgiveness and love all in vain."

"Jeff sounds like a wise man."

"He is," Alisha said. "So I'm trying to follow his advice. But it's hard, Momma. I'm trying to forgive you, for Daddy's sake, but I'm still very angry with you. I don't know when that's going to go away."

"You have every right to be angry, Alisha. I'm not asking you not to be. That you're thinking about forgiving me is enough."

"There are strings attached, though," Alisha said.

"What do you mean?"

"I mean we have to go forward as a family in honesty. There can't be any more lies or secrets between us. We're family. If we can't trust each other with our secrets, who *can* we trust?"

Delilah knew her youngest daughter was right, but she also knew that some secrets were necessary. She chose to keep that opinion to herself. "We'll have to get your sisters to agree as well," she said.

Alisha nodded. "We need a family meeting."

Chapter 54

$\mathcal{D}$elilah called to Veronica and Roxanne, beckoning them to join her and Alisha. "They would have been over here anyway had they realized you were here."

"That may be true, but I don't think they wanted their picnic turned into a family meeting." Alisha sat on the swing next to her mother, who had taken her up on her suggestion for a family meeting. Alisha just hadn't expected the meeting to happen today, right now. "It could get ugly."

"It won't get ugly," Delilah said. "It may get uncomfortable, but it won't get ugly."

"I hope you're right," Alisha said. She stood as her sisters came closer. Not waiting for them to get to her, she walked toward them. When they were close enough, she pulled both of them into a single embrace. She stood holding them close for a minute before she felt her mother join in the group hug.

When they all pulled back, Delilah, tears in her eyes, said, "It's been much too long since we've done that."

"You're right about that, Momma," Veronica said, her

eyes also full. "That's not all I've missed about y'all. I miss everything—the good and the bad."

"Well, it seems we've had more than our share of the bad lately," Roxanne said. "It's been a tough couple of months for Delilah and her daughters."

Alisha couldn't help but chuckle. "I'd say that's an understatement."

"What matters is that we're together now," Delilah said. "The past is the past."

Alisha glanced at her mom. "Except now the past has become the present and has major implications for the future." She turned to her sisters. "I told Momma we needed a family meeting. It's been a long time since we've had one."

Roxanne nodded. "It's time."

"I agree," Veronica chimed in.

"We couldn't have picked a better spot," Delilah said. "Let's go back to the gazebo; we can talk there. Tommy and Jeff will give us the privacy we need."

"Jeff?" Veronica asked.

"I remember Jeff," Roxanne said, a grin forming on her face. "He's one of the guys who helped Alisha move out of her apartment. I knew he had eyes for her then." She nudged her sister with her shoulder. "I guess you finally saw what I was trying to tell you."

"I'm seeing a lot of things these days," Alisha said. The evolution of her relationship with Jeff was only one of them. "When I needed somebody, I immediately turned to him. I guess I've been turning to him when I needed help for a while now."

"Good for you, Alisha," Veronica said.

When the four women were all seated in the gazebo, Alisha and Delilah on one swing and Roxanne and Veronica on the swing facing them, Delilah said, "I'm going to take one of the benefits of age and be the first one to speak, even though this meeting was Alisha's idea." She took a moment and made eye contact with each of her daughters. "I want to apologize again to each of you for the secret Rocky and I kept about Alisha's parentage. I hope you know that we kept it with the best of intentions. As it turns out, it was the wrong decision. This was the kind of secret that you needed to hear from both of us. Maybe Rocky and I would have realized this had he not died so unexpectedly, but we didn't get that chance. And now we all have to live with the consequences. It would still have been hard to hear and digest with Rocky here, but you would have had the support of both of us to get through it."

"I forgive you, Momma," Veronica said.

"So do I," Roxanne said, "but I'm not the one who's most affected, and neither is Veronica. This one really belongs to Alisha, and you have to give her the time she needs to make her way through it."

"Thanks, sis," Alisha said, reaching for her oldest sister's hand and giving it an affectionate squeeze. "Momma and I have talked this out already. And I'm trying to make my way through it. Morgan and I spent some time together the other day, so I'm making progress. I just need things to be all right with all of us. This family is my rock, my foundation, and always has been. When I learned about Morgan, I felt my foundation crumble, and I didn't have anywhere to stand. I don't like that feeling, and I don't want to experience it again."

"I'm with Alisha," Veronica said. "I've felt a bit rudderless lately myself, and it's not a good feeling at all. Unlike Alisha, though, I brought it all on myself." She glanced from her mother to her two sisters. "I need to apologize to each of you for the way I left Birmingham. I was wrong not to contact each of you to say good-bye. I know I can't speak for Dexter, but I need to apologize for his actions. First, for not inviting you all to the surprise going-away celebration he planned for me, and more recently, for deleting your phone messages."

Delilah took a deep breath. "Don't be so hard on yourself, Veronica. I have some responsibility in this as well. Maybe things would have turned out differently if I had told you girls about the Legends offer and allowed you to make the decision, instead of keeping it from you. It seems I have a bad habit of thinking 'mother knows best.' I promise to do better in the future. I have to start treating you three like the women you are, rather than the little girls you used to be."

"Unfortunately, we sometimes act like little girls," Roxanne said. She turned to Veronica. "Despite the ugly things I said to you about taking the Legends offer, I want only the best for you. Nothing would make me happier than to see Veronica Y hit the top of the charts."

"That goes double for me," Alisha said. "I'm sorry I wasn't more supportive either. I was so proud when I saw that picture of you and those three guys in the entertainment section of the Atlanta paper. That was my sister doing it up with Atlanta's finest! I called you then and left a message, which I now know you didn't get."

Veronica wiped at her eyes with her fingers. "I love you guys so much. The past is the past," she said. "I'm ready to leave it behind and move ahead."

"So am I," Alisha said, "but first I have another apology to get out." She turned to Roxanne. "I was way out of line in the things I said when you told me about you and Gavin. I didn't mean them. I couldn't handle what I was feeling about Morgan being my biological father, so I unloaded on you. It wasn't fair."

"But there was truth in the things you said, Alisha," Roxanne told her. She sighed deeply. "My relationship with Gavin didn't just affect me. You were right to remind me that it affected Delilah's Daughters and our family as well. I never meant to bring shame on the family."

Alisha reached out to her sister. "I was overreacting," she said. "Delilah's Daughters will survive, and so will the Monroe family."

Roxanne squeezed her sister's hand. "I'm not so sure," she said. "There's something else you need to know."

"What?" Alisha asked.

Roxanne glanced at Veronica, then back to Alisha. "Not only did I have an affair with a married man," she said, "I'm pregnant."

"Pregnant?" Alisha repeated.

Roxanne nodded. Then she turned to her mother. "I'm sorry. I should have told you earlier, but I couldn't add to the burden you were already carrying."

"I'm sorry you felt you couldn't tell me," Delilah said, tears in her eyes.

"Wait a minute," Alisha said, "I'm still on pregnant. You're really pregnant?"

Roxanne nodded. "You'll have proof in about seven months when you meet your niece or nephew."

Veronica chuckled. "She'll have proof long before then, when you blow up like a whale."

"Let's be honest," Roxanne said, her hand pressed across her stomach. "This pregnancy wasn't planned, and this baby wasn't conceived under anything close to ideal conditions. I never planned on being an unwed mother or a single parent, but that's what I'm going to be."

"You won't be alone," Delilah said. "You and the baby will have all of us. I'm going to be the best grandma ever. Just watch."

Roxanne wiped at her tears. "Thanks, Momma."

"And I'll be the best aunt," Veronica said.

"No, you won't," Alisha said, "because that will be me."

Roxanne sobered. Looking at Alisha, she said, "I can't be pregnant and be a member of Delilah's Daughters. I'm sorry I let you down."

"You have more important things to think about than the group," Alisha said, "and so do I."

"But what about the demo?" Roxanne asked.

Alisha waved the notion away with her hand. "I'm not sure," she said, "but don't worry about it. I'll talk to Mr. Tommy and Morgan and see what they think. You should focus on the baby. We can think about the demo later."

"She's right," Delilah said to Roxanne. "Putting all the plans for Delilah's Daughters on hold seems the right thing to do for now."

"I can't help but wonder what Daddy would think," Roxanne said. "I feel I've let him down even more than I've let you guys down."

"More than anything," Delilah said, "Rocky loved you

girls and wanted the best for you. He loved you more than he loved Delilah's Daughters. He may have been disappointed in the group not flourishing, but he would have understood that what was going on in each of your lives was more important than cutting a demo. Rocky had to make the choice between family and music himself, and he chose family. He'd want you to do the same."

"Where does that leave me?" Veronica said. "Does putting family first mean I should walk away from the Legends contract?"

"I don't think so," Roxanne said. "That contract was probably a godsend that we didn't recognize. If you hadn't taken it, we still would have lost the Magic City contract due to my pregnancy. If I were you, I'd look at that Legends contract as a blessing straight from God." She turned to Alisha. "I know this is hard for you to hear, but your relationship with Morgan opens new doors for you as well. It's probably a good thing that you aren't tied down with Delilah's Daughters."

"Roxanne's right," Delilah said. "Each of you has a new adventure ahead of you. You should each embrace them, without guilt, knowing that your family is fully behind you."

"What about you, Momma?" Alisha said. "What are you going to do now that Delilah's Daughters is on hold?"

Delilah smiled at her girls. "Don't worry about me," she said. "I have a new adventure ahead of me as well. I'm getting married."

Chapter 55

*R*oxanne sat in the living room of the suite she and Gavin had used on the occasions between cruises when they spent time together in Orlando. She didn't know what to expect from him when he heard her news today; she only knew she had to tell him. Her baby deserved the chance to have a father, though she knew it was also possible that Gavin would want nothing to do with the child. If he didn't, the rejection would be hers to deal with, not her child's burden. Thanks to Mr. Tommy and the legal documents she had in her purse, she was prepared for either outcome.

Her stomach knotted up when she heard the key card in the door. She was unsure whether to stand or remain seated. When they were in a relationship, it had been their custom to greet each other at the door with a kiss. Since those days were long gone, she decided to remain seated.

Her heart fluttered a tiny bit when Gavin stepped through the doorway and then almost stopped when his wife followed him into the room.

Darla laughed. "The look on your face says you didn't expect me."

Roxanne swallowed. "I didn't," she said, looking in Gavin's direction. When he refused to meet her gaze, she wondered if he had always been this weak. The Gavin she was seeing now and had last seen on that fateful night on the cruise ship was new to her. She wondered if she had ever known the real Gavin.

"So you wanted to meet with us?" Darla inquired, after making herself comfortable on the sofa a few feet away from Roxanne.

Roxanne turned her attention back to Darla since she was obviously the one in charge. "I have some news for Gavin."

Darla looked in her husband's direction. "I've bet him a thousand dollars that you're pregnant. Something tells me he's going to have to pay up." She looked back at Roxanne. "Did you bring us here to tell us that you're pregnant?"

Roxanne couldn't speak. How stupid had she been? Had Gavin gotten other women pregnant? Did he have other children out there? Maybe she shouldn't tell him about the baby, after all.

Before she could speak, Darla went on, "It doesn't matter. Not really. We're willing to give you a onetime lump-sum payment," she said as she opened the portfolio-sized bag she was holding and pulled out a legal-sized envelope. "In return, you have to agree to the terms outlined in the contract in that envelope." As Roxanne gazed at the envelope, Darla continued, "There's no rush," she said. "You can have your attorney look it over—if you have one, that is."

Roxanne wished she had some smart retort for the woman,

but she didn't. Darla's presence had thrown her off a bit, and this full-out attack had leveled her. She glanced over at Gavin, hoping against hope that she would find some semblance of the man who'd always been supportive of her.

"There's no use looking at him," Darla said. "In case you haven't figured it out by now, Gavin belongs to me and he likes it that way."

"I don't want your money," Roxanne finally said, after giving up on getting any support from Gavin.

Darla laughed. "You may not want it now," she said, "but you will. Trust me. We've been through this before." She turned to Gavin. "Haven't we, sweetheart?"

Gavin didn't have to answer. The look on his face was more than enough. Roxanne closed her eyes to block out the pain. She'd been a real fool. Gavin had never cared for her. While she'd always doubted his claims of love, she'd believed that there was some genuine caring between them. She'd been wrong.

Darla chuckled. "You're finally getting the picture. That's good. Apparently, you're smarter than some of the others. Then again, maybe you're not. Your best bet is to take the money. It's about the amount our attorneys say you would have been awarded had you filed an unlawful termination or sexual harassment complaint. Knowing that, you can tell yourself that you're getting what's coming to you and not selling your child's birthright. Just don't name the poor boy Jacob. That would be too much."

The biblical reference was cruel and unnecessary, but that seemed to be Darla's way. "How do you do it?" Roxanne asked.

Darla shrugged. "I've had lots of practice."

"Not that," Roxanne said. "How do you put up with Gavin? Why do you?"

Darla looked at her polished and sculptured nails. "I was a spoiled child who always got what she wanted. As an only child, I never learned to share. Those traits carried over into adulthood and into my marriage. What Gavin and I share works for me, and it will keep working. Gavin gets to do what he wants, and so do I. All the while, we maintain this loving front for my family. That front is important to them."

Roxanne nodded. "So it's about your family's money."

"Everything comes down to money, doesn't it?"

She glanced at Gavin again, finally seeing him for who he really was. "He's a serial adulterer. According to you, he's had children with multiple women. How do you even look at him, much less sleep with him?"

Darla snorted. "Who says I sleep with him?"

Roxanne opened her mouth, and then she closed it. There was nothing for her to say.

"You're pretty smart, aren't you?" Darla said, as if she'd wanted Roxanne to know her secret. "I should have known. Gavin and I both like them smart. And dark."

Roxanne reached out and slapped Darla right across the cheek. She covered her mouth in surprise after she landed the blow.

Darla stood. "Not bad," she said, a slow smile forming on her now-reddened face. "We both like them feisty as well." She glanced in Gavin's direction. "Our work here is done," she said. "I'll meet you downstairs. You can say your final good-bye in private." She turned back to Roxanne. "And you can have the suite for the weekend. After that, don't ever come back."

Roxanne heard Darla chuckling as she left the suite and closed the door behind her. Then she turned to Gavin. "No need for you to stay. There's nothing left to say."

Gavin stuffed his hands in his pockets. "I'm sorry, Roxanne," he said. "I really am."

"Yes, you are," she said. "I think you should go."

When he opened his mouth to speak, she said, "If you don't go, I'm going to call hotel security and make a scene. I'm pretty sure your wife doesn't like scenes. No, she lets you do your dirt, and then she cleans up after you." She shook her head in disgust at all of them, herself included. "What kind of man are you, Gavin? I don't even know who you are anymore. Was the man I knew a figment of my imagination?"

He averted his eyes. "I don't know anymore, Roxanne," he said. "I really don't know."

"Then I feel very sorry for you."

He nodded. "I am sorry."

"So am I," she said. Then she turned away from him to stare down at the envelope Darla had left for her. After she heard him open the door and close it behind him, she covered her face with her hands and let her tears fall. As she cried, she prayed for the strength to put this episode behind her and move on to a happy, full life with her child.

Chapter 56

*D*exter sat in his hotel room, wondering what he was going to do to get his wife back. He was supposed to return to Atlanta yesterday, but he couldn't go back without Veronica. He had hoped she'd reach out to him, but that had been false hope. His marriage was in more trouble than he'd imagined. What was he going to do?

When he heard the knock on the door of his room, he rushed to it. *It has to be Veronica,* he thought. Who else knew he was in town? He stopped short when he pulled open the door. "Delilah?"

She nodded, smiling as if they were old friends. "Veronica told me you were here. May I come in?"

Dexter looked at her long and hard, trying to figure out what his mother-in-law was doing here. Then he stepped back and beckoned her in. "Why did Veronica send you?"

Delilah sat on the club chair in the corner near the windows, making herself at home in his room. "Veronica didn't send me," she said, still smiling. "She doesn't even know I'm here."

Dexter sat on the side of the bed, facing her. Despite her smiles, Dexter knew Delilah didn't like him, and he had done nothing recently that would change her mind. In fact, he'd done just the opposite. He had no doubt Veronica had told her about the going-away celebration and the voice-mail messages. If anything, Delilah liked him even less now. "Then why are you here?" he asked.

Her smile turned serious. "I'm here to apologize and make amends."

Dexter couldn't believe his ears. "You're what?"

"I was wrong to keep the Legends deal from Veronica, and you did the right thing by bringing it to her attention."

Dexter wondered if someone or something had taken over Delilah's body. "I was right?"

She nodded. "I let my fears get the best of me," she said. "I was afraid of losing my girls when I should have been happy for Veronica. I should have trusted her sisters to be happy for her. If I had handled things differently, then the breach between me, Alisha, and Roxanne and Veronica and you wouldn't have happened. I know that now."

Dexter resisted the urge to shake his head to get rid of the cobwebs that seemed to be blocking his thinking. Was Delilah really apologizing to him? It certainly sounded like it. "Veronica needed your support," he said.

"Well, she has it now," Delilah said. "And as Veronica's husband, you have my support as well. You're an important part of this family, Dexter."

Dexter lifted a brow. "I am?"

"Yes, you are," she said. "I'm sorry I haven't always made you feel that way. I promise to do better in the future."

Unsure whether he should believe Delilah's proclamation, Dexter leaned forward and rested his elbows on his thighs. "What brings this on, Delilah?" he asked. "You've hardly tolerated me in the past, and now I'm an important part of the family. Forgive me for being a little bit skeptical."

"I don't blame you," she said. "Given our history, I'm not sure I would believe me either if I were you."

He sat back. Not sure what to say, he said nothing.

Delilah scooted to the edge of her chair. "Veronica loves you, Dexter, but she also loves me and her sisters. She shouldn't have to choose between us. It's not fair to her. So it seems to me the only answer is for the two of us to start over with a clean slate."

Dexter thought about his recent failed attempts to keep Veronica away from her mother and sisters. "A clean slate?"

Delilah nodded. "That includes putting the lie about the going-away celebration and the deleted voice-mail messages in the past. They were childish acts that are beneath you. I don't expect you to repeat them in the future."

"I only did what I thought was best for Veronica."

"But it wasn't best for her," Delilah said, her voice pleading. "I know you can see that. Veronica needs us as much as she needs you. We're willing to share her with you. Are you willing to share her with us?"

Dexter was a bit leery of what Delilah meant by sharing Veronica. "Are you saying you're on board with Veronica working with Legends?"

Delilah nodded. "Delilah's Daughters is going on hiatus

for a while. Legends is, and has always been, the perfect opportunity for Veronica. I couldn't see that initially, but I see it clearly now. Her sisters and I think she needs to make the best of the opportunity."

Dexter's spirits began to lift. "If she wants to make the best of it, she has to get back to Atlanta. She shouldn't have left in the first place."

Delilah reached out and rested a hand on his knee. "You're wrong," she said. "Veronica needed to come home. That's what you've got to see. She can have a life with you apart from me and her sisters, but she can't thrive when we're separated by strife and lies. She needs our support as much as she needs yours. If we want what's best for Veronica, we have to get along a lot better than we have in the past. I'm willing to make the changes necessary for that to happen. Are you?"

Dexter wrestled with the idea of sharing Veronica with her mother and sisters. He much preferred to have his wife to himself, but he was beginning to accept that this was impossible. Maybe it was even unnecessary. Maybe Veronica could love him and her family. He wasn't sure, but given recent events he really didn't have much choice. "Then you have to help me get Veronica back to Atlanta," he said.

Delilah sat back in her chair, shaking her head. "First, we have to show Veronica that we've reconciled. She needs to see her family united in support of her. That's the only way she's going to be free to give 110 percent to Legends. If you don't know that about her, then I'm not sure if you know my daughter at all."

Chapter 57

Alisha thought she'd shown a great deal of maturity when she called Morgan and told him she wanted to meet her half-sister and half-brother. Now she wondered if she'd made a mistake. Morgan might be her biological father, but she didn't know him at all. She should have kept things professional like he suggested. Why hadn't she?

Too late for questions now, she told herself. Then she smoothed her hands down her blue sheath and walked up to the maître d'. "I'm Alisha Monroe," she told him.

"Ms. Monroe," he said, "your party is waiting for you. Please follow me."

Alisha took practiced steps as she followed the man. As they rounded a couple of tables, she saw Morgan and Morgan Junior seated at a table along the windows. She wondered where Paige was. When she reached the table, the two men stood.

"You look beautiful, Alisha," Morgan said.

"That's an understatement," Junior said, with a broad smile. "But I'm a brother, so what do I know?"

His casual reference to himself as her brother helped to calm Alisha's nerves. "Thank you," she said.

The maître d' pulled out her chair and she sat across from her brother.

"Where's Paige?" she asked.

"She had a meeting," Junior said quickly. Too quickly.

Morgan cast a chiding eye at his son. "She didn't have a meeting," he said to Alisha. "She's not ready to meet you yet, so she decided to spend the evening with her mother."

Alisha appreciated his honesty. "I understand," she said.

"She'll come around," Junior said. "It's that MBA in her that's causing all the problems. When I see you, I don't see dollar signs the way she does. I hear your music and I'm sold. Delilah's Daughters made a strong impression on me during the *Sing for America* contest. Did Dad tell you that I brought him a copy of your performance on DVD?"

Recalling that Morgan had said his son had shown him the DVD of Delilah's Daughters, Alisha said, "I think I offered to give you my firstborn for doing that."

Junior chuckled. "I appreciate the offer, but I'll pass on the kid. I'd love to spend some time in the studio with you, though. I think we could do some exciting things together."

Alisha glanced at Morgan.

"Yes, Junior's serious," he said, answering her unasked question.

"Of course, I'm serious," Junior said. "Why wouldn't I be?"

Alisha met his eyes. "For one, you don't even know me."

Junior shrugged. "I know your music, so I feel I know you very well." He put down his napkin. "We're brother and sister. We both need some time to fully adjust to what that means. In the meantime, I don't see why we can't work together. I'm not just another pretty face," he said, grinning. "I know music. I know what works and what doesn't. Dad told me you were working on a demo with Magic City Studios in Birmingham. While I like Mr. Johns and all, I can probably do more with you and your demo than he can."

"Why is that?" Alisha asked, both intrigued and taken aback by his self-confidence.

"Because gospel-pop is who we are and what we do," he said. "That's who you and Delilah's Daughters are. That's never been Magic City's calling card."

Alisha knew Junior was right. Mr. Tommy was trying gospel-pop with their demo, but his work at Magic City typically fell along more traditional lines of gospel or pop, not both. "How would that work?" she asked. "Would you come to Birmingham?"

He shook his head. "You'd have to come to Los Angeles, to our studios."

"You wouldn't have to worry about a place to live," Morgan added. "You can stay with us."

Everything is moving so fast, she thought. "Move to Los Angeles? Stay with you?"

"We have a guesthouse on the property," Junior said. "You could stay there. Or you could bunk with me in my apartment."

"Trust me," Morgan said, casting a wary glance at his son, "the guest house is better."

She looked between them. "Are you two serious?"

Morgan nodded.

"Serious as a heart attack," Junior said. "I don't play when it comes to music."

Alisha had to admit that she was drawn to Junior. Though they didn't share any physical traits—he was tall and light-skinned like his father, while she was petite and dark like her mother—they had the same heart for music. Maybe they could work together on the music and see what happened. "I don't know," she said.

"You don't have to decide now," Morgan said. "Take your time."

"But don't take a lot of time," Junior said. "In this business, you have to strike while the iron is hot. In your case, that means while there's still some memory of Delilah's Daughters out there."

"A lot has changed with Delilah's Daughters," she told them. "The group is going on hiatus for a while."

Junior leaned forward. "That's even better," he said. "To be honest, I didn't like the idea of your mother joining the group. After your sister Veronica left, it really was time to think about doing something different."

She looked at Morgan with a raised brow.

He inclined his head toward his son. "I told him about your idea of revamping the group, and he didn't share my opinion of it. It wasn't the first time we've disagreed, and I'm sure it won't be the last."

Junior chuckled. "Everything I know, I learned from him."

"Right," Morgan said, his smirk evidence of his sarcasm.

"It's true, Dad, but that doesn't mean I have to see things the way you see them."

"Don't I know it," Morgan said.

Alisha smiled at the interaction between father and son. They were as relaxed and at ease with each other as she had been with Rocky. The love and respect they shared was obvious. She wondered if she'd ever have that with Morgan. She wondered if she even wanted it.

"So, Alisha," Morgan said, "what do you think?"

She looked from her father to her half-brother. "What about your mother and sister?" she asked Junior.

Junior sobered. "This is not an easy situation for them," he said, "but they're good people with good hearts. I know them, and I feel very sure that, given time, they'll come around. They need time to get to know you. We all do." He glanced at his dad. "They'll make it work because they love this guy like I do. They'll do it for him."

Alisha felt Junior's love for his father, mother, and sister. And she marveled at how much they all loved Morgan, especially given what they'd recently learned. *He must be a special husband and father,* she thought, the kind of man she'd like to get to know. "Okay," she said. "So when do you want to get started?"

Chapter 58

*V*eronica sat across from Dexter at breakfast drinking a glass of juice. He'd called last night and asked her to meet him at his hotel. She'd come because he was her husband and she loved him, but she still wasn't sure what their future held, professionally or personally.

"When are you coming back to Atlanta?" he asked her.

She wished his first question had been about them personally rather than about Legends. "I don't know," she said.

"You signed a contract," he reminded her.

She glanced down at her plate to keep him from seeing the disappointment she knew would be reflected in her eyes. She didn't need him to talk to her about contracts. She needed to hear heart things from her husband, but he seemed to be on another page altogether.

"If you don't want to go back," he continued, when she didn't respond, "we need to schedule a meeting with the attorney."

She looked up at him. "The attorney?"

He nodded. "We have to find a way to get out of the contract," he said.

"You're okay with me not going back?" she asked, a flutter of hope in her heart.

He reached for her hand. "I've had a lot of time to think about this over the last few days. And while I think Legends is a great opportunity for you, it has to be what you want. More than anything, I want you to be happy. If Legends doesn't make you happy, then it's not for us."

"But what about your book deal?"

He lifted his shoulders in a slight shrug. "It was one opportunity, and I was glad to get it, but I have to believe there will be others. We had always planned for me to go the traditional route to publishing anyway. I'll get a commercial fiction agent and go from there, the way most authors do."

Tears of happiness welled in the back of Veronica's eyes. This was the kind of support she'd wanted from her husband. "That won't be necessary," she said, feeling a hopefulness she hadn't felt since she'd taken the Legends contract. "I'm going back. You know I'm going back."

He shook his head, his eyes sad. "I don't know much of anything where you're concerned these days. You've said some pretty confusing things to me." He paused to clear his throat. "To be honest, I don't even know where I stand. Do you still love me, Veronica? Do you want our marriage to work?"

"Of course I love you," she said, "and I very much want our marriage to work. I've just been unsure of so many other things that our relationship got caught up in the uncertainty. I'm sorry for that."

"What things?" he asked.

She looked away, unsure how to tell him her fears.

He tugged on her hand. "You have to talk to me, Veronica," he said. "I can't read your mind."

When she turned back to him, there were tears in her eyes. "I'm afraid, Dexter," she said.

"What are you afraid of?" he asked, reaching out to wipe away her tears with his fingers.

"I don't know," she said as he pulled her close. "Everything."

"You shouldn't be afraid," he said, raining kisses along her brow.

Her arms tightened around him. "But I am," she said. "What if I'm not good enough? The folks at Legends practically told me that it's not my voice they want. If not that, then what do they want from me? What will they want in the future? How much will I have to give up?"

He pulled back, and she saw the love and confidence in his eyes. "You're good enough," he told her. "You're more than good enough. Legends is lucky to have you. They sought you out; you didn't seek them out. They want you."

"Then why do they want me to have this surgery?" she asked, unable to keep the pain out of her voice. "Why do you want me to have it? Why am I not good enough without having this surgery?"

He studied her face. "Is that what you think? That Legends doesn't think you're good enough as you are? That I don't think you're good enough?"

She lowered her eyes, taking small comfort in hearing her fears voiced aloud. "What else could I think?"

He tilted her face up to his. "I'm so sorry," he said. "I never meant to give you that impression, because that's not what I think. It's not even close." He cupped her face in his hands. "You're more than good enough, Veronica, so get those ideas out of your head. You have no reason to doubt yourself or your talent."

"If you believe that, then why do you want me to have the surgery?" she asked, finally having the courage to ask the question that had always nagged at her.

He closed his eyes briefly, as though the question pained him. When he opened them, he said, "Because I'm selfish. I only wanted you to do it because Legends wanted you to do it. I just wanted to stay on their good side. We have such a good setup with them that I was fearful of blowing it. I was only trying to go along to get along. I was wrong, Veronica, very wrong."

"So you don't think I should do the surgery?"

He shook his head. "You shouldn't do it if you don't want to do it. You have talent, Veronica. Legends is not going to drop you because you decide against the surgery, regardless of what Mr. Washington or Tia has said. We can take a stand on this."

"But what if they do drop me?"

"That contract goes both ways," he said. "You have an obligation to Legends, and they have an obligation to you. We have that entertainment lawyer, but maybe we need someone like Delilah as our advocate as well. I'll bet she'd be willing to act as your manager again. She handled Mr. Washington pretty well before you signed the contract. I'm sure she can handle him now. There's no reason for either of us to be walking around in fear of what Legends will and won't do. Delilah will make sure we don't have to."

Veronica felt the weight of the last few weeks slip away. "Are you really okay with bringing Momma back on board?" she asked.

He kissed her fingers. "Delilah came to see me the other day, and we cleared the air between us. It's like you tried to tell me. You need to be surrounded by folks who love and care for Veronica Monroe Timmons, not only folks who are concerned with the Veronica Y brand. I finally get it. I'm just sorry it took me so long to understand."

Veronica smiled into his eyes. "I love you, Dexter," she said. She made a mental note to thank her mother later for whatever she'd said to him.

He kissed her softly on her lips. "I love you more."

"Impossible."

"I can prove it," he said. Then he reached into his pocket, pulled out a square, white jeweler's box, and handed it to her.

"For me?" she said, taking the box. The last gift he'd given her had been the sterling silver choker with their names engraved on it.

He kissed her softly on her lips. "There's nobody for me but you."

She opened the box and pulled out a beautiful gold charm bracelet with six gemstone charms. "What's this?" she asked.

He took the bracelet from her and clasped it around her wrist. "It's a family charm bracelet," he said. "It has a birthstone charm for each member of your family."

She studied the bracelet, tears of happiness flowing down her cheeks.

"I guess that means you like it," he said.

She looked up at him. "I love it almost as much as I love you," she said. This charm bracelet was a tribute to the family they shared because he'd included a charm for himself. "But there's an extra charm. Are you trying to tell me you want a baby?"

He smiled down at her. "We need more than one charm for the babies we're going to have, but that'll be a separate bracelet."

Her heart bubbled over with joy at the prospect of the children they would someday have. "Then who's this one for?" she asked.

"It's Mr. Tommy's," he said, fingering the extra charm. "I figured he deserved a charm since he asked me to be his best man. I see it as my duty to welcome the next man into the Monroe family."

Epilogue

$\mathcal{R}$ocky Monroe wished Roxanne had stayed home today instead of trekking out to Gospelfest. Though her due date was more than a month away, he thought it was better to be safe than sorry. Babies were unpredictable, and he much preferred having his first grandchild born in a hospital, not in a pavilion at Gospelfest.

"Are you sure you're comfortable?" he heard her friend Judd ask her.

Of course she's not comfortable, Judd! Rocky shouted to no avail. *She's as big as a house. She won't be comfortable again until after she has the baby.*

"I'm fine," Roxanne said, patting Judd's hand. "You worry too much."

"I'm not sure you should have come today," he said.

Rocky agreed with him. He wished his daughters had found men who would make them toe the line. Instead, they seemed to have found men who indulged their every whim. It had taken nothing for Veronica to persuade Dexter to drop everything and follow her to Europe, where she was one of the opening acts for Beyoncé. Poor Jeff had taken a leave of absence from his job so he could spend a month with Alisha in Los Angeles, where she was working on a demo with Junior while she dealt with Morgan's death. And here was Judd Thompson, one of the three heirs to the impressive Thompson real estate portfolio, actually believing a heavily pregnant woman when she told him she was comfortable. *The boy might have business smarts,* Rocky thought, *but he obviously doesn't have much common sense.* He should have kept Roxanne at home with her feet up. As her father, he would have demanded that she stay home.

"She's fine, Judd," Delilah said, sitting on the other side of Roxanne. "Don't worry so."

Tommy, seated on the other side of Delilah, leaned forward so he could look down the row at Judd. "Give it up, son. She's here now. We just have to go with it."

Rocky took some comfort in the uncertainty on Judd's face. Maybe the boy wasn't as ignorant about pregnancies as he'd first thought.

Roxanne pressed a kiss against Judd's cheek. "I appreciate your concern," she said, "but it's not necessary. I've never missed a Gospelfest, and I wasn't about to let this pregnancy make me miss it this year."

Judd looked into her eyes. "I know it's important to you," he said, "but your father could have visited you at home."

She shook her head. "No, Gospelfest is where I feel his presence strongest. And I need to feel it today. I want the baby to feel his grandfather."

Some of Rocky's ire faded when he heard his daughter's

words. He leaned close and gave her a whispered *I love you,* a kiss on the cheek, and a soft caress of her tummy. Roxanne didn't have to worry about his grandchild feeling his presence, because he would make sure she did. That was one of the benefits of being dead that he appreciated.

"I feel him," she whispered to Judd, her hands rubbing her tummy. "I knew he'd be here. He's always here."

Judd's expression said he wasn't sure, but he was wise enough to keep his thoughts to himself.

Rocky moved from his daughter to his wife, who was now Tommy's wife. *Good-bye for now,* he whispered to Delilah. She had chosen well in Tommy, so he had no complaints. As he watched them take in the performance of Tommy's newest boy band, he knew they belonged together. Though they had never discussed it, Rocky had always known of Tommy's feelings for Delilah. Being the friend he was, Tommy had never crossed the line, content to love Delilah from afar.

As he watched Delilah whisper in Tommy's ear, Rocky knew this would be his last Gospelfest for a while. He no longer needed these annual visits with his family, and they no longer needed him hovering over them. He marveled at how far they had come in the four years since his death. Delilah had Tommy. Veronica had Dexter and her music career. Alisha had Jeff and a new brother and sister as well as a new career. Roxanne had Judd and soon she would have a new baby.

Yes, his four girls were moving on with their lives, and he had to move on with the new life he had in death. There were families other than his own who needed someone watching out for them. He'd take on one of those families and leave his

to one of his fellow angels. He already had somebody picked
out for the job.

"Uh-oh," he heard Roxanne say.

"What is it?" Judd asked.

She peered over at him, a shaky smile on her face. "I think
it's the baby."

Mor-gan! Rocky yelled for Morgan Sampson, the newly
minted angel who would take over the care of his family.
*You'd better get here quick. If you allow my grandchild to be born
in this pavilion, I'll—*

About the Author

ANGELA BENSON is a graduate of Spelman College and the author of thirteen novels, including the Christy Award–nominated *Awakening Mercy*, the *Essence* best-seller *The Amen Sisters*, as well as *Up Pops the Devil* and *Sins of the Father*. She is currently an associate professor at the University of Alabama and lives in Tuscaloosa.

BOOKS BY ANGELA BENSON

DELILAH'S DAUGHTERS
A Novel
Available in Paperback and eBook

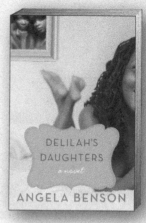

An inspirational family drama set against the backdrop of the music industry. Delilah Monroe and her husband, Rocky, always dreamed of their three daughters making it big in show business. After Rocky's death, Delilah's determination is even stronger. However, her daughters aren't so sure.

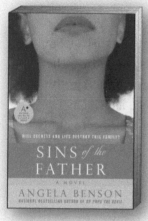

SINS OF THE FATHER
A Novel

Available in Paperback and eBook

Sins of the Father is a powerful story of a house bitterly divided—a wealthy black entrepreneur with two families and the catastrophic consequences when they both collide. It blends romance, drama, inspiration, and intrigue in an unforgettable tale of redemption and, ultimately, of love.

UP POPS THE DEVIL
A Novel

Available in Paperback and Ebook

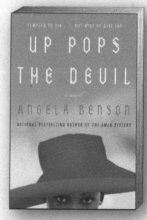

Two hard years in prison have changed Wilford "Preacher" Winters for the better. He did his time, now he's going to "do the right thing." But the women in his life have other ideas. With his world about to explode all around him, Preacher is going to need every ounce of his new-found faith to remain strong. Because it takes a lot to become a new man, sometimes even a miracle.

31901067385742

CPSIA information can be obtained
at www.ICGtesting.com
Printed in the USA
LVHW042028200821
695754LV00007B/137

9 780062 002716